BOUND
OF
BLOOD

BOOKS BY KRISTA STREET
SUPERNATURAL WORLD NOVELS

Fae of Snow & Ice

Court of Winter

Thorns of Frost

Wings of Snow

Crowns of Ice

Supernatural Curse

Wolf of Fire

Bound of Blood

Cursed of Moon

Forged of Bone

Supernatural Institute

Fated by Starlight

Born by Moonlight

Hunted by Firelight

Kissed by Shadowlight

Supernatural Community

Magic in Light

Power in Darkness

Dragons in Fire

Angel in Embers

Supernatural Standalones

Beast of Shadows

Links to all of Krista's books may be found on her website.

www.kristastreet.com

BOUND
OF
BLOOD

paranormal shifter romance
SUPERNATURAL CURSE
BOOK TWO

KRISTA STREET

PREFACE

Bound of Blood is a paranormal shifter romance and is the second book in the four-book *Supernatural Curse* series. The recommended reading age is 18+.

CHAPTER ONE

My ex and I stood outside of my apartment building, only one house down from my front door, when the Fire Wolf's portal emerged in a glowing circle as though from thin air. And once the hunter stepped through it and his nostrils flared, I knew he'd caught my scent on the wind.

"Well, this is shitty timing," I muttered to no one in particular, even though Carlos, my ex-boyfriend, stood right beside me.

My ex glanced behind him, his eyes widening at what was barreling toward us on the sidewalk.

The Fire Wolf, all six-four of him, strode our way, his features twisted into a wrathful expression that rivaled a violent tornado. And not one of those EF0 tornadoes. Nope, this dude was a full-blown EF5, intent on destroying everything in his path.

"Do you know him?" Carlos asked warily. Despite his

tone, my ex held his ground, but his shoulders tensed and his hands fisted.

"You could say that." I still clutched my jacket tightly around me as the cool autumn wind bit into my cheeks.

Carlos turned questioning eyes on me, but before he could ask anything further, the Fire Wolf was upon us.

The hunter's cedar and citrus scent clung to him when he stopped only a foot away. Dark hair ruffled across his forehead in the breeze, and his amber-hued eyes gazed down at me with a glinting emotion veiled within their depths.

Perhaps that was because I'd kicked him out of my bed earlier this morning. Just guessing here.

"Tala," he said, which I assumed was his form of greeting. *Hello* would be too simple for him, and *how's it going* no doubt required too much tongue work.

"Fire Wolf." I didn't back up even though the energy strumming off the huge hunter was getting apprehensive glances from the humans stepping around us on the sidewalk.

"I have your purse." The leather bag was draped over his shoulder, hanging from his massive frame like a piece of dental floss. "I thought you might like it back."

"You assumed right." I eyed my bag, and if this moment wasn't shrouded in so many unsaid emotions, I would have laughed. His huge frame made the medium-sized purse look like a small clutch. That and he looked entirely uncomfortable carrying it, as if such a feminine item didn't jive with his 'scourge of society' look.

But then I remembered how he'd pried my secret from me this morning—using seduction and an alpha command —and my amusement vanished.

I held out my hand.

Instead of handing my purse over, he studied me, a questioning look in his gaze.

I wasn't surprised. We hadn't exactly left on the best of terms a few hours ago. I rolled my eyes and waved my hand impatiently. "My purse? Can you just give it to me?"

The Fire Wolf frowned, his eyebrows pulling tightly together as Carlos watched us, but he finally held my bag out.

I snatched it from him before he could change his mind, then remembered that the strap had been torn by Hoodie Guy following the run-in outside of the Fire Wolf's man cave.

I inspected the strip of leather, searching for the tear.

"I fixed it," the Fire Wolf said gruffly. "I thought you'd want it repaired."

He must have used a tactile spell, because no trace of the damage remained. "Oh, thank you," I said begrudgingly. Fixing my purse was one less thing I would have to do today.

"You're welcome."

I slipped it over my shoulder, then checked to make sure my wallet and phone were still inside. They were. Lucky me. This day might not be completely shit after all.

"Should we go?" Carlos asked, his tone still wary. The wind blew his short black hair around his forehead as he

3

assessed the Fire Wolf, and then me. He was clearly brimming with questions, but I was in no mood to answer them even though Carlos had shown up to help me.

I sighed. "Yeah, we can go."

A low rumble came from the hunter. "Go where?"

"The SF," I replied dryly.

"Why are you going to the SF?"

"Um, because my sister was abducted? They kinda need to know about that."

"But they refused to help you."

"Actually, they only refused to help me for forty-eight hours. And that was only because they'd thought my sister had gone on another one of her impulsive disappearance escapades. But now that I have proof of her abduction, and the fact that her disappearance was related to something bigger—" My mouth grew dry when I thought about the other supernaturals that had been taken during the past few months. All of them had been so powerful. Could they all be linked? Because apparently someone named Jakub, and perhaps also someone named Damascus, was collecting intensely magical supernaturals. As for their reasons for that, I didn't know.

I quickly shook off those thoughts because they only put me on edge. After all, the power Jakub had been after when he'd abducted my sister was actually the power *I* possessed, not Tess.

"Shall we go?" Carlos gestured to the street corner. "I can call us a ride."

The Fire Wolf stepped into Carlos's path before my ex could guide me away. "Who are you?"

My ex's chin jutted up. "Carlos Lopez."

Flames surged in the hunter's eyes. "Tala's former boyfriend?"

"That would be me. Who are you?"

The Fire Wolf took a step closer to my ex, malice rolling off him in waves. "The man who made Tala scream in pleasure this morning."

I blanched just as Carlos blinked.

"Dude, TMI," I hissed under my breath.

The Fire Wolf scowled. "It's true," he said to me. "I've thought about it several times since I left this morning."

Carlos's jaw worked, but he remained quiet.

The Fire Wolf rounded on Carlos again, a growl rumbling from his throat. "You're her *ex*-boyfriend, are you not?"

Carlos's lips thinned. "I don't see how that's any of your business."

"I second that," I added, although in all honesty, I was somewhat thankful that the hunter's attention remained on Carlos since it meant that we were no longer talking about my orgasms.

"Is he not an ex?" the hunter demanded, the power off him climbing up another notch.

I rolled my eyes. "You know what? Carlos is right. This *isn't* any of your business."

A muscle ticked in his jaw. "How can you say that after we—"

"You know, I have a bone to pick with you." I planted my hands on my hips and figured that now was as good a time as any to bring this up, since I had no intention of speaking to the hunter after today. If I wanted to know if my theory was correct, now was my only chance. Besides, it stopped the Fire Wolf from divulging what he'd been about to reveal of our . . . ahem . . . *extracurricular activities* this morning.

The hunter's gaze narrowed. "What bone to pick?"

"Who's Katarina Varga?"

"Why do you ask?" he asked haltingly.

"Because I'm curious to know if you've been lying to me the entire time I've known you."

Carlos's eyes widened. Yep, shit was about to get real.

The hunter cast Carlos an irritated glare before saying quietly to me, "What makes you think I was lying to you?"

"Because I've come to the conclusion that the only reason you offered to find Tessa was to help you with another job you'd taken. So tell me, were you hired to find Katarina Varga?"

That unreadable mask descended over his face.

"I'm right, aren't I? You didn't come to my apartment because you had a change of heart after I'd tried to hire you in the Shadow Zone. You came because you knew Katarina and Tessa were most likely abducted by the same person, and that was because I'd mentioned Star Tattoo Guy's tatt to you just before you disappeared into your portal."

His jaw clenched, but he still didn't reply.

Gods, I am right. I crossed my arms, then shook my head at how easily I'd been duped. "Were you ever going to tell me that you'd been hired by Matija to find his daughter? And that you were using Tessa's magical footprint as a way to find her?"

His expression faltered for the merest second. "How do you know all of that?"

"Because I'm smart. I heard things, and Tessa told me enough that I figured it out. So tell me, were you ever going to come clean and admit why you'd taken my job?"

"Why does this feel like a trick question?"

I scoffed. "So it's really true. I'm right. You only took my job because Katarina's trail had grown cold and you knew you could find her by scrying for Tessa."

His mask slipped again as a trace of worry rolled across his features, before he bit out, "It was a smart business decision."

I crossed my arms. "Is that the closest I'll get to a confession?"

"Tala—" He growled, then raked a hand through his hair. His growl increased when he caught Carlos eyeing us. I had to admit, my ex was looking a bit too intrigued by this conversation.

The hunter glared at him again, then gave my ex his back, blocking us from Carlos's view, before saying softly to me, "Why are you making it sound like I did something wrong?"

Because you did. You should have been honest with me. And you never should have alpha-compelled me to tell you my secret.

7

Or seduced me. Or given me two earth-shattering orgasms, 'cause now every time I look at you—

I took a deep breath, willing myself to gain control of my emotions. Thankfully, my practical side kicked in. I remembered again that the hunter had probably made the decision to take my job based on calculated risk, pure and simple, because he'd needed to find Katarina. Following Tessa's trail was the easiest and quickest way to do that. *And* he would make twice the profit since I'd offered to pay him too. Win-win. I couldn't blame him for that, but it still hurt.

It hurt that he hadn't been honest with me. It hurt that he'd seduced me so easily and pried my secret from my lips like child's play. And all of that pain told me I was too emotionally invested in this—in him—and needed to take a huge step back. A clean break was the only way to untangle myself from this messed-up mating shit that had been born between us.

I tilted my chin up, looking him in the eye. "Just answer, will you? Was I right? Did you take my job because scrying for Katarina wasn't working anymore? Did you think that you could find Katarina *and* Tessa, since Tessa's trail was still fresh?"

He frowned, and I could see the wheels turning in his mind. A hint of demon fire rolled in his irises before he said, "Yes, that was the reason I took your job."

"So the part about having a change of heart was a total lie?"

His frown increased before he replied hesitantly, "It might have been."

"And when that blue-haired fairy said they got a heads-up about you coming, was that from Matija?"

"No, but it was from somebody in Matija's camp. I'd sent Matija a text to tell him where I thought his daughter was before we left, which means that he has a traitor in his mix. That's how they knew I was coming and were able to ambush me, and it's probably how his daughter got abducted in the first place. Matija's aware and is working to correct that."

I placed my hands on my hips. "And were you ever going to tell me any of this?"

This time, the dude studied me for a full ten seconds before he responded. "No. I didn't see a reason to."

I made myself not react, but inside, my heart cracked. Dammit, it *cracked*.

Too invested. I'm too invested in this.

"Thanks for answering honestly." I wrapped my coat tighter around me and turned my back on him. It was time to make my getaway and be done with the Fire Wolf. Our business was officially over.

I took off at a brisk pace down the sidewalk, and Carlos hurriedly fell into step beside me.

In the next moment, the hunter was walking on my other side. "What do you think you're doing?" he snarled over my head to my ex.

Carlos stiffened. "Escorting Tala to the Supernatural Forces. I'm here to help her." Carlos's hand drifted to my waist, as if he were intent on propelling me away from the menace of the Shadow Zone, but . . . sigh . . . that was a mistake.

Before I could blink, the hunter had Carlos pinned to a tree three yards away. I stopped dead in my tracks, my jaw dropping even though I knew this was normal mating behavior for an alpha whose chosen female hadn't accepted him. The dude was simply acting on instinct and my earlier suspicion was turning out to be entirely accurate. The hunter was territorial as fuck.

The scent of the Fire Wolf's illusion spell drifted around me. Thank the gods. At least he was sane enough to hide what he was doing from the humans walking by on the sidewalk.

"Don't. Touch. Her." A low growl rumbled in the hunter's chest.

Okay, maybe he wasn't that sane . . .

Carlos's eyes widened, but then they narrowed. "It doesn't look like she wants you touching her either. From what I can see, you have no claim on her."

The hunter's nostrils flared before he slammed my ex into the tree again.

Carlos groaned. "She's okay with me walking her, though." The corner of his mouth kicked up.

Oh, for fuck's sake. This was worse than I'd thought it would be. Both of them were now occupied in a pissing contest. Werewolves, seriously, but ah-ha! Silver lining.

I used the opportunity to make a beeline for the street corner. As much as Carlos had intended to help me today, I wasn't so stupid as not to see what he was really doing. Yes, he was honest in his intentions to help me, but given his recent text messages, he was also looking to rekindle our relationship, which wasn't something I was interested in.

And if the dude felt like pushing the Fire Wolf's buttons, I wouldn't get in his way, but that was on him, not me. I had shit I needed to get done today.

I whipped my phone out and began furiously tapping. With any luck, I would be in a hired ride, driving away, before either of them had put their dicks back into their pants.

I was one tap away from confirming my ride when the sound of footsteps came from behind me. I hurriedly finished the request, before swinging around to find *both* men staring at me. Carlos was now keeping his distance, and he kept giving the hunter wary glances.

So much for a quick getaway.

"I'll escort you to the SF." The Fire Wolf's hands fisted.

"I don't need an escort."

His gaze flashed to Carlos, then back to me, as if saying, *you were going to let* him *escort you.*

I merely raised my eyebrows. *Clean break.* We needed a clean break.

The hunter glowered but something flashed in his eyes. Worry maybe? "Tala," he growled, before he prowled closer to me.

I jumped back. "Keep your distance, please."

He stopped, his frown turning into a glacial scowl.

Carlos's lips twitched, and the hunter shot him a

murderous glare at which my ex wisely wiped his face clean.

"Tala, I can help you." The hunter's plea came out through gritted teeth.

"I don't need your help, thanks. I'm just fine on my own."

"Tala," he snapped. "Why are you being so difficult?"

"I'm not being difficult. If anything, *you're* being difficult. I'm merely stating the obvious. I don't need you to escort me to the SF. I'm a big girl."

His scowl grew even darker, especially when Carlos took another step in my direction. "So you're going to let *him* escort you?" the Fire Wolf demanded.

I resisted the urge to pinch the bridge of my nose, because I had no doubt the hunter was currently experiencing an overriding urge to claim me and mark me as his. The mating instinct was obviously sinking its teeth into him so deeply that he couldn't have fought that bitch off if he'd wanted to. Right now, he just wanted to stamp his ownership of me, and that reaction was only being heightened because my ex was present.

I bundled my coat tighter around me as I imagined what said ownership would look like. The dude would probably insist on tattooing my forehead with something like, *Property of Fire Wolf. Do not touch. If you do, I'll dismember you. And if that doesn't get the point across, I'll burn you in my black flames 'cause I'm a demon werewolf who's also something else as I have magic, but my chosen mate doesn't know what that other part is because we just met. But anyway, beware. She's mine.*

Yeah, no thanks. Because despite my undeniable attraction to the hunter, I wasn't going down that path. Any attraction he felt toward me was one hundred percent driven by his wolf, and well, I wanted more than that. The Fire Wolf's interest in me had only started after his wolf had gotten a whiff of my true scent. Prior to that, my arousal had merely amused him. *Amused* him. Hence, he wasn't *actually* attracted to me. He only wanted me now 'cause his wolf told him to, and I wasn't interested in getting wrapped up in that mating crap. I wanted something real.

My long blond hair blew over my shoulder while I continued waiting for my ride as the Fire Wolf's and Carlos's energies barreled into me from behind. I could only imagine what my ex was thinking right now.

I sighed and shot the hunter another annoyed stare. "Okay, seriously. I don't have the energy for this right now, so can you just go away? Please?"

"Why are you standing on a street corner?" He frowned, completely ignoring my request. Shocker.

"Because I'm waiting for my ride."

Carlos ran a hand through his hair, then asked hesitantly, "So just to clarify, am I understanding this right? He's interested in you, but you're not interested in him despite what he claimed he did to you this morning?"

Right, we were back to the subject of my orgasms. *Le sigh . . .*

The Fire Wolf made a discontented sound when I replied, "Something like that. Now, please, can I just wait for my ride in peace?" I gave my ex an apologetic look.

Carlos straightened his jacket and took a step toward me, although he eyed the hunter warily. As a werewolf who'd grown up in a pack, Carlos knew better than to push an alpha, which the Fire Wolf obviously was. Still, as a mid-level, Carlos was also used to having dominance over some, so he wasn't a complete pushover. "I can still come with you. I'm going there anyway."

Right. The whole reason my ex had shown up on my doorstep was because the Supernatural Forces was now willing to search for my sister. And since Carlos had begun working for the SF again, he'd offered to deliver that news to me personally. Only thing was, the Fire Wolf and I had already found Tessa. Still, the SF needed to know that Tessa's abduction was actually part of a much larger kidnapping ring.

A warning snarl erupted from the hunter. Apparently, my ex was standing too close to me again.

I muttered a curse at the hunter's animalistic behavior. I needed to nip this in the bud, because the Fire Wolf looked seconds away from shifting. And considering I'd seen how fiery his wolf could get, that was the last thing I needed. I kinda wanted my neighborhood to stay standing, not burned to the ground, because being homeless on top of everything else I was dealing with would be the icing on the cake.

Speaking of being homeless…

I planted my hands on my hips again and cocked my head at the hunter. "Do you know how Declan is?"

My question forced the Fire Wolf's attention to shift from my ex to me. His shoulders were still tensed, though, but he took a deep breath and some of the fire receded from his eyes. "He's fine."

"Are you sure? Did you actually check on him?"

The Fire Wolf nodded tightly and gave Carlos a side-eye again. "Actually, I did. I promised you I would, didn't I? Miranda's got him placed in one of their rehabilitation centers. Declan's got his own room and a roof over his head. He won't be back on the streets again."

Some of the ire died inside me. Because of the hunter, one less homeless kid was walking the streets in Portland, but that didn't mean the Fire Wolf and I would ever mate.

Carlos's gaze drifted from me to the Fire Wolf and back again. "Who's Declan?"

I shook my head. "Long story." I shivered again as I waited on the sidewalk. According to my app, my ride was still five minutes out. *FML, seriously.*

The Fire Wolf stepped closer, until he stood right beside me. "You know, I can take you there." He pulled his yellow crystal from his pocket. "You don't need to wait for a ride."

"No thanks."

"But you're cold."

"As I'm aware."

He growled and slammed a hand through his hair.

"Dammit, Tala, I could see your shivers a mile away. I'm just offering you a free and quick form of transportation."

I nibbled my lip. He was right. I was freakin' freezing, and a ride to the SF would probably cost me at least twenty bucks, but a clean break was the only way to do this. It was best to hold firm and not muddy expectations. "Thanks, but I'll wait for my ride."

His nostrils flared, but he made no move to leave, and when my hired ride finally pulled up, he opened the door for me. So he was back to being the gentleman. This was full-blown Courting Shit 101.

Once inside the warm cab, I was about to reach out for the door to close it, but the hunter was suddenly there, sinking onto the seat beside me before slamming the door.

"Um, what?" I sputtered. But then the door on my other side opened and Carlos slipped in.

I tilted my head back and sighed.

"Do you mind?" Carlos asked. At least my ex had the decency to ask.

"Whatever."

The Fire Wolf angled his body, his huge chest brushing mine, and my damned libido perked up. *Ugh.*

A sharp intake of breath came from both werewolves. Yep, my arousal was that obvious, but then the hunter growled a warning at my ex, his hand creeping possessively toward my thigh.

I brushed his hand away even though the contact made my nerves tingle. May the gods save me. I just couldn't win.

The driver cast the three of us an uneasy look in the

rearview mirror before pulling away from the curb. Even though the driver was human, it was obvious his instincts had detected predators in his midst.

I leaned my head back against the seat again as the car picked up speed. Because apparently all three of us were going to the SF . . . in *my* ride.

CHAPTER TWO

When we reached the Supernatural Forces' office, both men tried to reimburse me for my hired ride.

I rolled my eyes. "Put your wallets away. I'm not a damsel in distress."

The Fire Wolf's lips curved up while Carlos awkwardly stuffed his wallet back into his pocket.

Without waiting for either to reply, I strode toward what appeared to be a mom-and-pop barbershop but was in actuality the Supernatural Forces' office.

Their office sat on a street corner in the midst of a middle-class neighborhood. Two-story houses sprawled only a block down from the supposed barbershop. Nobody would have guessed that this was actually the gateway to the supernatural community's elite law enforcement and military.

The Fire Wolf and Carlos followed behind me, their

footsteps quiet. They hadn't argued on the ride over, but the tension strumming between the two was palpable.

I pinched the bridge of my nose and hoped that this would be a quick stop. My stomach was growling, and I still had to go to Practically Perfect and possibly work the rest of the day. Not to mention, whether I liked it or not, I needed to talk to Tess and learn what she'd disclosed to Jakub's people about my abilities. I wasn't looking forward to any of those things.

I stepped over the SF's threshold and the wash of magic tingled across my skin. The illusion of salon chairs and mirrors disappeared as the Supernatural Forces' office materialized in front of me.

Seated at the front desk was a familiar face. When I approached Jeff, he looked up from his computer screen, then rolled his eyes when he spotted me, but when he took in the Fire Wolf, that smirk wiped clean off his face, and he sat up straighter.

The hunter wore a blank mask as he assessed the office interior, yet Jeff's attention stayed on the Fire Wolf even when Carlos asked, "Is Commander Klebus free? There's been a development in the case regarding Tessa Davenport. It's important that we speak with her immediately."

Jeff nodded, attention still on the hunter. "She's in her office."

"Follow me," Carlos said.

The Fire Wolf silently prowled at my side as we followed Carlos toward the back offices. Jeff watched us the entire way. *Um . . . okaaaaaay.*

I shrugged off the receptionist's strange interest in the hunter as we wove through the halls, the turns familiar. Even though I wasn't a Supernatural Forces' member, I was no stranger to this building. I'd been seated in front of Commander Klebus more times than I wanted to remember, thanks to Tessa.

When we crossed the threshold into the commander's office, she looked up from her desk, her eyes like sapphire jewels. When she was human, I would have bet money her complexion had been a rich brown, but now it was as bright as molten gold, due to her vampire transformation.

A surprised expression formed on her face. "Tala?" She pushed to a stand, cocking her head, but when she beheld the scourge of society, a hopeful smile danced across her lips.

My brow puckered. And what the hell was that all about?

"Hello, Mr. King." The commander dipped around her desk, her eyes on the Fire Wolf and him only. "What a surprise to see you here."

Mr. King?

The hunter crossed his arms. "That makes two of us."

She didn't react to his disinterested tone. "What can I help you with?"

And just like that, she glided right past me with her vampire speed, as if I wasn't even there. *Um, what the hell?*

My mouth fell open as she avidly assessed the hunter.

"I'm not here to speak with you about *that*," the Fire Wolf said with bite. "I'm only here because of Tala."

That? There was a *that?* I frowned. What kind of secret was he hiding now? And what in all the realms? Were he and Commander Klebus an item or something? I tried to picture the two of them together and just . . . couldn't. As for the slight flare of jealousy that suddenly coursed through me, well, I was just going to completely ignore that.

"I see." The SF commander frowned. "Then what can I do for you, Ms. Davenport?"

"Her sister was abducted," Carlos replied for me. "We need to launch a full investigation. It sounds like it goes deeper than any of us have estimated."

"Is that right?" The commander gave another wistful glance in the hunter's direction—and now my curiosity was seriously piqued—before she glided back behind her desk and waved at the two chairs across from her.

"Have a seat."

Since there were only two chairs, Carlos took one and I the other. The hunter drifted closer and positioned himself directly behind me. Not so close that he was smothering my personal space, but close enough that it was obvious he was here for me.

A warm feeling drifted through my belly, and I wanted to kick myself for it. I reminded myself that the Fire Wolf's interest in me was only because of his damn wolf, and then I forced myself to remember the numerous times in the past forty-eight hours that I'd embarrassed myself when he'd detected my desire. Each time he'd looked amused. Amusement wasn't really something I was looking for in a life partner. So best to remember that and squash these ridiculous reactions.

"So you've confirmed that Tessa Davenport was indeed abducted?" the commander asked Carlos.

He gave a swift nod.

"Where is she now?"

"At our apartment," I cut in before Carlos could answer. "The Fire Wolf—err, Mr. King—and I rescued her last night from a dance club in New York."

The commander's eyebrows raised. "Rescued her how?"

I took a deep breath and glanced at the hunter. His eyes burned into me, those red flames appearing again. Just thinking about last night, about how close we'd both come to being killed, about how we would have been if my forbidden power hadn't saved us . . . I shivered.

The Fire Wolf placed a hand on my shoulder. It felt hot and heavy, yet also strangely comforting.

Despite the warm and fuzzy sensations his touch was giving me, I shrugged him off and shifted my attention back to Commander Klebus. "The Fire Wolf tracked her there, and then when he'd been inside the club for what I thought was too long, I went in too. I found him surrounded by six supernaturals in their underground rooms. They were talking about someone named Jakub, and we know someone named Damascus is also involved due to another incident. Long story short, we think the European mafia might be involved, or it could all be a cover to hide who really is involved. But anyway, a fight ensued, and we managed to get the upper hand. From there, we—or rather, the Fire Wolf—freed the other supernaturals also held imprisoned. There were seven total."

"There were others?" the commander asked sharply.

The Fire Wolf grunted. "Six others beside Tessa."

"Where are they now?"

"Back at their homes."

"Do you have names and locations?"

"I do," he replied dryly.

"I'll need that information."

"Of course you will."

The commander ignored that jab. "And you say that two men—Jakub and Damascus—are responsible for their capture?"

"Not Damascus," the Fire Wolf cut in. "He's unrelated."

I frowned. "But in that alleyway in the Shadow Zone with the half-demons, you were asking them about him and Katarina, and—"

"That was a bad lead." The hunter's jaw tightened. "Damascus is a known pedophile involved in illegal gambling rings. I tracked him because Katarina was underage and someone he would have coveted, but he isn't involved in the abduction ring led by Jakub."

That information hit me like a pile of bricks. And then it all made sense. Of course, Damascus wasn't involved. Because when I'd first encountered the Fire Wolf, with the half-demons beating him bloody outside of the Black Underbelly, the hunter had been trying every avenue he could think of to find Katarina Varga—all because she'd been gone for too long and his scrying was no longer accurate. Damascus must have been a lead he was grasping for, but when that lead proved fruitless, and I'd told him about Star Tattoo Guy's constellation tattoo, the hunter had decided to come knocking on my door. Or rather, not knocking, but breaking into my apartment.

I turned in my seat to face the commander as I clenched my teeth. Once again, I was reminded that the hunter had lied to me.

"So you believe that the only supernatural behind Tessa's abduction is a person named Jakub?" The commander's expression was calculating as her attention drifted between me and the hunter.

When I didn't reply, the Fire Wolf gave a curt nod.

"Have you confirmed that Tessa is safe?" Commander Klebus asked Carlos.

My ex's lips parted before a sheepish expression overtook his face. "I meant to, but things got rather"—he looked at the hunter—"complicated," he finished.

"She's at our apartment now," I added.

The commander picked up her tablet. "I'll dispatch a team to confirm her whereabouts. She'll also need to be brought in for questioning in order to learn as much about her abduction as she can recall." The commander sent off a message, then her attention shifted to the hunter again. "You tracked Tessa single-handedly to this club in New York?"

"I did."

She sat back in her chair, a contemplative look forming on her face, before she straightened and pulled a crystal sphere from her drawer. "I'll need a full write-up of what occurred during the past few days, down to every detail of what happened in that club. Mr. King?" She slid the crystal toward the hunter, bypassing me completely.

He scowled and crossed his arms. "Not interested. I'm only here because of Tala. She can tell you what she wishes to disclose."

The commander's nostrils flared, but after a lengthy staring contest, in which the Fire Wolf didn't even blink, she finally slid the crystal in my direction. "Tala, would you please assist?"

I lifted my hand but before placing it on the crystal, I cocked my head and said, "You were wrong, you know, not to believe me about my sister being abducted. I hope you remember that if she's ever in trouble again."

The commander inclined her head, although she looked far from contrite. "Noted."

I barely suppressed my eye roll. With a shake of my head, I set my hand on the crystal. Magic activated, tugging on my mind and memories, and then words began flowing across the commander's digital tablet as the crystal charm extracted my memories quickly and efficiently. Not even a minute passed before the report was complete, the majority of the last few days' events translated into a flawless digital format.

I hid some of the details, though, namely everything about the hunter's man cave, since he didn't want that location known. And, of course, all details of what had occurred inside said man cave, specifically my night spent in the hunter's bed, in which he'd uncovered my true scent. That particular moment was when the hunter's wolf side had taken a very keen interest in me. So that embarrassing encounter was definitely *not* something I wanted to share.

And another was the scorching kiss the hunter and I had experienced in the alleyway before he'd launched himself inside the club to rescue Tessa. Oh, and then this morning when he'd made me scream a second time. Yep, definitely hadn't disclosed those moments either.

And last but not least, I'd hid all things associated with my forbidden power. It was bad enough that some of the fights I'd been engaged in divulged just how diverse my witch powers were, but it was another matter entirely to announce to the world that I harbored a power that no other supernatural could claim.

The commander began swiping through the pages on her tablet, speed-reading the six-page report. Several times her brow furrowed, and she darted glances at me and the hunter.

When she finished, she set her tablet down and pursed her lips. "So it sounds like you believe the European mafia may be involved, and somebody by the name of Jakub is running this abduction ring?"

"Correct," I replied.

"And what's this about a key?" She frowned.

I shrugged. "I'm not sure. It's something the blue-haired fairy said. That Jakub is looking for a key."

"A key to what?"

I shrugged again. "Your guess is as good as mine."

I was about to ask what her plans were going forward, but she turned to the Fire Wolf. "You were really able to track her sister twice with perfect precision?"

The hunter's jaw locked, but his face remained blank. "I was."

"And that tracking ability is something you're able to do on all of your hired jobs?"

He didn't reply, but his eyes became hooded, guarded almost.

The commander sighed and clasped her hands. "I wish you would reconsider our offer. The Supernatural Forces would pay you highly for your time and abilities. I can have the contract drawn up—"

"As I've said before, I'm not interested."

"But surely with the right price, we could reach some sort of agree—"

"Not happening."

The commander's nostrils flared. "Very well, but I'll still need the names of the others held captive in that club."

The Fire Wolf grumbled but snatched the crystal charm. The names of those he'd rescued, along with their cities, appeared on the commander's tablet, but that was it. The hunter didn't divulge any other details.

When finished, he tossed the charm back onto her desk. It thumped and rolled across the surface before she caught it from tumbling off the edge.

She gave the hunter a pointed look, then tucked the charm back into her drawer before addressing me. "We'll be in touch if more information is needed. We'll take it from here."

"Take it from here?" My eyebrows shot up. "What does that mean?"

"It means the SF will be investigating this further. As Private Lopez has probably told you, the SF will open a full investigation into this matter. It does indeed sound like it's more complicated than your sister's sole abduction."

"Yeah, it is, especially when—" I bit my lip. I'd been about to say *especially when Jakub wanted me, not Tess*, but then realized that would shine the spotlight on moi. Commander Klebus would undoubtedly want to know why I was such a prize, and that would literally put me back in my original predicament of not wanting the SF or the supernatural community to know about my forbidden power. It was bad enough that the hunter knew, but hopefully it stopped there.

I frowned, still not feeling as if the matter had been put to bed, because the reality hadn't changed—Jakub had wanted *me*. But did he know it was me who harbored the powers he craved? Or did he still believe Tessa owned them? I grumbled internally as I stood from the chair. I still didn't know, because I wasn't aware of what Tessa had revealed since I'd been too mad at her to get to the bottom of it.

But despite our fight, I needed to find out, because if Jakub knew . . .

Well, who was to say he wouldn't come hunting for me or Tessa a second time?

CHAPTER THREE

"Thank you again for bringing this to our attention, Ms. Davenport. We do appreciate it. I'll walk you to the front." The commander waved toward the hall.

Right, I was being dismissed. I followed her out of her office, the hunter right behind me and Carlos behind him. When we got to the waiting area, the commander dipped her head. "Have a good afternoon. Thank you again."

"Same to you, but wait—" I made a move to touch her arm, but with vampire speed she rounded on me.

"Yes?"

"Will you keep me informed about what you find?"

Her lips pursed. "That is highly irregular. The SF does not share information with civilians."

I rolled my eyes. "Even civilians who bring you the information that opens up an investigation?"

Her expression turned glacial. "If we uncover something that directly affects you, we will inform you. Otherwise, no, Ms. Davenport, I will not be sharing our intel."

I sighed, not entirely surprised by the commander's response, but it felt weird to be actively hunting for my sister one minute and then sitting on the sidelines the next.

"I suggest you return to your daily life and do your best to forget this nasty experience," she added. "The SF will get to the bottom of this. You can rest assured."

I almost replied, *if you say so*, but managed to bite my tongue. Not trusting myself to contain further snarky comebacks, I simply nodded.

I expected the commander to retreat to her office, or some other area where they conducted super-secret and uber-important magical meetings, but instead she sidestepped to the Fire Wolf.

"Mr. King, in case you ever change your mind." She held out a card. Even from the two yards of distance between us, I could see that it held her contact details.

The Fire Wolf's hands stayed at his sides. "I already know how to reach you."

The commander arched an eyebrow. I could tell that she was about to launch into another speech about why he should accept whatever they were offering him when Carlos drifted to my side.

"Please tell me you're not really involved with that guy," he said under his breath.

My eyebrows rose. Carlos stared down at me, his expression pleading.

"And if I was?"

A flash of anger flickered across his face before it disappeared. "That guy is bad news, Tala. I'm worried about you."

"How do you know he's bad news?"

"We've all heard of him. The SF has been trying to recruit him for years. I have no idea why. The guy has a questionable reputation. That's not the kind of person we need in our organization."

I crossed my arms. "Is that what she was talking about when we first got here? When he said something about not being here for *that*?"

"Yeah, she and a few other commanders have tried to get him to work for us, even though in my opinion they never should have started."

"So you're too good for him?"

"No, it's not that." He raked a hand through his hair as Commander Klebus kept talking behind us, but then he angled his body so that I couldn't see the hunter or commander and was forced to focus entirely on him. "It's not just his questionable practices when it comes to his occupation. It's also how he conducts himself. The man's part demon. That right there says you need to watch yourself."

I laughed, unable to help it. "The SF has plenty of half-demons on staff."

"But half-demons that are also womanizers? He's known for being one. Did you know that?"

"Why would that matter?" I tried to keep my tone light and disinterested, but a quiver ran through my belly. "I'm not with him."

"I hope it stays that way, for your sake," he added quickly. His dark eyes filled with concern. "Look, I'm not trying to tell you what to do, but I'd stay away from him, Tala. I would hate to see you caught up in something in which you're only going to get hurt. From the little I've seen, I can tell that he's already done something to unnerve you." He took a step closer. "Did he hurt you?"

Anger laced his tone, and while I appreciated that he cared, I wasn't a child. "First off, I'm a big girl who is perfectly capable of making her own decisions even if you're worried. And second off, I don't think it's that simple. Did you not see his reaction to me?" I lowered my voice more, practically hissing, "He thinks I'm his *mate*. Until he gets over that, I have a feeling he's going to keep pursuing me."

Carlos's nostrils flared, and his gaze drifted over his shoulder to where the commander had cornered the hunter. Given the energy pulsing toward us, I didn't know how much longer the Fire Wolf would stay there. I was surprised he'd allowed himself to be cornered at all, but then wondered if the commander was upping her ante. Maybe she was now offering him a deal he couldn't refuse.

Swinging his attention back to me, Carlos took a shallow breath. "I don't know what the hell that was back at your place when he stepped through his portal, but he's not a normal werewolf. I don't know how he can feel you're his mate. The guy doesn't even have a pack, yet he's never turned rogue, so that tells you something. You know that all werewolves who avoid other wolves eventually turn rogue, so whatever he feels for you, it can't be the normal mate instinct. It's probably something more fucked up, so be careful. I don't want to see you get wrapped up in something that leaves you . . ."

My lips parted at his implication. *That leaves you hurt.* That was what Carlos had almost said.

Carlos knew how hurt I'd been when he'd left me three years ago, but I'd gotten over it. I was *still* over it, even if he was interested in rekindling our relationship. But something else he'd said made me pause. *Can't be a normal mate instinct.*

While I knew Carlos wanted the Fire Wolf gone 'cause *he* was interested in pursuing me again, I also knew that Carlos wasn't the manipulative type. He was truly worried for my safety and well-being, even if he did want to hookup again.

So I mulled over his comment instead of replying. *Can't be a normal mate instinct.*

Carlos squeezed my hand, then leaned down to whisper softly in my ear, "I hope to see you again soon," before he pressed a soft kiss to my cheek.

Heavy footsteps suddenly came from behind me, and in my next blink, the hunter was at my side, scowling at my ex. Carlos took a step back, releasing my hand as his throat bobbed in a swallow, but then defiance shined in his eyes. "You have no claim to her."

"Back off, pup. She's not interested in you." The Fire Wolf took a menacing step closer to my ex.

Carlos shot me a glance as if to say, *See? This is what I'm talking about.*

However, I knew that if Carlos was more dominant and had decided I was his mate, then he'd be acting the same way, so I wasn't really digging his self-righteousness either. Werewolves were notorious for being possessive and territorial around their females, and since the hunter had decided I was his female, well, his behavior was par for the course.

The hunter gave my ex another warning glare before saying to me, "Are you ready to go?" His words were deep yet filled with a coolness that bordered on icy even though he'd addressed me, but then he bared his teeth at Carlos.

Ah, so my ex had stepped too close to me again. I rolled my eyes. Even if the Fire Wolf wasn't a normal werewolf, he was certainly territorial as hell and *that* trait was one hundred percent wolf-driven even if Carlos claimed otherwise.

Carlos mumbled a curse before giving me another weighted look.

I shook it all off, my head beginning to pound. It was only midday, I was hungry, and I hadn't been to the store yet. And all of this possessive cock-preening? It was giving me a headache.

"Tala?" the hunter said, his warmth drifting to me when he stepped closer to my side. "Are you ready to go?" His palm settled on my lower back. The heat from it penetrated my shirt, and even though it felt blissfully warm and tingles danced up my spine, I stepped away from his touch and pulled my jacket on. *Clean break.* It was the only way.

"Yeah, I'm ready to go, but I'm good on my own. Thanks for everything you did for my sister. I'll wire you the rest of your money this afternoon, but our business is done, okay?"

I met his gaze, not allowing myself to react when flames leapt to life in his irises. He held eye contact with me, not moving.

"Is that what you want?" he finally asked roughly.

I released a breath, not realizing I'd been holding it. A pang of remorse filled me, but I shoved it down. I wanted something real, not a mate-driven relationship in which the male had never genuinely wanted me before Mother Nature pushed him into it.

"It is." Before he could say anything else, I strode out the front door.

I didn't glance over my shoulder—I didn't dare to—but considering the heavy energy barreling into my back, and the low growl of discontent, I knew the hunter wasn't happy. But he didn't follow me or try to stop me. For once, the hunter respected my wishes, even though I knew he was fighting his wolf fang and claw.

I KEPT UP A SWIFT PACE. Block after block passed me until I reached the L train. I jumped through the doors right before they closed, then finally glanced behind me to see if the hunter had followed after all.

He hadn't.

Nothing but bare sidewalk and the platform greeted me.

I sank low into a seat, nibbling on my lip. *Can't be a normal mate instinct.* Carlos may be right. Or he may not be. Whatever the case, it didn't change my decision. A clean break was the only way for me to quash these feelings and continue on with my life.

I pulled out my phone. A few old texts from Carlos waited. He'd tried to reach me several times while my purse had been in the hunter's man cave. Each text conveyed concern, even more so when Carlos had become aware of my report filed with the SF.

Since I didn't see any point in replying now, I didn't. Instead, I pulled up my banking app. I owed the hunter ten thousand dollars, and it was the last tie I had to him. Once I paid him, our business would officially be over.

A wave of nausea swept through me when I watched the remaining money in my retirement account melt away. When the transfer was complete, I stared at what remained.

A hundred and thirty-eight dollars.

After years of saving, doing my best to be responsible for the years ahead—since I knew Tessa wouldn't be—that was what I had left. A hundred and thirty-eight dollars.

Needing a pick-me-up, I texted Prish.

> So much to tell you. I'm back in Chicago. We rescued Tess. The SF is aware of everything. Meet up tomorrow? I gotta work tonight.

Her response came a moment later.

> Yes! Gods, I have so many questions. If I wasn't with my mother right now, I'd be calling you.

> I promise to tell you everything tomorrow.

> Okay, see you then. Love you. xx

> Love you too. xo

After stuffing my phone back into my purse, I wrapped my arms around myself and watched the city drift by. I tried to think about the store, the conversation I would need to have with my sister, and my upcoming get-together with Prisha, but as much as I tried to distract myself, my thoughts kept circling back to flame-filled eyes and the tightness around the hunter's jaw when I'd run away from him at the Supernatural Forces.

But I'd done it. I'd made a clean break, and now, it was time to get on with my life.

CHAPTER FOUR

Somehow, I managed to lose myself in work that afternoon. While Nicole and Sajid had kept the shop afloat over the past few days, a number of deliveries had come in that still needed to be processed.

I spent a few hours cataloging and inventorying everything. Tessa never showed. While that wasn't surprising given what she'd been through, a tiny bit of resentment filled me. The last few days hadn't exactly been peachy for me either, yet here I was, elbow deep in boxes doing the grunt work that kept our business afloat. But perhaps Tessa was at the SF answering questions so legitimately couldn't be here.

One good thing did come from the afternoon. I offered Nicole a manager position, complete with extra pay and added bonuses, and she'd accepted. She'd actually been ecstatic, thankfully, so now I could start delegating more work to her, which would hopefully lighten my load, even if that meant my pay would need to take a cut.

"You sure you don't need any more help?" Nicole asked as she flipped off the lights at the front of the store. Nine o'clock had arrived so quitting time was finally here.

"I'm fine, really, I am," I assured her.

Behind her, Selena was straightening items on a few of the shelves. As one of our newer part-time employees, Selena was still learning the ropes, but she showed up for each shift and had a willingness to learn. I appreciated her so much for that.

"All right, if you're sure." Nicole slung her bag over her shoulder. "Selena and I are gonna split. I got class in the morning, so I won't be here to open, but Alex is on too, so he'll be here with you."

It wasn't lost on me that she didn't mention Tessa. Practically Perfect's employees were so used to my sister being unreliable, that half the time, they acted like she wasn't also a part owner.

"Thanks, Nicky. Now go on and get outta here, and thanks again for everything. I don't know what I would have done without you over the past few days."

She beamed, a large grin splitting her lips. "I was totally happy to do it. I've been waiting for you to offer me a management position."

I laughed. "I should have done it sooner."

She sauntered back to the front and grabbed Selena before both disappeared out the door. Hearing the bell jingle reminded me that I'd have to craft a new illusion enchantment since the Fire Wolf had destroyed the original one.

"Just add it to the list," I mumbled to myself with a sigh, before returning to what I was doing.

TESSA WAS ALREADY ASLEEP when I got home. Not surprising since it was after ten o'clock. Her cracked door greeted me when I tiptoed down the hallway, and I peered inside her room.

Her hair was splayed across her pillow, and a soft snore drifted up from her. Despite our fight, a fierce wave of love bloomed through me. A part of me was terrified that she'd be taken again. Jakub was still out there, and it suddenly struck me that I needed to place some serious protective wards around our apartment. Prisha and her father had offered to do it for me years ago, but I'd never seen a need for it. Now, I wished I had. I had no idea if the bad dudes knew where we lived, but if they did . . .

I should do it now.

A heavy feeling filled my head when I contemplated how much magic that would take and how time-consuming it would be. I wasn't proficient in protective wards around something as large as an apartment, so it would no doubt take several attempts before I got it right, and I was already freakin' exhausted.

Tomorrow. First thing tomorrow.

With that decision firmly in place, I took a short

shower, brushed my teeth, and put my pjs on before crawling into bed. A quick check of my phone had my heart leaping when a text appeared from an unknown number.

Convinced it was Jakub, I swiped it open with a knot of dread balling in my stomach.

> Hope you sleep well tonight. Kaillen

My breath rushed out of me. Not Jakub, but the Fire Wolf.

I looked at those words as I sat in stunned silence. The Fire Wolf had kept his distance since I'd fled the SF, but he was still wide awake considering his text came through only twenty minutes ago. He also didn't seem to be taking the hint that we had no reason to communicate anymore.

As for how he'd gotten my phone number, I wasn't sure I wanted to know.

But *Kaillen,* hmm? That was what Miranda, his vampire collaborator in Portland, had called him. So the Fire Wolf's given name truly was Kaillen. And Commander Klebus had called him Mr. King.

Kaillen King.

So that was his birth name? And it was a name he'd now given to me to use, except I didn't have any intention of keeping in touch.

Nibbling my lip, my stupid stomach flipped when another text came through from him.

Thinking of you.

Oh. My. Gods. He did *not* just say that, and my heart-beat did *not* just trip.

This was ridiculous. *His wolf was ruling him.* Two days ago, the man had found my arousal amusing. Now he wanted to bang my brains out. *'Cause his wolf told him to.*

"Gods." I flopped onto my pillows. *Put your phone away.*

I picked my phone back up and studied his number. It was an area code I didn't recognize. A quick internet search placed the area code in Montana. Huh, who would have thought. I had assumed it would be Portland, Oregon, but it wasn't, so what did that mean? Did he have another man cave in Montana?

Of course, I didn't know, 'cause I'd only known the dude for three days.

But I *did* smirk that the menace of society had a cell phone and he texted. A few days ago, after I'd called Jenkins for a contact following Tessa's abduction, Prisha had insisted that the Fire Wolf would have a phone despite Jenkins' assurances that the Fire Wolf *didn't* have a contact number.

Smart lady, my bestie.

But while replying to Mr. King was bad idea #1, I *could* save his number, which was actually a smart thing to do in case Jakub came knocking and took Tessa again. Even though I didn't have the money to hire the hunter a second time, I could find a way to pay him again, somehow, if needed.

My ridiculous stomach did another dip when I saved his number in my contacts, although I didn't call him Kaillen. That felt too familiar. Instead, I programed him in as I knew him—Fire Wolf.

I was about to put my phone away when another text rolled through.

> Check your bank account.

Say what? Frowning, I did as he said and pulled it up. My mouth dropped, like seriously *dropped*, just like a cartoon character's, when I saw that twenty thousand dollars had just been returned to my retirement account.

I sputtered and before I knew what I was doing, I was replying to his text.

> Why did you give me the money back?

His response came immediately.

> I don't want it.

> Why?

> Because I enjoyed working with you.

That declaration hit me right in the gut. I put my phone on silent as fast as I could and flipped it over on my bedside table so the screen wouldn't glow if he texted again. So many emotions were rolling through me. This was anything but a clean break, and despite my imagination wanting nothing more than to fantasize about a scorching fuck-fest with the scourge of society, I didn't allow myself the luxury.

It was over between us, even if he'd returned the money. His wolf would move on, and when he did, the Fire Wolf would realize he'd never wanted me in the first place and would no doubt be freakin' ecstatic that I'd saved him from the old ball and chain.

Reminding myself *again* that nothing good would come from an affair with the hunter—so *no*, I couldn't pleasure myself by thinking about him—I pulled my covers up around me and rolled to my side.

"Do you like that?" the Fire Wolf rumbled as he kissed along my neck, his erection rubbing against my entrance. The hunter straightened, still kneeling behind me as my body quivered on all fours. He palmed his length and rubbed me again, then slid the tip in.

I gasped.

"I take it that's a yes." I could hear the smile in his voice, and when I glanced over my shoulder, lust making my gaze clouded, he grinned.

He slid in deeper until I was moaning so low that the sound vibrated my entire body. His large frame leaned over me again, until his chest rubbed on my back and his mouth brushed against my ear. "I can make you come a dozen times between now and sunrise," he whispered. "All you have to do is ask." He pushed in more, his thick girth stretching me.

I arched, grinding my ass against him, begging him to enter me fully. My body felt so hot with need for him that my belly was aching.

"Please!" I panted. "Fuck me! Please!"

He chuckled, a deep, knowing rumble that rippled through my belly and went straight to my core.

"Anything for my mate." He slammed his length inside me, his huge erection filling me to the hilt.

I screamed, then writhed and gyrated against him, wanting more, more, more, as he began to pound me in earnest. Oh, fuck, YES! This was what I wanted, what I needed, what I craved—

A scratching noise came from behind the hunter, and the dream began to fizzle.

No! Gods, this dream was amazing. I didn't want it to end, but my ears pricked when I heard the noise again. A splintering sound?

The dream faded further. I reached out for the Fire Wolf, wanting the dream-fucking to continue, especially since a part of my conscience knew this was the only fucking I'd ever be getting from him.

But then the sound of my window creaking snapped my eyes wide open.

What the hell? I bolted upright, the dream disappearing completely just as two figures dove through my window, executing perfect somersaults before leaping with catlike grace toward me.

My foggy brain didn't even know what was happening

until they were on top of me. A lash of pain ensnared my limbs when one whipped a binding spell around me. The other slapped a hand over my mouth when I tried to scream.

I cried out in a muffled tone as I attempted to claw at his hand, but the binding spell held.

"No!" It was the only word I got out before all sounds died from my lips. Acid hit my tongue. My voice was *gone*. I screamed, or wanted to, but nothing came out. They'd *taken* my voice with a gag spell.

Oh fuck, oh fuck, oh fuck.

My heart pounded as I became *very* awake.

"Take her out the window," one of the men growled in a low voice.

I fought against the binding spell more, calling upon my magic. I tried to cry out too, but no sound came, and the acid taste grew. Fucking gag spell.

I was carried halfway across the room when reality hit me. These were Jakub's men, and I was being taken. Just like Tessa had been. Without a doubt, the same outcome was the intention. I would be transported to a distant cage with Jakub as my master, which meant they knew that *I* held all the power. Not Tessa.

FUCK!

Panic exploded in my veins, and my magic erupted. It cut through the binding spell, and in a tidal wave of power, it shattered. I lashed out, my legs kicked, my entire body flailed as the binding spell cracked around me in a shower of sparks.

A rush of power shot through my veins, and I kicked out over and over again at the two men attempting to abduct me.

"Hold her!" one of them barked.

The bigger one pinned me from behind, his thick arms wrapping around me, and a memory flashed in front of my eyes. Tessa being taken. Meaty hands on her. Star Tattoo Guy overpowering her and holding her down.

I tried to cry out, but despite the binding spell shattering, the gag spell still held.

But just as that spell began to falter, too, the one holding me slapped a band of cuffs around my wrists. Zinging pain sliced through my hands and forearms, and a draining sensation pulled at my witch magic, but the gag spell had already faltered. A small yelp escaped me.

I tried to call on my witch powers again, but they had me at the window now, both of them pushing and grunting as I fought, and I couldn't concentrate enough to harness it. My eyes bugged out when I saw a carpet hovering just outside of my third-floor bedroom.

An enchanted carpet. From the fae lands. Hovering in mid-air here on earth. And it was *outside of my bedroom window.*

We would literally be flying away in seconds. My home would be gone. No trace of my struggle would be left. Tessa would simply think I spent the night at Prisha's because she hadn't seen me come back tonight.

I can't get on that carpet. I can't get on that carpet. I can't get on that carpet.

The intruder at my back shoved me hard toward the window, but I slammed my feet against the wall as fresh terror hit me like a million volts of electricity. I tried again to call upon my witch powers, but the cuffs' buzzing magic had wilted them to nothing.

"Bind her!" the one holding me grunted.

The other sorcerer whipped out a spell, and then . . . all of my movements stopped.

The new binding spell held, the power of the cuffs draining my witch magic so much that I couldn't fight through it.

They're going to kill me.

And knowing *that* . . . terror like I'd never felt before *consumed* me.

Out of nowhere, gushing black magic rushed into me as the two supernaturals threw my lower half through the window. A sliver of my still functioning mind recognized what was happening. *My new power.*

But that thought was there one second and then gone the next because *my legs were dangling outside.*

More black magic rushed into me. A surge of raw fury sliced my insides. Foreign magic pummeled me, so dark and angry, as the man holding me from behind groaned and staggered. His grip slipped, and my upper half fell backward.

"Rigger?" the other one said.

My legs flopped. I couldn't move with the new binding spell in place. The carpet hovered only feet away as the first supernatural struggled to hold his grip while his magic barreled into me.

My vision grew dark as whatever this awakening power was inside me unleashed itself. *Please not now.*

So *much* angry magic. Too much.

"Rigger, get the fuck up!" the first one yelled in a thick accent.

But Rigger's magic continued slamming into me, the large supernatural growing weaker by the second. His power filled my soul like a snarling beast. His sorcerer magic mixed with my witch magic until it felt as if lightning coursed through my veins, but I couldn't unleash it. Not with the cuffs' containing my power.

I tried again to move my arms, to break the cuffs as I focused on the first supernatural, but the binding spell held.

But the cuffs didn't contain my awakening power.

Invisible tentacles of my new magic slithered from me toward him. I could *feel* them. They felt like strands of light intermixed with zapping power. Sweat dripped into my eyes, and my vision blurred again.

Just stay conscious. Don't pass out!

Concentrating on those tentacles of power, I begged them to listen to me and imagined wrapping them around the first intruder like an octopus's arms.

They responded, and a jolt of power hit me when they clamped onto him like the jaws of a shark, jagged teeth serrating through his magic. A brief swell of victory hit me even though my hands were still cuffed, and my body was like a rag doll. *You're mine.*

His rage hit me first. Then his fear. I sank my claws deeper into him. He cried out as his magic bubbled out of him like a cauldron blowing its lid. It poured into me, soaking all of my cells. So much. *Too* much.

My vision darkened again. I couldn't hold on.

The smaller man also fell to my bedroom floor. Both were down now, and writhing around in pain, as my heart beat so fast it felt as though it would stop. My legs were still outside, my back awkwardly arched over the windowsill with my arms behind me. My hands were still cuffed, but at least the intruders had stopped trying to get me through the window.

Another blast of power hit me. Nausea made my stomach heave as the magic pummeling me doubled. So much magic. *Too much. Too much. Can't breathe. Can't think. Must get inside.*

Rigger bucked, which shoved me upward, and I slid out of the window farther, my butt now barely perched on the ledge. He continued to twitch like a flopping fish, every movement from his large body propelling me closer to the edge.

Oh gods.

I struggled internally against the cuffs again, anything to pull myself back inside, but the binding spell held as the sorcerers' potent magic hit me again and again and again.

Power. Gods, so *much* power. I was drowning in it. Their magic was suffocating, knifing through me in never-ending slashes. I screamed in agony—a loud scream as my voice finally broke free from the remnants of the gag spell.

I fell another inch.

"Help!"

I tried to propel myself back in as gravity threatened to claim me, but my limbs wouldn't respond, and the tremendous magic hitting me over and over was like being smacked into by a freight train in unrelenting punches.

Blackness danced across my vision as my heart *pounded*.

A moan came from one of the men just as more cold air caressed my skin.

I'm going to fall.

My door whipped open. "Tala!" Tessa screamed.

I felt my twin, felt our bond stretch and pull toward her as she leaped across the room, but then a large hand grabbed my shoulder, but it didn't pull me inside.

It pushed.

And despite all of the power that I'd stolen from the two men, despite the ocean of magic surging through my veins, I couldn't fly.

That final shove broke what little hold I had on the windowsill. I slid out.

Coldness greeted me first, and then air.

A scream followed, but it wasn't my scream.

Tessa.

The air rushed past me as my stomach shot into my throat. I plummeted downward as the second story windows sped by. The ground was careening toward me. So incredibly fast.

My body tumbled of its own accord. I twisted upward at the last moment and saw the magic carpet hovering above me, then the flash of a waxing crescent moon, and then Tessa's horrified expression as she strained out of the window, her arms extended as though trying to reach me.

It was all over in a heartbeat. So incredibly *fast*.

My body made a sickening crunch when I hit the concrete alleyway below.

Then I heard nothing at all.

CHAPTER FIVE

"Tala!"

The rough voice came from far away. So far away. As if in a tunnel. As if beckoning me from a distant nether world as I hovered on the precipice above it.

"Drink for me, Tala! Drink!"

My eyelids cracked, slitting open. I tried to open them fully, but they wouldn't obey. It was as though my lids weighed a thousand pounds.

"That's it. Stay with me."

When I finally cleaved them open a bit more, I saw darkness, and a sliver of pale moon. Then a pitiful sounding moan filled my ears before a blurry face appeared in my line of vision. A man hovered above me.

My eyelids slammed closed when the pain hit me. Such *pain*. Burning, aching, stabbing pain. It was everywhere.

I'm dying.

"Tala, fucking drink!" the voice snarled.

A hand tightly gripped my neck and yanked me forward as hazy darkness filled my mind. Something warm and wet pressed against my lips. The thick wetness coated my face, and a bead of it slipped into my mouth.

Rich, decadent spice rolled across my tongue in that one single drop.

"Tala, you need to drink."

I was floating. Hovering. Between this world and the next. But that rich liquid beckoned to me.

"Drink, Tala. *Drink!*" That voice called to me with so much agony but that last word was imbued with *power*. Alpha power. Commanding power.

Obey. You must obey.

I opened my mouth, my tongue lazily darting out, sluggishly, but then another drop of that sweet nectar hit my senses. A thimbleful of life flared inside me. I cracked my mouth open more, then lapped slowly at the rich liquid that was being held against my mouth. I swallowed. The liquid warmth coated my throat, burning down into my body as more of the sweet nectar filled me.

"That's it. *Drink again.*" The man's command was filled with razor-sharp precision and rippled with power. It was the voice of a general, a warrior, an alpha leading a pack of thousands, a force to be reckoned with.

Fire Wolf.

I faintly recognized him in the floating darkness. He forced me to drink, commanded it of me, over and over, so I did.

I didn't know where I was. None of this made sense because it felt as if I hovered between worlds. On one side, pain-free bliss stretched for eternity, only a hair's breadth away. All I would have to do is reach for it, *touch* it, and this pain would vanish. It would be so easy, so peaceful, because on the other side was a world of icy coldness, never-ending darkness, and such raw pain.

"Tala!" the Fire Wolf snarled again. "Don't you dare die on me, you hear me? You're not dying today. *Drink more!*"

His thick hand cupping my neck squeezed. My jaw hinged open, and a gush of rich nectar flowed into my mouth again. Gods, its taste was addictive, like honey wrapped in decadent chocolate with the zing of berries. It *consumed* me.

More of the liquid rushed forward as I swallowed, and another surge of strength flowed into me, the need to devour the liquid suddenly entrancing me.

I clamped onto the source, my lips wrapping around it as I sucked and pulled desperately. The nectar sprang forth under my greedy lips, rushing into my mouth like a fast-flowing river as I drank mouthful after blissful mouthful.

"Yes," the Fire Wolf said in relief. "That's it."

I drank and drank and drank. It was only after my belly sloshed with the liquid that I realized somebody was holding me. The beckoning scent of citrusy cedar wafted toward me. Strong arms enveloped me.

The pain began to ebb as I became more aware of my body. The hunter held me. No, he *cradled* me to his chest, and the pain didn't hurt as sharply as it had before. My lungs filled more easily with each breath, and the throbbing in my head eased. As my sucking became languid on the liquid's sweet source, my bones shifted. The sounds of cracking and snapping followed. Brief flares of pain accompanied those, but then they were gone and a dash of soothing coolness followed. All the while, the sweet nectar continued to gush forward and I lapped and sucked at it like a woman dying of thirst.

"How much more does she need? Is she going to be okay?" a woman asked.

"She'll live," the Fire Wolf replied.

"What about you? How much have you lost?" *Tessa.* That voice belonged to my sister. She was here too.

"I'll lose as much as she needs," the Fire Wolf rumbled against me.

I swallowed more as the aching and stabbing pains lifted from my body, as though an angel had descended from heaven and was healing all of my wounds.

Another man said, "Her bruises are disappearing, and her legs are no longer bent at odd angles."

That voice. I knew that voice too. *Carlos.*

But I kept my eyes closed, letting myself fall back into the fog of the sweet nectar, relishing every second of the sustenance filling me and the feel of the Fire Wolf's warm hard body pressed against mine.

"Is she healed?" Tessa asked in a small, scared voice.

Another deep rumble vibrated against me, the sound reminding me of a giant purring cat. "Almost."

I wrapped my arms around the hunter, pressing my

body flush against his. Whatever he was feeding me was like nothing I'd ever tasted. A swell of magic accompanied it, wrapping me in a cloud, caressing me in its warmth. I wanted to drink and drink and never stop. I wanted it, *craved* it, needed it to continue for eternity.

It was only as the pain completely abated that I became aware of myself straddling the hunter. My legs were wrapped around his waist, my arms entwined around his neck. He sat on the ground holding me as my head was dipped below his ear, just above his collarbone, and my mouth was—

My mouth was on his neck.

The decadent drink was coming from his skin. It was coming from the hunter's . . . *neck*.

My eyes flashed open as I took in my surroundings. My body felt strangely energized, as if I could climb a hundred mountains or run a thousand miles. Strength flowed through my veins, and amazingly, the pain had completely evaporated.

I broke contact with his skin as my head whipped back. "What the hell?" I whispered. I was in the middle of a concrete alleyway between two buildings in the dead of night. A carpet lay on the ground to my left, along with shattered metallic pieces that were a dull blue. I blinked. Above me, the sliver of moon hovered in the sky. "Where am I?"

"In the alley outside of our apartment," Tessa said quietly. A shiver struck her. "You . . . you fell from your window."

My head cocked, the movement not hurting in the slightest as my gaze flew upward.

Three stories up, my bedroom window was open, the curtains fluttering in the breeze through the open pane.

It all came flooding back then.

Waking from the delicious dream with Fire Wolf. Two figures diving into my room. The struggle as they tried to abduct me.

My eyes widened in horror. Carlos and Tessa stared down at me. Concern twisted their features.

I was still wrapped around the Fire Wolf. He continued to hold me in his arms as my limbs folded around him, but he was bleeding. A trickle of blood streamed down his neck, and my nostrils flared.

I could smell it. I could *scent* his blood—rich honey, molten chocolate, decadent berries.

I brought a fingertip to my lips, feeling wet stickiness coating my skin. I looked back at the Fire Wolf's neck, at the cut that was sealing over as I stared at it. "Did I . . . Did you . . ."

But I couldn't get the sentence out. I couldn't believe what I was seeing.

No, I had to know if this was *real*. "Did I just drink your *blood*?"

The Fire Wolf's blazing eyes flamed to life, the irises glowing like embers as his arms refused to loosen their grip. He was like a rock, a heavy immobile mountain that had positioned itself around me and was refusing to budge.

"Yes," he replied quietly.

I gasped and wiped at my mouth. Blood. I'd drunk his *blood*. Crimson droplets were smeared along my hand.

But I'd never heard of such a thing. The only supernaturals that gave blood were vampires who were transforming another. No other species did that, and the hunter wasn't a vampire. Or was he? *No.* He wasn't. I hadn't seen any vampiric traits in him.

"Why?" I whispered.

His jaw worked. "Because if you didn't, you would've died."

I shook my head. Disbelief coursed through me. His blood healed me? How was that possible? But then I remembered the Black Underbelly and how he'd healed after the half-demon attack. Healing like that shouldn't be possible.

I tried to push him away, especially when I realized how intimately we were entwined, but a memory of that rich liquid pouring down my throat, and the absolute bliss it had created, made me grow completely still.

He'd just saved me.

"I don't understand," I finally said. "You weren't here."

"I called him to help." My twin sister twisted her hands and glanced at us, then at my ex- boyfriend.

Carlos stood immobile at her side, his gaze shifting between me and the hunter. An unreadable expression covered his face.

Tessa wrung her hands more. "I didn't know what to do, so I called everybody."

"What happened?" I didn't know why I asked. I knew

what had happened. I remembered it, but none of this could be true. Surely this was all just another dream. No, a nightmare. Not a dream. The dream I'd had before, when the Fire Wolf had been holding me, *fucking* me, that had been a dream. That was fantasy, but surely this was too fantastical to be reality. His blood had *healed* me.

"I heard you scream," Tessa said quietly. Her body slackened, her hands falling to her sides. "I stumbled out of my bed into your room, but when I opened the door—" Her eyes grew distant, her expression haggard. "Two men were shoving you out the window, but something was happening to them. I didn't understand it, but all I saw was you being shoved out the window and you were so close to falling." Her face twisted, her lips turning into a grimace. "But I was too late. One of them pushed you, and then you were gone." Her voice broke in a sob. "I ran to the window hoping that I could grab you, but I was too late. There was nothing I could do."

The Fire Wolf stiffened, his arms tightening around me.

Tessa looked down, her chest heaving, and her lips trembled as she continued. "Those two men stopped moving after you hit the ground. I could *hear* when your body hit." She shuddered. "And when that happened those men just . . . died." A haunted look flashed across her face. "And I knew you were going to die too. I was frantic. I was in a panic, but then I saw your phone. I unlocked it, and the Fire Wolf's contact was on your screen." She looked at the hunter. "I called him and told him what had happened. And then I called Carlos because I knew he was in town too.

And then I called the Supernatural Forces. I was going to call an ambulance, but then the Fire Wolf was just *here*. He was in your room, and when he saw you, he leapt out of the window, so I rushed downstairs, and I was going to call for more help, but he said he would take care of you."

The Fire Wolf's arms grew warmer around me.

I lifted my gaze to his, to the fire in his eyes, to the strength in his features. I licked my lips, and some of his blood coated the tip of my tongue. That luxurious burst of flavors again hit my senses. "But how does your blood heal?"

"I have exceptional healing abilities, but I can't heal others. The only way for me to do that is to share my blood."

Is that something you do regularly, I wanted to ask, but I didn't voice the burning question.

I shifted slightly, testing my limbs and joints. Everything rolled and moved smoothly, as though I hadn't just fallen three stories, landed on concrete, and shattered everything. "And the men that attacked me? Where are they?"

"Still in your room," Carlos replied. He stood off to the side, watching my every move. "The SF will dispose of the bodies after we've studied them. We'll want to check their identities in the database and decipher what magic they used to gain access to your apartment. Three stories up along a smooth wall is a feat even a skilled supernatural would struggle with."

"They had an enchanted carpet." The image of the thick

fabric hovering outside of my window popped to the front of my mind.

"They did? On earth?" Carlos frowned. "Are you sure? Maybe you're not remembering—"

I waved at the carpet lying beside me. "It's right there." Admittedly, the carpet now looked like a used, discarded old rug. There didn't appear to be anything magical about it.

Carlos's frown grew.

I brought a hand to my head, then realized I was moving my hands. But they'd *cuffed* me.

"What happened to the cuffs?" My gaze skittered to the shattered metallic pieces on the ground. Tiny shards lay everywhere. A fractured memory returned of hitting the ground on my back with the cuffs beneath me. Had the impact shattered them or had the magic from the sorcerers being snuffed out nulled the cuffs' power, making them easily breakable?

I had no idea.

I waited for a headache to begin, to throb in my temples, given all that had happened, but I still felt *good*. So normal. No, not normal. I felt energized, invincible.

"I think the men who broke into my room are tied to Jakub," I said to the hunter.

Flames erupted in his eyes. "I'd assumed so. I'm guessing these metallic blue shards on the ground were the cuffs?"

I nodded, then cursed my stupidity. "I should've put protective wards around our apartment before I went to bed. I knew it, but I was so tired. All I wanted to do was go to sleep so I didn't, and look what happened because of it."

Tessa rushed forward, collapsing onto the ground beside me just as a flurry of activity erupted near the mouth of the alleyway. The SF had arrived.

"You couldn't have known," she said in a soothing voice as she placed her hand on my shoulder. "None of us could have."

The familiar touch and feel of her helped quell some of the uneasiness that was blazing through me. I grasped her hand, unable to believe that we'd argued yesterday. How could we be fighting when twice now our lives had nearly been snatched from us?

I shifted, unwrapping my legs from around the hunter, but he still held on to me in his lap, as though reluctant to let me go.

The group of Supernatural Forces' members strode briskly toward us as I pulled my sister into a hug. "I'm sorry about yesterday," I whispered.

She gripped me tighter, the familiar feel of her making my heart ache. "I'm sorry too."

Hearing her apologize made my eyes scrunch closed. Tessa very rarely apologized for anything. It seemed the both of us were realizing how closely we'd come to losing each other.

I pulled back and licked my lips. "But I have to ask you something. Did you tell Jakub about—" I eyed Carlos. Even he didn't know the extent of my power. He knew I was more magical than I let on, but he didn't know about all of it.

But I didn't need to continue. Tessa knew I was asking if she'd told the supernaturals in New York that it was actually *me* who harbored what they craved.

She shook her head vigorously. "No, I didn't. I swear I didn't, not even when they were threatening me."

When I saw the sincerity in her eyes, I knew she wasn't lying. "Then they must have mixed us up, thinking I was you." It wouldn't be the first time something like that had happened. Being identical meant it was hard for others to tell us apart, but this was certainly the most dangerous mix-up we'd ever been in.

I pulled back from her when Commander Klebus reached us. She led a group of six squad members. They had weapons drawn and glowing devices around their wrists. They all wore the signature black SF suits, the obsidian fabric gleaming like night.

"We had a call about another abduction," she said briskly, her astute attention appearing to assess everything at once.

"That was me!" Tessa squeaked. "I called you. Those men came back, but they tried to take Tala this time, not me."

The entire squad studied me, which wasn't surprising considering that I still sat on the Fire Wolf's lap.

"We need to secure the area," the commander said brusquely.

"The area's secure to the best of my knowledge, Commander Klebus," Carlos said, his spine straightening.

"You're sure?"

He nodded. "I am, ma'am."

"Very well. Thank you, Private." Her eyes narrowed as her gaze landed on the Fire Wolf. "Mr. King. Twice in one day. That's a first."

He grunted but didn't say anything further.

"If the area's secure, we'll need to start collecting evidence. Patterson and Wokawitz, check the back alley. Lopez, grab your supplies from the chest and check for magical signatures. Cheng and Merrick . . ."

She continued giving commands, but I tuned her out as a buzzing sensation filled my skull. "This really isn't a dream, is it?" I muttered more to myself than anything.

The Fire Wolf's arms tightened, and I suddenly became aware that he still had an arm snagged around my waist. Even though I'd released him to hug my sister, he hadn't let go, and it struck me that not once, in all the time that I'd been hovering between life and death, had he let go.

CHAPTER SIX

I stood in my bedroom, as SF members combed through my apartment. Cloaking and illusion spells shimmered everywhere, hiding all of this from my human neighbors. The magic that surrounded the area was enough to make my head spin.

My arms stayed wrapped around myself, disbelief now settling upon me like a heavy, soaking rain. I'd nearly *died*, and that realization was only now fully hitting me.

Commander Klebus and the Fire Wolf were in the room too. The hunter's heavy energy strummed toward me as the commander grilled him about what he'd seen.

The other SF members worked around the building, collecting evidence, studying magical footprints, and assessing for remnant energy. It all felt like a dream, a horrible twisted dream that I couldn't wake from.

Tessa's tinkling laugh drifted to me from the living room, startling me in its sharpness. A male laugh followed.

Of course, she'd charmed one of the SF members. I was pretty sure he was going to ask her on a date just as soon as his shift finished.

I felt the Fire Wolf's eyes land on me again. I couldn't stop myself from returning a glance in his direction. Nor could I stop my attention from fluttering down his body, taking in his broad shoulders, firm waist, and muscled thighs.

He stood tall and unyielding. Defined muscles strained against his shirt, his dark hair was a tousled mess, and his amber-hued eyes swirled with barely controlled violence. His chiseled features clenched, a muscle continually ticking in the corner of his jaw. An aura of menace clouded around him, and I had a feeling that he was barely holding himself in check. He was angry. I'd known that from the moment my head began to clear as the high from his potent blood dissipated. Not angry with me, but angry at what had happened to me.

The hunter had positioned himself near my bedroom wall, like a giant predator ready to pounce. His gaze left me to follow a new SF member who hurried into the room to join those studying the sorcerers' bodies.

The Fire Wolf had been like that for the past hour, scrutinizing everyone who entered and exited my room even though his conversation with the commander was ongoing.

My heart rate sped up, and his gaze cut to mine again. The dude had probably heard the sudden uptick.

Tapping a finger on my forearm, I wondered how much

longer this was going to take. Now that the effects of the hunter's blood were wearing off, and the adrenaline of my potential abduction had faded away, fatigue was rolling in. And damn if I wasn't bone-weary.

Commander Klebus frowned as she crouched beside the two dead men in my bedroom, her brown skin shining like gold. "This is the one thing I can't make sense of. *How* did they die?"

For a moment, I thought she was asking herself the question, but then realized she was looking at me. Despite my exhaustion, *that* question snapped me upright. "Cause of death?"

"Yes." The commander's lips pursed. "I don't see any obvious trauma."

I did my best to maintain a cool expression as I frantically searched for a way to explain their sudden demise. It needed to be a convincing one, because the two men who lay sprawled across my bedroom floor had such grotesque expressions on their faces, it was as if they'd seen the devil himself right before they'd passed.

But they hadn't seen Lucifer. Only me.

I swallowed the unease that crawled up my throat. I'd literally just spent twenty thousand dollars to keep my forbidden power a secret, and even though that money had been returned to me, that wasn't the point. And now I had this *new* power erupting inside me that I neither understood nor knew how to wield. The only thing I knew was that it was good at killing people who were trying to kill me.

But I didn't really want that info spread around either . . . Damn, this whole secret-keeping business was becoming quite a headache.

I shifted my weight to my other foot. "Um, they—"

"I killed them," the Fire Wolf cut in.

My eyes widened, but his expression gave away nothing.

The commander straightened, and placed her arms akimbo. "How?"

"A death curse."

"But there's no trauma."

He shrugged. "Not all curses have outward trauma."

Her eyes narrowed, but he was right. Most death curses left a crater in a person's chest—most, but not all. Some were like a poison, killing you instantly without any sign of infection.

The vamp commander's nostrils flared. "You know you can't go around killing supernaturals as you please. You aren't above the law."

"As I'm aware," the hunter drawled, "but last I heard, it was within my rights to kill any supernatural that attacked my mate with intent to maim or harm."

He did not just say that . . .

The commander's lips parted. I'd never seen the vampire looked so stunned. Given the expression on her face, it looked as if she'd just been told she won the Powerball.

"I—" She cleared her throat. "I didn't realize you'd been mated."

"I am now." His expression didn't waver.

I didn't know if he'd finally recognized what was happening to him or if he was grabbing at the one law that would allow him to kill on my behalf. I wouldn't put it past the shady fucker. Thanks to some law written in the 1800s, which allowed mated male werewolves to defend their mate even if that led to the death of another, many male wolves had avoided prison time. If not for that law, pretty sure most of them would be in there now.

But by claiming *me* as his mate to help me avoid any fallout? A tiny thread of gratitude wove through me. Once again, he was saving my ass.

"Very well," the commander said after she'd smoothed her shocked expression. "But we still have one very important question left to answer."

I stood up straighter. "What's that?"

She turned her full attention on me, her eyes piercing. "Why did they try to abduct you? I thought it was Tessa they wanted."

I cleared my throat. So that wee, tiny detail wasn't going to go unnoticed after all. "Keep in mind that Tessa and I are twins. They probably thought I was my sister."

The commander made a noncommittal noise. "That does make sense." She studied me a moment longer, as though dissecting me. I had a feeling she knew I was hiding something, but she hadn't figured it out yet. She signaled a few SF members over. "Please take the bodies to the processing lab."

"Yes, ma'am," they replied in unison.

Once the dead intruders were packed up and removed from my bedroom, I looked at my bed and wondered how I would ever sleep in it again. I'd felt safe here. This was my home. How many times had I gone to sleep in that bed without a second thought as to whether or not I would be harmed during the night? Now, even if I placed protective wards around our apartment, I didn't know if I'd ever feel safe here again. My hands curled into fists. *Fucking Jakub.*

"Ms. Davenport?" Commander Klebus called from my doorway.

I startled, my hands relaxing. "Yes?"

"The SF would like to offer you and your sister protective custody. Would you like to venture to Boise to stay at headquarters?"

I swear the vamp could read minds. Or maybe it was just the twisting expression on my face as I'd stared at my bed that did it. But Boise?

"Thanks. I really appreciate the offer, but we have a business here. We can't just up and leave."

She dipped her head, her short hair brushing her chin. "I understand that, but if your sister's safety is in jeopardy, and by association yours too, then that's another matter. However, if you decline to stay at headquarters, the SF can provide two squad members to guard the premises, but I can't guarantee your safety. If the supernaturals who broke in through your window were using an enchanted carpet on earth, then I do question the extent of their magical capabilities."

Translation—even two fully trained SF members may

not be enough protection against another attack. Like Carlos, Commander Klebus had been gobsmacked when I'd told her about the enchanted carpet, and for good reason. Those didn't work outside of the fae lands. It required too much magic to power them here on earth, so whoever was pulling the strings with these abductions . . .

They were hella powerful.

I ran a hand through my hair. "We can stay with my friend, Prish—"

"They can stay with me," the Fire Wolf cut in.

They? He was going to allow my sister to stay at his man cave too? But Portland was even more of a commute than Boise. "Thanks, but we still need to stay local. Our business really can't be left for weeks on end."

The commander arched an eyebrow, probably thinking a lover's quarrel was on the horizon. *Oh gods. Talk about mortifying.*

She gave me a wan smile. "I'll leave you to make your decision. The offer for two squad members stands firm. Let me know what you decide."

"Will do, thanks," I replied.

The Fire Wolf didn't make any attempt to leave. He stood tall and brooding-looking as the SF finally cleared out, then he followed me into the living room. His steps remained silent, yet I could feel his energy. It was heavy and dark, matching his mood.

Carlos had lingered, unlike his squad members. He pulled me aside at the front door as the hunter and my sister stood by the couch. Tess began trying to charm the Fire Wolf, but considering the hunter seemed more interested in Agent Orange, who was swimming lazily in his tank, I didn't think her charms were working.

"You shouldn't stay here," Carlos said in a low tone. "It's not safe."

I nodded, smothering a yawn. It was almost four in the morning, and I was beginning to wonder if I would ever get a full night's sleep again without something disastrous looming over me.

"I know. We won't."

I expected my ex to nod and leave, but instead his head dipped. "The squad was saying that you're mated to *him*. Is that really what you told Commander Klebus?"

"I never said that."

In the living room, the Fire Wolf stiffened. His back was still turned to us, but I knew he could hear everything we were saying despite Tessa prattling on.

"That's what they all think."

I shrugged, irritation prickling me. "So? Let them think what they want."

"Are you saying that doesn't bother you? To know that the community will believe you're *mated* to him?" Carlos sneered the word, letting me know perfectly well how he felt about that.

I crossed my arms just as the hunter began prowling toward us. Yep, he'd definitely heard everything. "I didn't realize you'd become so interested in what others thought of me."

Carlos scowled. "Of course I care what people think of you. I care about you."

"Could have fooled me."

"What's that supposed to mean?"

But he had to know. When he'd been gallivanting around the world and I'd been here, pining away for him, he hadn't exactly given two shits about how I was doing or what people were thinking. But that was all water under the bridge now. There was no point in rehashing the past.

"Never mind." I sighed when the hunter appeared at my side.

"Tala, is this one bothering you?" the hunter asked, his gaze promising retribution.

"Yes, he's a threat to be eliminated."

Carlos's jaw dropped.

"I'm kidding," I added in a hurry.

Carlos gave the Fire Wolf a withering stare. "You should mind your own business. I was speaking with Tala privately."

The hunter crossed his arms.

Gods. A pissing match was on the horizon again.

"She's not your girlfriend," Carlos added.

The Fire Wolf's eyes narrowed. "She's not your girl-friend either."

"Guys, seriously." I held my hands up between the two men. "As cute as this little duel is, can we not? It's like four in the morning, and I don't know about you two, but I have to work tomorrow."

They continued staring at each other, but when a push

of power exuded from the hunter, Carlos let out a furious snarl and bared his neck.

Yep, one point for the Fire Wolf. He was bigger, badder, and more dominant. Whoop-dee-do.

"You can both see yourself out," I added.

Carlos shook his head and went out the door, but the Fire Wolf didn't budge. "You can't stay here," he said with a frown.

"As I'm aware."

"Then where are you going?"

"We'll stay at my best friend's house, you know, Prisha? You met her in the Shadow Zone when I tried to hire you to find Tessa, and you told me to fuck off."

"I didn't tell you to fuck off."

"You kinda did."

He sighed heavily. "Well that was then, and this is now. You should stay with me. I can keep you safe."

"Where? In your man cave? Don't you think that'd be kinda crowded?"

"I don't live there. It's just a base."

"So where do you live?"

His jaw locked, and a flash of something shone in his eyes. When he didn't reply readily, I was reminded that the dude was as secretive as hell. He didn't even want me, his supposed mate, to know.

Clean break. Once again, I needed to establish a clear boundary.

I shook my head. "Just forget it, okay? We'll go to

Prisha's. Come on, Tessa," I called over my shoulder. "We'll crash at Prisha's until we figure out what to do."

"Let me get my things," she called as she finished feeding our goldfish.

When she zipped back to the bedroom area, I finally faced the hunter again. Blazing fiery eyes met mine.

"Why are you looking at me like that?" I asked mildly.

"Because you're refusing to come with me."

"Um . . . 'cause I don't even know where we're going. Remember how you refused to tell me?"

"I didn't refuse, I just—" He raked a hand through his hair.

When he didn't continue, I arched an eyebrow.

He cursed quietly. "I live in Montana, okay? I have a home there."

So the area code on his phone was his actual residence. "Why didn't you just say that in the first place?"

"Because I don't share that information with many. That location is private."

Ah, so the big bad wolf didn't like people knowing his postal address. I got that. He was the scourge of society after all. "Fair enough, but you do know my sister has one of the biggest mouths in the world, right? If you took us there, half of the community would know by the end of the week where your digs are."

He cast a dark glance toward the bedroom area. "As I'm coming to see. It's amazing you two are related. You're nothing alike."

I shrugged. "True. Even though we're identical twins,

our personalities are quite different, but while I appreciate the offer to whisk us away to the Rockies, we still need to stay here. I wasn't lying when I told Klebus that we need to stay close for our business."

He frowned. "I could transport you every day."

My eyebrows shot up. "Through your personal portal?" That was quite a commitment.

Luckily, Tessa interrupted with two suitcases in tow. She huffed, looking winded even though she'd only carried them twenty feet from her bedroom.

"Will you carry these?" She dropped them at the hunter's feet. "They're so heavy."

He didn't reply but easily picked them up. "Where are your bags?" he asked me.

"Not packed yet. Be right back." I hurried to my room and threw some clothes and toiletries into a backpack. When I returned to the living room, I had it slung over my shoulder.

The Fire Wolf looked between my small bag and the two massive contraptions my sister had packed. He held out his hand to take my pack too.

"I'm good." I kept the backpack strap over my shoulder. "And thanks again for offering to put us up, but we'll stay with Prish. It'll be safe there." My bestie's family always had protective wards around their homes. Too bad I hadn't taken them up on the offer to ward mine.

"Are you sure she's okay with that?" the hunter pushed.

I rolled my eyes. "I've already texted her to give her a heads-up." Since Prish hadn't responded, I knew she was sleeping and her phone was on silent, but we both had open door policies with each other, so I was confident she wouldn't mind me staying. But as for my sister . . . That one I wasn't so sure about. I'd have to ask Prish tomorrow if she was okay with Tessa crashing at her place too.

The hunter was scowling when I looked back at him. I had a feeling he wasn't used to being denied anything.

"Thank you again for . . . saving me." Even to my ears, that statement sounded lame, but I had to end this—whatever *this* was—between me and the hunter once and for all, because we were yet again getting tangled up in each other, and even though it was possible he was finally recognizing that I was his mate, it needed to stop.

CHAPTER SEVEN

Despite my not-so-subtle hint that things were once again over between us, the Fire Wolf accompanied Tessa and me outside. I figured when the ride I'd hired pulled up to the curb, I could bar his entry to the vehicle, but considering how well that had gone earlier today, I didn't know if he'd take no for an answer.

So we all stood on the sidewalk as cold night wind whipped around us. I tried to put distance between myself and the hunter, tried to make it clear that even though I was appreciative of all that he had done, that this *thing* between us couldn't continue.

But he kept drifting toward me, as though the wind blew him in my direction. I finally stopped trying to avoid him.

"What?" I asked with a sigh. "You obviously want to say something."

"I do." His eyes burned brighter. "You need to train."

Okay, *that* was a comment I hadn't been expecting. I straightened. "I do train, and I train pretty damn well, thank you very much."

"Not the kind of training you've been doing, but *new* training."

Despite telling myself not to ask, I found myself saying, "What do you mean?"

"Finally!" Tessa squealed. She rushed to the curb and waved at our approaching ride, which left me and the Fire Wolf alone on the sidewalk.

His amber-hued eyes blazed into mine. The joking expressions and seductive grins that he'd sported when we'd been looking for Tessa were nowhere to be seen. In their place, tight lines surrounded his mouth, and his energy ran high. "I mean that the power that's awakening in you is raw and unfiltered. You need to learn how to control it. To train it. It's incredibly powerful. Twice, it's saved you. And considering we haven't caught Jakub, you need to be strong enough to defend yourself if he sends someone to take you again. Your new power is the key to that."

Tessa opened the front door to the car. Puffs of exhaust swirled from the tailpipe. "Can you grab my bags?" she called to the hunter. She didn't wait for his reply before sinking into her seat and closing the door.

I waved the fumes away as the Fire Wolf made no move to help with my sister's suitcases. He continued staring down at me, his eyes now brimming with crimson fire.

"I know," I finally said. "Okay, yes, you're right. I need to learn how to control whatever's awakening inside me, but I don't know if now's the right time. I'm perfectly capable of defending myself without this new power. It's probably more important that I learn how to suppress it, so it stops interfering with my magic. Because training it will only draw attention to myself, and that's not something I want." Like my forbidden power, this new one was unique too. Neither was good to advertise.

"Tala," the hunter said in a low warning tone. "Have you stopped to think that maybe Jakub and his cohorts *know* about this new power of yours?"

I stilled as the Fire Wolf lifted my sister's suitcases and put them in the trunk. A part of me wanted to tell him to mind his own business. I was supposed to be making it clear we no longer had any reasons to associate, but I couldn't stop my biting curiosity.

I joined him by the back of the car. "But how could they?" I said, keeping my voice quiet. "Nobody knew about my new power before this week. Not even *I* knew what was happening."

Even though I'd had strange magical reactions during the past month, none of them were as powerful as what had unleashed itself on the warlocks in the insane asylum or the sorcerers who'd tried to abduct me tonight. During the past few weeks, I'd merely thought I was coming down with something and that was why my magic had been misfiring. Now, I realized it was actually the beginning of my awakening power manifesting.

He slammed the trunk closed, his expression grim. "There were cameras at that club in all of the rooms. It's possible there were witnesses to what you did to me when you sucked my power and then enhanced it."

My eyes widened. "But the fire you created—"

"It destroyed the cameras *after* the building went down, but if those cameras had live feed rolling somewhere, it's possible somebody was watching."

I just stared at him, unable to believe what I was hearing, as the scent of exhaust curled around us. So it was possible that Jakub not only knew about my forbidden power if he'd witnessed it on the cameras, but it was also possible that he knew about my *new* power too since it had briefly sucked the Fire Wolf's magic from him.

"You're saying that you don't think they mixed Tessa and me up tonight." I shook my head, frowning. "You think they know that the powers they're after belong to me and not her, even though she didn't tell them."

"Yes."

"But could they have known what was happening in the club—with my new power and forbidden power? How could they have known that I took your power by accident and then enhanced it?" But then I remembered what Tessa had told me. She'd bragged about my forbidden power to Star Tattoo Guy. They'd known about my forbidden power from the beginning. It was why they'd taken her. But now their cameras had revealed that it was *me* who held that power, not her.

In a rush, I explained to him what Tessa had told me

that morning—all of it. I didn't know why I was telling him. I knew that I was supposed to be pushing him away, telling him that everything was over between us, but icy fear now filled my stomach, and the thought of dealing with this threat on my own after almost being abducted . . . I suddenly didn't want him to leave.

He was scowling by the time I finished. "So they definitely know about your forbidden power." His jaw worked. "And I don't know what kind of cameras they had, but if they were enchanted, it's possible they were able to register your magical footprint, and during that encounter, your magic was off the charts. The logical conclusion is that they saw everything, including your use of your new power. It explains why they came for you and not your sister." The hunter dipped his voice even more. "And it would explain why they attempted to abduct you immediately after you fled, because they know what you are. They know that *you* hold all of the power, and they really want you."

Oh gods. I felt the blood drain from my face. Could he be right? That my secret, the one I'd spent *my entire life* hiding away, had been blown wide open for the entire community to know about? It was my worst fear.

I shook my head, not wanting to believe that Jakub and his men could know that much about me . . .

The Fire Wolf stepped closer to my side. "I can help you learn to control your new power and wield it."

My eyes shot to his.

Burning embers rolled in his irises. "I could train you."

"How could you possibly know how to train me?"

"I've seen your new power in action. I've felt it. I have a few ideas."

But I couldn't train with the hunter, with the wolf who wanted to claim me as his, and with the demon-born who my legs wanted to wrap themselves around at every second of every day.

If I thought I'd been pale before, that was nothing compared to the cold realization sweeping over my blood-less cheeks. Because all of the touching required during training, the magical flares, the erupting power . . . I could just see it all happening between us. We would be like two tornadoes colliding, an epic storm of unheard-of proportions.

In other words, we'd be fucking in no time, probably right on the mat in the middle of the training room. And then where would that leave me? I'd always wonder if what we had was real or merely the hunter's wolf driving him. And worse, what if I fell for him—really, truly *fell* for him—while his emotions for me were only a result of the stupid mate bond, not actual lasting love.

I remained silent as I studied the asphalt beneath my toes. This was why I'd wanted a clean break.

"We should go," I mumbled. I took a big step away from him, my heart pounding.

A questioning look burned on his face, but I swung away and hurried to the side door of the cab.

I slipped inside the car, and from the front seat Tessa

sighed and rolled her eyes at me. "About time. You guys were yakking back there for an eternity."

The driver grunted in agreement.

"Sorry," I replied in a clipped tone just as the hunter slipped inside using the other door.

So much for making an escape.

The sedan sagged when it took the brunt of the Fire Wolf's full weight. I felt him looking at me—his gaze ever watchful and assessing—but I didn't have the energy to say anything further. So I kept my attention firmly focused out my window as I bit my fingernails while the driver pulled away from the curb.

The entire drive, the energy crackling between me and the hunter rose, and I was surprised that sparks weren't flying in the air. Still, I refused to look at him.

When we pulled up to Prisha's high-rise, I bolted from my seat, welcoming the cold wind outside as it met my flushed skin.

I already had Tessa's massive suitcases on the sidewalk, with my smaller bag strapped to my back, when the hunter appeared silently beside me.

"Tala?"

I slammed the trunk closed as Tessa tipped the driver.

A harsh sigh came from the hunter. "Tala, we need to think about what's to come, even if it's upsetting you."

I paused, my back to him. Oh, so that was what he thought. That I'd gone all silent from fear of Jakub, not from fear of how my body would betray me if I allowed myself to train with him.

I finally faced him and did my best to sound confident. "Are you still going on about the *we* thing?" I met his gaze, unflinching. It was the closest I'd come to asking him about his *mate* comment earlier. "News flash. There is no *we*. I can handle this on my own." The truth was I totally couldn't, but maybe Prish could help me figure it out. At least I didn't want to bang her brains out when we trained . . .

Fire roared within the hunter's eyes, but I ignored it and spun around, then marched toward the door.

CHAPTER EIGHT

S o, my grand plan had been to leave the Fire Wolf in the dust. Of course, he didn't allow that.

After my harsh reminder that we were *not* a couple, the hunter's lips pressed into a thin line, but he still rode the elevator with us to Prisha's apartment. And from the elevator, he escorted us to her front door all the while watching our surroundings, his attention forever shifting to take in any threats which could potentially lay hidden in the well-lit hallways and beautifully decorated potted plants.

"They have good security here," I said when I pulled my key out to Prisha's apartment. "The potted hibiscus aren't going to harm me, and Prisha's entire apartment is warded. We'll be safe."

"Why wasn't your apartment warded?"

I shrugged as Tessa watched us. A curious expression was growing on her face.

"Never saw a need for it," I replied. The hunter glowered, and I rolled my eyes. "Until last week, I was an unknown supernatural just minding her own business in Chicago."

I gave my sister a firm glare, 'cause if she hadn't opened her big mouth, it would have stayed that way.

"Um, I'm just going to go inside." Tessa bumped into me in her haste to escape.

Once my sister was gone and it was only the hunter and me, I pocketed the spare key and stepped inside the foyer. The warded magic surrounding Prisha's apartment prickled my skin.

"When do you want to start training?" he asked, still in the hallway.

"I'm not training with you." I paused, and it struck me that I was acting like a complete bitch to someone who had just saved my life.

Really, Tala? But damn, I didn't know what else to do. I *needed* to keep my walls up with him. If I didn't, I'd probably fall so hard and fast that I'd face plant. Still . . . being an ass to him wasn't the best alternative either.

Taking a deep breath, I softened my tone. "I'm sorry, but I can't train with you. Thank you for the offer though, and for what you did earlier. For saving me when Tessa called you. For returning the money to me. For all of it. Seriously, thank you."

An unreadable expression descended over his face. "Why does this feel like goodbye?"

"Because it is."

The bright lights above him highlighted his dark hair that I knew felt silky soft. It was so tempting to reach for those strands on the nape of his neck, to thread my fingers through them, and pull him in for another—

Nope! Not thinking about that.

I nibbled my lip as anxiety bubbled in my stomach. *Why* was he still just looking at me and not saying anything?

His nostrils flared, and he toed the line of the doorway, halting when the wards flashed. His gaze drifted to my mouth, to where I nibbled my lip. A flash of heat blazed in his eyes, and I abruptly stopped chewing it.

"You need to train. The offer stands."

"Good night." My heart hammered to life as I shut the door. And *dammit*, from there, I stood on my tiptoes and looked through the peephole.

In the hall, the hunter raised his gaze skyward before his lips thinned. He shook his head, then withdrew his yellow crystal. In seconds, his portal was swirling like a cosmic void before he stepped through it and disappeared.

A MOVEMENT on the mattress woke me. I peeled an eye open to see my bestie sitting cross-legged on the bed beside me, an inquiring smile on her face. Despite the curtains being drawn in the guestroom I'd nabbed last night, sunlight flooded the room, letting me know that morning had arrived.

Prisha's brown eyes were full of mischief, her dark hair

shining like obsidian. "Got your text about needing a place to crash for a few days. Does this have anything to do with a lover's spat? I heard the Fire Wolf offered his shack."

I groaned and pushed my face into the pillow. "Not you too."

Even though I wasn't looking at her, I could hear the grin in her reply. "Tessa filled me in. Mate, huh? Is that really what he called you?"

"Can we *not* talk about that?" I muffled into the pillow. I hadn't brought that up with the hunter last night, even though I'd been curious to know if he truly understood the bond now. But if he was aware, it didn't change anything. We were done.

I cracked an eye open again, grimacing at the light in the room. I figured it was still way too early to be waking up. Our store didn't open until eleven today, which meant I should still be sleeping right now.

But Prisha continued. "Tessa also said that two asshats tried to abduct you last night." All joking and smiles left her face. "And your text said you need to get wards around your apartment. I'm guessing the two are related?"

I rolled onto my side, blowing hair out of my eyes as I faced her. "Sounds like you got the full story."

"Yeah, I've already called my dad. He'll start crafting the wards tonight and have them done in a few days, but I need to know what's going on, so spill it. *All* of it."

I sighed. "Okay, fine, but can I at least have a cup of coffee first?"

She scrambled off the bed. "Coming right up."

An hour later, I finally finished telling Prisha everything that had happened. We still sat on my bed in one of her guestrooms. Yep, my bestie had multiple guestrooms in her ginormous penthouse.

The coffee was long gone, but she now knew about Portland and Declan, although I'd kept the hunter's man cave location a secret. She also knew about the insane asylum and the warlocks we'd encountered, and everything about Tessa's rescue and the scorching encounters the Fire Wolf and I had shared and how he now thought I was his mate because of my true scent. And, of course, I told her how two sorcerers had crept into my bedroom last night and had been killed with my new power, which was essentially why we were here in her apartment now.

But all of that was par for the course. The big thing I told her though—the *real* thing, the only thing that truly mattered—was the truth about my forbidden power. It was something I'd hid from everyone, even her, until now.

When I finished, Prisha blinked. Then blinked again. She shook her head, her black hair shining in the light as her expression remained clouded. "Wait, so you can enhance another supernatural's powers, which is something you've been able to do your entire life, and now you can also *suck* their magic from them?"

I dipped my head, shame washing through me. "I'm sorry I hid my forbidden power from you for so many years."

A moment of silence passed between us, and I could

feel her hurt and her questioning. It pulled at me like the tides. We'd never hidden anything from each other.

"I'm sorry," I whispered again. "I should have told you, but my mom made me promise—"

"It's okay. I get it, I do." She sighed. "Your mom told you to keep it a secret, so you did, but just so you know, I *never* would have told anyone."

I looked up, meeting her gaze, and I wondered why I hadn't just told her years ago. If Tessa knew—and, admittedly, she was someone who wasn't the greatest at keeping secrets—then how come I hadn't told Prish?

"I know you wouldn't have. I shouldn't have kept it from you."

"It's fine. I'm glad you've told me now." She plucked at a thread on the bedspread, then took a deep breath. I could tell she was still processing everything I'd told her.

"It's a lot. I know."

She laughed softly. "No shit." Her gaze grew curious, and she cocked her head. "And you really know how to use your forbidden power?"

"I do. I've been practicing in secret since I was a kid."

"And your mom didn't want you to tell anyone because of the Bone Eaters?"

"Yes."

Her nose scrunched up. "Who the hell are they?"

"No idea. I've never been able to discover anything about them despite trying to over the years, but she was seriously concerned about them, so I've kept my promise because of that."

"Do you think we should try to find out who or what they are? If the Bone Eaters are the entire reason your mother didn't want you telling anyone about your extra powers, maybe that's worth pursuing."

"You're right. It is worth figuring out, even more so now, since my powers are no longer a secret. I'll add that to the list of shit I need to do."

She gave a wry smile. "Especially if you now have some new power erupting inside you, and you don't know if those douchebags in New York know about that one too. Maybe they have ties to the Bone Eaters."

I stilled. I hadn't even considered that, but then I shook my head. I hadn't had nearly enough caffeine for this kind of talk. "This is a really uplifting conversation for eight in the morning, just sayin'."

She gave me a playful shove. "Just keepin' it real. And it's nine o'clock already, not eight."

I made a show of lifting my empty coffee cup. "Despite being severely de-caffeinated, you're right. I should be more concerned about whoever the Bone Eaters are, but honestly, that's the least of my immediate concerns since in twenty-five years, they've never shown up. And I never heard any mention of them from those douchebags in New York, and Tessa hasn't said anything about them. So right now, what I'm most worried about is Jakub-Dipshit, because if those cameras in the club did stream the live feed somewhere and were able to gauge magical footprints, it's possible Jakub-Dipshit and his minions know all about my forbidden power and awakening one."

"Jakub-Dipshit?"

"It's the name I've given him."

"It's quite fitting."

"I think so too."

She chewed on her lip, her skin glowing a light-brown in the morning sunlight spilling into the room. "And the Fire Wolf thinks you need to train this new power?"

"He does. It only ever comes out when I'm stressed or frightened, but it does just as much damage to me as it does to the people I hurt. I almost passed out several times last night when those two tried to abduct me."

"But you're still alive, and they're not."

I cocked my head. "True, it hasn't killed me, but each time it's erupted, it feels like I'm going to die."

A contemplative look came over her face. "And you have no idea where this magic comes from?"

"No, none, and like my forbidden power, Tessa doesn't have it either, only me."

"I wonder if my father would know anything about this."

I grimaced. "Then even more people would know the truth about me."

"My father's trustworthy. You know that."

"Yeah, you're right. It's just . . ." I thought about what my mother had warned me of when I was a child, to never tell anyone. "The last clear memory I have of my mom, is her telling me not to speak to *anyone* about this."

Prisha squeezed my arm. "You don't have to share it

with him if you don't want to. I'm honored that you shared it with me."

I hugged her, loving her so much it hurt. "You're family to me. I should have told you sooner."

Her arms tightened around me. "And you're family to me, the sister I never had."

I pulled back and thought about everything that Azad had taught me throughout my childhood—fighting, magical manipulation, discipline. Maybe telling him about these powers wasn't the wrong move. Maybe my parents would have wanted that since they were no longer here to help train me themselves.

I angled my head. "You know what? Let's do it. Maybe it's time I stop hiding who I really am from those I love."

Prisha's lips split into a grin. "It's been a while since we trained together. This may be fun."

"And I don't want to bang you, so it's really a win-win."

"Huh?"

"Never mind. Just a Fire Wolf joke."

She snorted. "Okay, so it's settled then. My dad and I are gonna help you figure this stuff out."

"I'm so relieved to hear that." And I was. It literally felt as if a huge weight had been lifted from my shoulders.

Because training with Prisha was a lot safer than training with the hunter. No sinewy muscles or chiseled abs for my fingers to wander across. Yep, training with Prisha and her father was definitely the right move.

Prisha and I accompanied Tessa to Practically Perfect since none of us thought it was safe for her to go anywhere alone anymore. Thankfully, my sister understood my request not to work with her today so that I could train with Prisha and her father instead.

I called the SF en route to the marketplace downtown and requested the two squad members that Commander Klebus had offered last night. A text message from the Fire Wolf lingered on my phone, but considering who it was from, I hadn't opened it yet.

When I finished the call, I gave Tessa a hug as we flipped over the *Open* sign on the front door. "Are you sure you'll be okay here today?"

She smiled, all cheer and happiness. It was the version of my sister I loved the most. At times, she was the most positive person I'd ever met, and her bubbling energy made it impossible not to smile. "Of course, I will be. Nicole will be here with me, and Selena's supposed to come in later too."

My eyebrows rose. My sister actually knew the schedule.

She curled a strand of hair around her finger. "Did the commander say which SF members were coming to be with me today?"

I cocked my head, scrunching my forehead up. "I think she said Private Patterson and Merrick."

Tessa beamed. I figured one of them who she'd been flirting with last night. I sighed. Only my sister would flirt with SF members after her twin had fallen three stories from a window.

I gave her an exasperated look. "Try to behave. And no disappearing today. I mean it."

Some of the happiness died from her eyes. "I won't. I promise."

Strangely, it was the first time I actually believed that she meant it.

Prish and I hung around until the cavalry arrived. Yep, Private Merrick was *definitely* the hottie my sister had been flirting with. She smiled coyly when he entered the store, and the crooked grin that lifted his lips told me he'd happily stay close to my sister's side all day.

"Guard her with your life, Private," I said to him before Prisha and I left. "I mean it."

He dipped his head. "Ma'am, it's an honor to do so."

I bit back my smile, because like most supes in our local area, he thought Tessa was the witch behind our magical concoctions and brews, and I was still fine to leave it that way. Just because some crazy dude in New York, or wherever the hell he lived, knew it was me and not Tess who held those powers, didn't mean that I was going to start advertising it. As unlikely as it seemed that my anonymity would remain, I figured I'd enjoy the remainder of it while I could.

"Bye!" Tessa said with a wave.

Prisha and I both gestured an arm in farewell before hurrying outside.

Thankfully, it was an uneventful trip to the facility we

trained in. Still, both of us kept our guards up, constantly checking behind and above us for potential threats.

But they never came.

"Do you think it's because I killed the two last night?" I asked Prisha when we stepped into her family's warded training facility, the familiar magic sparking along my skin.

She shrugged. "Or it's because it's broad daylight and there are too many witnesses."

"Yeah, could be that too."

"Betis!" Prisha's father, Azad, called to us before making his way over. Even though I wasn't his blood daughter, he still treated me as one.

"Hello, Pita." Prisha hugged him, then I did the same.

He clapped his hands, his mustache lifting when he smiled. "My daughters have come to train with me today. Tell me what sparks this fortuitous occasion?"

Prisha and I shared a glance. I twisted my hands. "Well, where do I begin?"

CHAPTER NINE

P risha wielded her sword in a blur of blue fire. I dipped and danced, sliding out of the way every time it arced my way. She'd been coming at me for over an hour, and sweat dripped from my forehead in a steady stream.

"Pull from her, Tala! Reach inside her and rip it out!" Azad stood to the side of the mat, the large gymnasium-like arena open and airy.

A scowl tugged at my features as I searched inside me for the area where my new magic lay. Unlike my forbidden power, which I kept carefully stored and could easily access, my new magic wasn't there to find. It'd only ever emerged when I'd been panicked or stressed. All other times, I could have sworn that it wasn't even inside me.

Hence, why my best friend was currently trying to kill me. It appeared that a near-death experience was the only thing it responded to.

"Faster!" Azad coached.

Prisha turned into a flash of fire and grace. Her figure lunged, coming at me again and again until she'd backed me into a corner.

I had to duck and roll to avoid being sliced open.

"Tala, *feel* for it, beti."

I grimaced and dodged the other way. "I can't." I gritted my teeth. "I don't feel anything!" I dove again at the last minute, then was finally able to leap away from my corner when Prisha's sword swung too low.

We were both panting when I held up my arm in the signal that told her to stop.

"I can't," I said through pants. "I can't find it, and even if I could, I don't know how to call it."

The blue flames rolling across Prisha's sword dimmed, and then died. Heavy breaths lifted her chest. "Now you tell me."

We both laughed.

Azad shook his head, then rubbed his chin. "Well, beti, your power continues to elude us. I am unsure how to continue, especially since I've never seen this new magic of yours in action."

I nodded, too winded to speak. We had jumped right into training after Azad confirmed that he also had never heard of any group called the Bone Eaters. I was beginning to think that whatever that group was, they were either long gone or had never existed, unless Jakub had ties to them . . .

"Shall we have you girls try again?" he asked. "Or

perhaps I could stage an attack when you're least expecting it. Perhaps that would pry it from you."

Prisha and I shared expressions of mixed emotions. If my new power hadn't appeared after hours of swordplay, what was to say another hour would help? And a staged attack? Eek, what if someone called the SF, thinking the staged attack was real? Then the SF would engage, and innocent people could get hurt.

From the uneasy expression forming on my best friend's face, she'd reached the same conclusions, but in the end, she shrugged and deferred to me. "It's up to you."

My mind drifted to the Fire Wolf, to his offer to train with me and how he had ideas on how to train my new magic. A tingle of awareness vibrated through me. Images of his bare chest, broad shoulders, and corded muscles came next.

Nope, training with him wasn't an option, even if he was the only one who'd seen my new magic in action.

"No, to the staged attack," I finally told Prisha's father.

Azad nodded respectfully.

"But Prish, you and I could go again." With any luck, something would change and my magic would finally manifest even though that now seemed doubtful. Still, I had to try.

Prisha nodded and took a step back. Magic began shimmering around her, and a blue flame erupted across her sword. She lifted the weapon, positioning herself in a fighter's stance before coming at me in endless strikes.

PRISHA and I carried on for another two hours, until we both became so tired that our muscles were quivering and our arms shaking.

When we finally stopped, my clothes were soaked with sweat and my legs felt like jelly. All I had to show for our efforts was a nicked forearm, which had stopped bleeding since Prisha's flame hadn't been soaked in her venom, only her enhanced magic.

"Are you sure you have a new power?" Prisha said in a joking tone between pants.

I bent over and cupped my knees, taking in huge gulps of air. "It seems questionable right now, doesn't it?"

She laughed, and I joined her. It was either that or cry. My new power had made zero appearances despite our endeavors to do everything we could think of to provoke it. If I hadn't been through so much in the past few days, I would be questioning if I'd imagined its existence.

Azad crossed his arms as he stood several yards away and watched us with a frown. I knew he was thinking the same thing. That this *new power* I claimed to have could very well be a figment of my imagination. I groaned. How embarrassing.

"We shall try again tomorrow." Azad clapped his hands together. "Until then, you should rest."

"Sounds good to me." Prisha straightened just as two servants appeared in the gymnasium corner.

They rushed forward, each carrying towels and refreshments. They held them out to us on silver trays. Yep, it was *that* kind of place.

Even though I'd grown up training with my best friend, I still felt awkward being waited on. Because outside of here, that never happened. I didn't think I would ever get used to the lavish lifestyle that Prisha led. To her, however, it was a normal way of existence. Not that I was judging. Prisha's family was not only incredibly wealthy, but they were also unique and respected throughout the world's supernatural communities, and for good reason. They were one of a kind. Nobody else in the world had fighting magic like theirs.

"Are you going to head back to the store?" Prisha took a long pull of the sweet drink infused with lemon and pomegranate.

The beverage fizzed slightly, tickling my nose. "I should."

"Or you can hang with me for the rest of the day. You're entitled to a day off every now and then. And after all the crap you've been through, now seems like a good time."

I sighed, because being a small business owner meant little time to relax. I was lucky if I got a day off each week. Some weeks I didn't even have that.

"I should really check in with Tess at the store first, but then I can meet you back at your place. Do you want to grab dinner at that new sushi restaurant tonight? I know you've been dying to try it."

Prish grinned. "Sure, sounds good. See you in a few."

AZAD SENT two of his servants with me to the supernatural marketplace, and he insisted that I take his private car. Like everybody he employed, the three men traveling with me were all trained in battle. The chauffeur, the butler, all of the servants—every single one of them—could hold their own in a fight.

I truly felt sorry for anybody that ever got the hare-brained idea to attack the Kumars' estate. They probably wouldn't make it past the front gates without being fried.

Sitting in the back of the spacious sedan, I finally pulled out my phone to check the Fire Wolf's text message that I'd been avoiding.

> I'm free this afternoon if you want to train.

My breath sucked in when I imagined the Fire Wolf shirtless with sweat dripping down his chiseled chest. Of course, that was where my mind went.

Perving fantasies aside, I would give him credit for one thing—the dude was as persistent as hell, even though I'd declined his offer to train and had made it clear that things were over between us.

But I wasn't surprised. As I'd come to learn, *relentless* was how many described him in the community, and it appeared that I was getting a very hefty dose of that trait right now.

Well, my relentless hunter, I happen to be quite stubborn, so it appears you've met your match.

I swiped his message closed without replying, because the reality was, cutting all strings was the only way to treat this going forward. It was what I would have done if the attack hadn't happened last night. And even though he'd saved me from death, I wasn't obligated to him.

I was about to put my phone away when another text dinged. My heartbeat kicked up, but when I saw the name on my screen, my breathing calmed. Just Carlos.

> Can you come in today? Commander Klebus would like to discuss something with you.

I straightened, then wondered why the commander hadn't told me she wanted to see me when we'd spoken this morning. I tapped in a reply to my ex.

> I can. What does she want to talk about?

His response came back immediately.

> There's been a new development.

My eyebrows drew together. It hadn't even been a day since I'd been attacked in my bedroom. I leaned forward in my seat, then tapped the driver on his shoulder. "Do you mind changing course? I actually need to go to the Supernatural Forces' office."

"Of course, ma'am." He swerved at the next corner, heading west instead of downtown. Cars buzzed around us as he expertly wove in and out of traffic. Twenty minutes later, we pulled up to the barbershop that fronted as the SF's office.

"Thank you so much for the ride."

"My pleasure," the driver replied.

The two men who had ridden along to guard me stepped out of the vehicle. They accompanied me inside, until I was safely encased within the SF's walls, before returning to the vehicle and smoothly pulling away.

I hurried to the front desk and was relieved to see that Jeff wasn't working today. Instead, Shelley was on. She and I usually got along pretty well.

"Private Lopez told me that Commander Klebus wanted to see me." I pushed some loose strands of hair behind my ears and hoped I didn't look like a sweaty mess, even though I was pretty sure I did.

Shelley smiled brightly. "She does. Right this way."

Unlike Jeff, she didn't wave me to the back offices. Instead, she rose swiftly from her chair and took off at a clipped pace down the hall.

I struggled to catch up only because my legs were still throbbing from training. Despite doing my best to keep in shape, today's session had been particularly brutal.

Commander Klebus was seated behind her desk, looking as fresh as a daisy, when I stepped into the room. One of the benefits to being a vampire was that they never needed to sleep. Those lucky ducks could work twenty-four hours a day and never tire.

"Oh good, you're here." The commander waved at the seat across from her. "I see that you're done with training."

I raised my eyebrows. "You knew I was training?"

"Of course, I did. You're now part of an active investigation. The SF knows your whereabouts at all times."

My jaw dropped. So now I was being stalked by the SF? Huh, wonder why nobody had told me that. I bit back the irritation that provoked, even though I knew they had my best interests at heart. "Is that why you didn't call me about whatever's going on?"

She dipped her head. "Private Lopez said that he would be happy to contact you, and since we knew you were training and well-guarded, I didn't feel the need to rush things." She watched me carefully, and I knew what she was thinking. She was wondering why a nobody shop owner was training with the elite Krishnalanthala warriors. And she was probably also wondering why my ex-boyfriend was back in my life if I was supposedly mated to the menace of the Shadow Zone. Male wolves weren't exactly known for being the sharing type.

Well, fuck me sideways. If my simple life wasn't being blown wide open now, I imagined it would be soon. But she could just keep on wondering. I felt no need to divulge my private life to her or anybody else for that matter, even if red flags had been raised.

I smiled sweetly. "Oh, Carlos offered that, did he? That

was very nice of Private Lopez." I kept my smile pasted on, just for good measure.

The commander blinked, and I swear she was about to grumble in irritation since I wasn't spilling the beans, but a mask of professionalism descended over her face instead. "The reason I needed to speak with you is because there was another break-in attempt at your apartment."

The pasted smile melted off my face. "What? Is Tessa—"

"Your sister is safe," Commander Klebus added in a hurry. "She's still at Practically Perfect and being guarded by SF members. I've kept firm locates on her all day, but when I informed her of another break-in attempt, she said I should defer all information to you."

I managed a jerky nod. "How did you know they'd returned?"

"I left several squad members on the premises, to monitor for further activity. Just before lunch, four new supernaturals arrived, but as soon as my squad members engaged, they vanished."

"So you didn't catch them?"

She shook her head. "I'm afraid not."

"Holy shit." I stared at her, gaping. "They're *really* trying to get me—I mean, Tessa," I corrected in a hurry.

Her eyes gleamed, but whatever was veiled in their depths disappeared in a blink. "They are, which is why I no longer think it's safe for either of you to stay in Chicago in any capacity."

"Whoa, what?" I reeled back in my chair. "But Tessa and I are staying at my friend's house. It's a heavily warded high-rise. It's more than safe, and tonight we'll be having protective wards put around our apartment. It should be secure in a few days."

The commander's lips pursed. "I don't think you're understanding the gravity of the situation. I don't think protective wards will be enough."

"Why not?"

"Because we're fighting a very intelligent and sophisticated organization. We've already uncovered that this goes beyond a single man—Jakub as you called him. Whoever he is, he's not new to this game. He's walking around our society, capturing supernaturals from their daily lives, and taking them to various locations throughout the globe without any trackable means of finding them—until Mr. King got involved." She steepled her fingers. "The other supernaturals that Jakub abducted, and whom Mr. King rescued, all had protective wards in place, but it didn't stop their abductions." Her words dripped with ice, and even though vamps were known for being indifferent to most things in our society, Commander Klebus was an exception. She was clearly furious at such atrocities.

"Is this all linked to the European mafia?" I asked.

"Possibly."

"So this isn't just the club in New York? There are more places?"

She nodded slowly. "I can't reveal too much given the sensitive nature of this information, but yes. That club in New York was only one location where we believe captives are being held. We believe there are more locations as we still have a dozen powerful supernaturals unaccounted for." She leveled me with a hard stare. "And next time you see your mate, will you please remind him not to set any more facilities on fire? It does do a number on our evidence."

For a moment, I didn't reply. She'd just referred to the Fire Wolf as my mate, as if such a thing were perfectly normal. I was so tempted to tell her that he *wasn't* my mate, but then remembered the only reason I was off the hook for explaining how those two supernaturals died in my bedroom was because the hunter had claimed responsibility for it *as my mate*.

I gave her a weak smile.

"Anyway, as I was saying," she continued, "you and your sister will need to leave Chicago. Since we can't trust this group to tell you and your sister apart, you're both in danger."

"But what about our shop?"

"Do you have employees who can manage your business while you're away?"

I gaped. "Well, I guess so, but that's asking a lot of them."

"If you explain the gravity of the situation, I'm sure they'll understand."

I leaned back in my chair. "So you're convinced that this group will eventually get my sister again?"

That gleam in her eyes returned. "On the contrary, Ms. Davenport, we now firmly believe that these men are only looking for you, and we've come to the conclusion that you were the intended target all along. However, your sister could be used as leverage, so she won't be left open. She will be protected too."

My eyes bugged out. She *knew*. The SF commander knew that *I* had been the intended target all along, not my sister. But how did she know? I figured it was either that damn report I'd given her which had pretty much spelled out how strong I was, or it was something they'd uncovered in their investigation.

I settled further into my chair, letting it all sink in. Inside, a little part of me withered. The SF officially knew about the strength of my witch powers, but did they also know about my forbidden one?

I was too afraid to ask.

My shoulders slumped. So many changes were happening so quickly. Just last week, I'd been doing my own thing, enjoying life, creating potions, crafting spells, and now this week my secret was being revealed to more and more people, I'd nearly died in my apartment, and now I was being kicked out of my hometown and asked to abandon my business. And all to avoid being kidnapped by some psychotic supernatural with an agenda we still didn't understand. *Fuck that guy.*

Rage bubbled up inside me. Hot, scorching, and consuming *rage*.

Fuming, I straightened. More than anything, I wanted to break something. Preferably Jakub's head. Yes, that would do nicely. I could take his noggin and crack it against the sidewalk like an egg splattering open on a frying pan. A dark smile spread across my face.

"Ms. Davenport?"

My smile wiped clean. "Yes?"

The commander placed her forearms on her desk. "We have several safe houses available. All of them would ensure your safety."

My jaw dropped. "Safe houses?" *Oh gods. This is real.*

She waved toward the far wall, and with the push of a button, a magical holograph of earth appeared. The globe spun, the continents ablaze with color. Shimmering cities appeared throughout the countries.

Several times, the holograph changed, zooming into various locations, but moving too fast for me to see what country or continent it had landed on. A mixture of terrains and buildings, all heavily guarded with Supernatural Forces members patrolling the perimeters, appeared in each display.

"What are those?" I asked.

"The SF commands several secure facilities throughout the globe—safe houses for supernaturals in dangerous situations such as yourself. Seven are currently open. Do you have a climate preference for where you go?"

I sputtered. "Wait, are you saying that I have no choice in this? That the SF is going to force me to leave Chicago no matter what?"

"Of course, you have a choice, but the question is, how much do you value your life and your freedom? Staying in Chicago leaves you in grave jeopardy."

I blinked, not able to believe what I was hearing. Just four days ago, this woman hadn't believed me when I'd said there was a threat. Now, she was telling me I had to leave the country. Or not. I had no idea where any of the safe houses were located.

A heavy dose of silence passed between us before the commander sighed. "There is one other option, if you don't want to be in SF custody."

"There is?"

Her face gave away nothing when she said, "Your mate has offered to provide protection for you amongst his pack."

My mate? His pack? Okay, there was no way I'd heard her correctly. She'd just said that the Fire Wolf had a pack, but he clearly didn't. He'd told me so. "Come again?"

"Mr. King has offered you refuge in his wolf pack. Would you rather accept that offer or would you prefer what the Supernatural Forces is offering? The choice is yours." She watched me, and I knew this was a trick question. Any female who was truly mated would choose to stay with her mate, so if I refused to go with the hunter, she could demand to know more about the two dead men in my apartment.

And then what would I say? Since the commander was aware that Jakub was after me and not my sister, she clearly knew that *I* held all of the magic behind the products at Practically Perfect, but as for my forbidden power and new power, she might still be clueless about those.

I couldn't win. If I didn't accept, she would undoubtedly

learn about my secret powers after digging further into those two deaths. And if I did accept, I would be with the Fire Wolf.

Sweat beaded on my upper lip when I thought of his text. *I'm free this afternoon if you want to train.* Those words swirled through my mind as did a dawning sense of understanding.

The Fire Wolf had engineered this. Somehow, someway, he'd known I would end up in this position—being asked to leave Chicago—so he'd already suggested a safe place for me to go to the commander, who was obviously keen to please him since she'd been trying to recruit him for who knew how long.

He was working ahead, thinking ahead, always two moves in front of me. It was probably why he'd claimed to be my mate, so that he'd have leverage on me. Damn. He was smart. *Really* smart. And relentless.

But I was just as stubborn.

I cocked an eyebrow at the commander. "Why do I feel like a toddler who's being given two choices? I can either have my milk in the red cup or the blue cup, but either way, I'm drinking the milk."

Her eyebrows drew together. "I'm not sure what you're referring to, Ms. Davenport."

Right, and the sky's purple.

"Ms. Davenport?" The commander's tone softened. "I know it's been a trying week for you, and I truly am sorry about that. But it's in your best interest to either accept a safe house provided by the Supernatural Forces or to stay safely within Mr. King's pack."

My breathing grew faster as my thoughts shifted rapidly. I could ask Azad for help. Perhaps he could spare bodyguards. No. I couldn't ask that of him. What if that put Prisha's family in harm's way?

"This is really happening," I whispered. I was either being shipped off to Timbuktu to a secret SF house, or to wherever the Fire Wolf's supposed pack was. So now the question became, did I want to spend my time with squad members or with the hunter?

But I already knew my answer, just like that smart fucker had known how I'd answer. I couldn't accept the safe house without giving up an explanation for how those men had been killed in my bedroom. For all intents and purposes, I needed to be seen as the Fire Wolf's mate.

He'd played this perfectly.

I chewed on my lip, and the commander raised an eyebrow.

Obviously, the amount of time I was putting into making this decision was raising even more red flags.

"Can I ask one thing?" I asked.

"Of course."

"How did . . . Kaillen . . . know about the break-in?"

"He called earlier to check in, wanting an update. Since he's your mate, I told him."

Of course she did. Because mates had rights in our society. It was how the supernatural community worked.

I gave her a brittle smile, knowing I couldn't put this off any longer.

I pushed to a stand, my chair scraping along the carpet. "I'll need to pack my stuff and help my sister arrange a few business details at the store." I swallowed the thickness in my throat, barely able to get the rest of my sentence out. "Then I'll be ready to transfer to my mate's pack as I'm sure Mr. King is expecting me."

CHAPTER TEN

The second I see that manipulative fucker, I'm giving him a piece of my mind.

Thinking about that was the only thing that kept me functioning and not raving like a lunatic for the rest of the day. Of course, I couldn't lose my temper at the store, not with two SF members trailing me.

I knew I could have refused their protection, but I wasn't stupid. If Jakub-Dipshit was after me, I would be an idiot to turn down bodyguards just because I was pissed at the hunter.

My mood was only further aggravated when Tessa had squealed in happiness when she'd learned she was being shipped off to a safe house. Seriously, only my sister would be excited about that.

She'd left Practically Perfect immediately, saying she needed to pack. Poor Private Merrick had looked crestfallen. Apparently, he wasn't getting his date with my sister after all, because Tess had already moved on to bigger and better things—an exciting safe house adventure—and her latest crush was already forgotten.

I imagined the young SF member wasn't the only one left in the wake that was my sister's tornado. My twin's entire closet had undoubtedly been emptied and was waiting in huge bags in Prisha's foyer, something I'm sure my bestie *really* appreciated.

I sighed. My sister was truly one of a kind.

With Tess gone, that had left only me to tie up all loose ends at the store. Thankfully, Nicole stepped up to the plate again. After promising to check in regularly with her, replenish inventory as needed, and give her another huge bonus, everything was ready to go for my departure, so I hightailed it back to Prisha's high-rise to where she and Tessa were waiting.

Sure enough, the foyer was packed with bags.

"You're back!" Prisha leaped from the couch in her living room when I entered her apartment. I nearly stumbled over a huge suitcase on my way to greet her.

"Tala!" Tessa called from down the hall. She appeared looking freshly showered and in stylish clothes. Of course, I was still a mess from training that morning. I hadn't even had time for a shower or change of clothes yet.

A flare of excitement danced in my sister's dark-blue eyes, especially when she saw the SF members who'd been assigned to me. They'd plastered themselves to the wall since space was so limited around the front door.

Irritation washed through me when I beheld my sister's radiant expression. "You don't have to look so excited."

She just clapped her hands. "Oh pooh, don't be like that. Because even you have to admit this *is* exciting. You're going off to one location and me another. Think of all the hot SF members that will be there." She gave a little happy dance, then eyed the two by the wall.

One of them gave her a crooked grin.

Rolling my eyes, I propelled her away from the SF members as Prisha followed. "Tess, our lives have just been turned upside down because *you* didn't keep your mouth shut about my magic, and all you can talk about is hot SF guys?"

She frowned. "You know it wouldn't hurt to embrace some impulsiveness every now and then. You're too uptight."

"Uptight?" I growled and advanced more, but Prisha intercepted.

"Not now," she said under her breath. "Someone's just arrived to collect you."

"What do you mean?"

She nodded toward the foyer. "The wards just flared. Your *mate* is here."

My heart felt as if it stopped. "He's here? Already?"

She nodded. "In the hall."

My mate. The Fire Wolf. The scourge of society. *He* was here to collect me and whisk me away to his pack.

Seriously. *FML.*

I walked on stiff legs to the front door as Prisha handed

me my purse. "You promise to write and keep me updated?"

"You know I will," I replied automatically. Keeping my whereabouts hidden also meant that the Supernatural Forces had confiscated my mobile, since phones could be tracked. From here on, it would be old-fashioned pen and paper as a means to communicate, with the SF transporting those letters.

Prisha pulled me into a fierce hug, then Tessa did the same, but both looked quite different when I pulled back. Sadness and concern tugged on Prisha's features whereas my sister looked ecstatic, as if she couldn't wait to also be whisked away.

I sighed. "Stay out of trouble," I said to my twin.

She winked. "Always."

I groaned. "If only that were true."

The Fire Wolf was pacing when I stepped into the hall, my bags in tow. The overhead lights glinted off his dark hair, and his shirt stretched over his broad shoulders as he flexed and moved.

Since I'd never unpacked at Prisha's, my backpack was already set to go, and in a rare show of thoughtfulness, Tessa had packed more of my things when she'd returned home to collect the rest of her stuff. I now resembled her with my embarrassing amount of heavy luggage.

The hunter stopped short when the door closed behind me. He stood as still as a statue as a golden glow flared in his eyes.

"I've got it from here," he said curtly to the two SF members behind me.

They gave brief nods before returning inside.

When we were alone, heat flashed in the hunter's eyes, and a predatory expression stretched across his face.

My belly quivered—dammit, it *quivered*—but then I remembered how he'd tricked me and my fingers curled into fists.

He prowled forward, his hands loose, but his swagger told me how triumphant he felt.

He'd won.

I recalled my earlier promise to slug him the next time I saw him, but his next words stopped my hand from drawing back.

"You look lovely."

For a moment, all I could do was blink. "What?"

"I said you look lovely."

I scoffed and looked down at my workout clothes. "Um, I was training most of the day, I haven't showered, and I stink, so nope, not gonna buy that." I crossed my arms. "And by the way, I pegged you for many things, but outright liar wasn't one of them."

He frowned. "I'm not a liar."

"Yes, you are. You said you didn't have a pack."

"I don't."

"Then where are we going?"

"To my family's pack."

Oh, for the love of the gods. "How is that any different from being *your* pack?"

"Because I don't associate with my family."

I stared at him for a moment, but his expression appeared guileless. "I don't understand."

"You don't need to, but I'm not a liar. I don't consider them my pack, but I will use their protection to guard you while we track down Jakub."

"We?"

"The SF."

My eyes narrowed. "What are you hiding from me now?"

He stepped closer, and his citrusy cedar scent wafted toward me. "Why do you look so sexy when you're irritated with me?"

I took a step away until my back touched the wall but already my heart was racing. "I'm not sure. Perhaps you should see a psychiatrist."

His gaze lowered to my mouth just as he pulled his yellow crystal from his pocket. "Have I told you how much I enjoy your wit?"

"I don't believe you have."

"In that case." He moved in more and dipped his head until his lips were pressed just below my ear. "I find it delectable."

I somehow managed to say, "You don't say," even though my toes were curling.

He inhaled, and nerves shot straight to my stomach. A low rumble came from his chest. "Your scent just changed. If I didn't know better, I'd say you're growing aroused."

"Good thing you know better then," I replied breathlessly.

His hand found my hip. He squeezed it before snaking his arm around my waist. "Ready?"

I pushed him back 'cause my heart was hammering a million times a minute and I was already melting into him.

Fuck, this was a bad idea. The man *knew* how to turn me on. How the hell was I supposed to survive the next few weeks while the SF did their job?

"Being that close isn't needed for portal transfers," I reminded him, then pointed at his crystal. "Let's just get on with it. Take me to your pack-that's-not-your-pack."

A devious smile twisted his lips as he began to swirl his crystal, then he held out his hand, his portal whirling behind him. "Ready?"

I brushed past him, not bothering to answer. I picked up my heavy bags, tossing them into the portal before I stepped in after them and his portal swallowed me in its wind.

The feeling of popping, falling, and being pulled apart hit me all at once. I kept my mouth firmly closed even though my insides were churning.

But a split second into the transfer, I felt something brush against me. A hard body. A warm hand. The scent of citrus and cedar.

The portal spat us out a second later, and I was in the Fire Wolf's arms—legit, *in his arms*—with my bags at my feet.

The dude was carrying me like I was Cinderella, as

though those ridiculous glass slippers had broken on my feet, cut my soles, and made my ability to walk impossible.

"Put me down."

A smile streaked across his face. "You're not very heavy."

"Your point being?"

"I thought you would be. Muscle weighs far more than fat."

"Is that your way of saying I'm not fat? Or that I am fat? I'm not sure."

He chuckled and finally set me on my feet. But he didn't let go, instead he kept an arm hooked around my waist. "You're toned and strong. I thought that meant you'd be heavier than most women."

Most women. As if he had a lot of practice carrying females. A memory of what Carlos had told me—no, of what he'd *warned* me about—flitted through my mind. He'd said the hunter was a womanizer, and there had certainly been plenty of women at the Black Underbelly who would have loved to give the hunter's dick a run for their money.

A flare of jealousy streaked through me. *Ugh.* I did *not* just feel that.

I disentangled myself from his arms, my fingers dancing across his smooth skin and chiseled forearms. A low grumble came from the hunter at my unintended light touch. My belly fluttered at that sound, but I forced myself to step well away from him and look around.

We were in a meadow, nestled in a valley between rolling hills covered in trees. Cool air flowed over my skin as a smattering of clouds drifted across the sky. The sound of running water reached my ears. Behind us, not even twenty yards away, a narrow stream flowed until farther away it reached a small lake. It was idyllic looking—quite picturesque—like something you'd see on a postcard for a destination that promised leisurely autumn walks, cups of hot cider, and lakeside picnics.

"Where are we?" I asked, genuinely curious.

"My family's pack territory. We're just outside Oak Trembler, Ontario." He nodded behind us. "I have a cabin here, and the pack town—Oak Trembler—is only a mile east."

I squinted in the direction he'd nodded. Just through the trees, I could make out the outline of a wooden cabin. It blended so well into the landscape, though, I never would have seen it if he hadn't pointed it out.

I shook my head, not able to believe any of this. "How can you have a cabin here if you don't associate with your family?"

He shrugged. "My father insisted that it's mine even though I never use it."

"When was the last time you were here?"

"A while."

I huffed. A vague answer. *Imagine that.*

I was about to open my mouth, to insist that he tell me —hell, the dude had basically tricked me into coming here, it was the least he could do—but then the sound of a slamming door reached my ears followed by a shriek of happiness.

"Kaillen!"

I swirled around to see a woman sprinting right for us. Given the direction she was coming from, I guessed that she'd emerged from his cabin.

She flew across the meadow, her dark hair whipping behind her. She was dressed simply in jeans and a chunky knit sweater, but even from the distance, I could see that she was beautiful.

A grin split across the hunter's face, and he held his arms open wide. When she reached us, she didn't even slow. She barreled right into him, wrapping her arms around his neck, as he swept her off her feet.

"Oh my gods, I've missed you!" she squealed.

He laughed. "Me too."

He swung her around, her feet flying through the air, and I backed up, shock rippling through me. *What in the actual fuck? Does this dude think I'm joining his harem or something?*

Rage sliced through me, as sharp as a knife, but the two of them just carried on, laughing and hugging.

When he finally set the woman down, joy radiated from his face. Pure, unadulterated *joy*. I'd never seen him look like that.

I bit the inside of my cheek, anything to stop the pain that was cleaving me open. *I don't care. I don't care. I don't care.* I kept telling myself that, over and over. Because he obviously loved this woman. Really loved her.

And for some reason, that made me want to claw her eyes out.

"Tala?" The Fire Wolf finally turned my way, his stupid grin still in place. But the second he got a look at me, his smile vanished. "What's wrong?"

"Nothing," I replied automatically.

The woman continued to gaze lovingly up at my hunter. Yes. *My* hunter. I'd really just thought that.

She finally faced me, and shards of emerald shone from her gaze, her eyes as lovely and beautiful as the precious gem.

"You must be Tala." Her smile didn't slip, not once, even though I was pretty sure I was scowling.

I nodded curtly, hating myself for despising this woman so intensely. It was an asinine way to feel. I didn't even know her. She could be lovely, or kind, or generous, or funny. She could have a million traits that would make her somebody I *should* like.

But my stupid head was still caressing images of me ripping her face off.

Gods, this was fucked up.

The Fire Wolf cocked his head, then a knowing glint lit his eyes. His smirk came next. "She's not my woman," he said simply.

My head whipped to his just as the woman gasped.

"You think—" Her hand flew to her mouth, then she laughed. "Oh gods, no!" she shrieked. "He and I aren't together. Eww." She made a face.

The corner of the Fire Wolf's mouth kicked up. "Tala, this is Ocean, my *sister*."

His sister. The Fire Wolf had a sister. In his non-pack. In Canada.

Fuck a duck. What else don't I know?

Humiliation burned inside me as hot as the sun. Because I'd just gotten jealous over his *sister*. Never mind that I'd gotten jealous. That was irrelevant. What was relevant was that, once again, I realized this hunter and I knew nothing about each other. I hadn't even known he had siblings.

"I thought you didn't associate with your family?"

His grin disappeared. "I don't. Not with the others. My sister's the exception."

"I suppose I have you to thank then," Ocean said, clasping her hands behind her back.

Somehow, I managed to sound halfway intelligent when I replied, "Thank me for what?"

"For bringing my brother home. It's been nearly ten years since he's been here."

"Oh?" With a startling realization, it hit me that I didn't even know the hunter's age.

She nodded. "He left when he was eighteen. He hasn't been back here since then, and the only times I've seen him are when I've visited him in the States or somewhere off pack territory. Until now, he's refused to step foot on this land."

"He has?" I snuck a glance at the hunter.

His face was devoid of emotion, but a heavy energy strummed around him despite his stoic mask. Something must have happened here to make him run away.

Brushing that thought off, I concentrated on what else his sister had said. *Eighteen.* If the hunter hadn't been here since then, and it had been ten years, that meant he was twenty-eight now, just a few years older than my twenty-five.

I side-eyed him. He was still watching me, except now a slow smile was spreading across his face, an infuriating smug smirk that only grew as his nostrils flared. Yep, he was once again scenting my jealousy even though that emotion had worn off. Apparently, it'd been potent, though, 'cause he seemed to be enjoying its lingering traces.

Seeing that self-satisfied expression on his face and knowing that *he knew* how much I'd been affected by the thought of him with another woman, well, I just couldn't help myself.

I whacked him in the stomach.

He stumbled back, his smug smile turning into an all-out grin as he coughed from my vicious jab. And it had been vicious. I'd thrown a bit of telekinetic magic into it, but of course, the hunter stayed on his feet, easily recovering from my impulsive display of violence.

"You'll have to excuse her," the hunter remarked to his sister. Ocean's eyes widened as she glanced between the two of us. He coughed again while laughing at the same time. "She enjoys hurting people."

"Not people, just you," I corrected.

But instead of that comment disturbing him—as it would to any *sane* individual—his grin only broadened.

Stupid, insane demon wolf.

I reminded myself that he'd tricked me into coming here. And I wasn't accepting his wolf's desire to make me his mate. As long as I held my ground, his wolf would have to eventually accept that. Then, the bond would wear off— or whatever happened when a female said no—and things would go back to as they had been. The Fire Wolf would brush me off as he had at the Underbelly, probably laughing as my vagina continued pining for him, and I would move on with my life, never once looking back.

Yes. Best to remember that.

Ocean glanced between the two of us, a small smile curving her lips, but she smoothed it when I planted my hands on my hips. "Well, if you're not needing to get settled in," she said, "would you care to join me?"

I cocked my head. "Join you where?"

"In town. The entire pack is dying to meet you."

CHAPTER ELEVEN

The Fire Wolf's non-pack wanted to meet me? My eyes bugged out. What did they think this was, the next alpha returning to his lair with his mate in tow? News flash. I was not birthing any pups to rule the Lord Underbelly's kingdom.

Thankfully, I didn't have to decline Ocean's invitation since the hunter beat me to it.

"Not right now." The Fire Wolf placed a hand on his sister's shoulder. "Tala and I have to work a few things out. As you know, she's here for her own safety, so I want to show her the property first."

"Oh, of course." Ocean shook her head. "Tomorrow then?"

The hunter gave a pacifying smile. "We'll see."

My ears pricked up. *We'll see?* What did that mean? Was he hiding me from his non-pack or his non-pack from me?

And how did that make any sense? If I was here for his pack's protection, shouldn't I be, you know, with his pack?

But before I could voice those questions, the hunter clamped his hand around my arm and scooped my bags up with the other before hauling me toward the cabin.

"I'll talk to you tomorrow," he called to his sister. "Promise."

She sighed before nodding, then jogged down the meadow and around a bend.

"Wait, what?" I said, digging my heels in. "Aren't you going to at least get her home or whatever if she doesn't live here?"

The sound of a car engine starting reached my ears.

The Fire Wolf didn't stop. "She has a car. She'll be fine."

Sure enough, tires spinning on gravel reached my ears next, and a second later, a car zipped into view with Ocean behind the wheel. She gunned down a narrow gravel road, which I assumed was the Fire Wolf's driveway, before disappearing from view when she reached the main road.

When it was just me and the hunter again, I planted my feet and wrestled my arm from his grip. "Hold up. Time out here."

He stopped and turned those blazing amber eyes on me.

"What exactly am I doing here?" I demanded.

A smile tugged at his lips. "Staying safe. Remember? Or has your adequate memory finally failed you?"

I didn't rise to the bait. Instead, I glanced around the wide-open valley. It was seriously beautiful in this slice of Canada, and the air was fresh, the view spectacular. Why the hell did he leave this place? "I thought I came here for the benefit of your *pack's* protection."

"You did."

I raised my eyebrows, not believing that I actually had to spell this out. "Then where's your pack? Or your non-pack?"

He raised a hand and pointed. "Gunnerson's positioned at the northwest corner. Underwood's at the north. Matter's to the northeast . . ."

One by one, he made a slow circle, pointing out each pack member that was guarding us.

I squinted. "I don't see anyone."

"Good. Then they're doing their job."

"But how do you know they're there?"

"I can scent them."

I cocked my head. "But how can you scent people if you haven't been here in ten years? How do you know what they smell like?"

He stepped closer to me, that cocky swagger back in his step. "So many questions. But to answer you, I came by earlier today to ensure that you would have adequate protection here. I scented all of the pack members I've assigned to guard you and informed them what would happen if they *didn't* keep you safe."

For some reason, that threat brought to mind images of being hung, drawn, and quartered, and then barbecued over a roasting fire.

But then something else he said caught my attention. He'd come *here* after I'd left the SF this morning. I crossed my arms, shaking my head in disbelief. "You've had all this planned from the beginning, haven't you?"

That stoic mask fell into place. "I don't know what you're talking about."

"Oh yes, you do. You knew that Jakub-Dipshit wouldn't leave me alone, so you very conveniently offered your non-pack's services as a way for me to stay safe."

He quirked an eyebrow. "So?"

I snorted. "So?" I threw my hands up. "Why didn't you tell me?"

His expression turned contemplative. "Why does this feel like another trick question?"

"Just answer, dammit."

"Fine. Because you would know soon enough. I didn't see why I'd need to spell it out for you. As you've demonstrated several times now, you're an intelligent woman."

A growl of frustration clawed up my throat before I stalked away from him.

The sound of long grass being parted came from behind me. "Tala? Why are you mad again?"

I stopped mid-stride and swung around. "You know, while we're in the middle of being honest, I have another question for you. Why did you tell Commander Klebus that I'm your mate?"

He stilled.

"Do you actually believe that?" I held my breath. Yesterday, I would have said that he didn't know I was his mate, that he didn't understand what he was feeling for me. But now? I didn't know. The dude had grown up in a pack. He would know all about werewolf mating.

"What if I did?" he finally answered.

I crossed my arms. "Are you capable of answering questions like a normal person? You seem to have a habit of answering a question with a question."

His lips twitched. "I could say the same about you."

Despite myself, I almost smiled, but I smoothed my mouth before the expression could form. "Will you just tell me if you actually think I'm your mate?"

He regarded me for a moment, his expression still impossible to decipher. "I don't think I will."

My jaw dropped. "And why not?"

"I quite like seeing you squirm."

"Oh, you—"

But before I could finish, he brushed past me. "Are you coming?"

Seething, I stomped after him, and I could have sworn that the fucker was laughing.

Picking up my pace, I passed him, and even though I'd never been to his cabin before, I kept walking. I needed some space from the hot-as-fuck but frustrating-as-hell hunter, and it seemed his little abode was the only place I could turn to.

The meadow took the brunt of my anger, the brown stalks of grass breaking and snapping underfoot, but once I reached the woods, the dead grass gave way to fallen leaves on soft ground.

Ahead, the cabin waited.

I stalked toward it, barely noticing the small porch and tiny two-story home. My boots stomped up the steps and when I reached the door, I yanked it open, not even slowing.

The scent of cinnamon hit me first. A single large candle burned on the kitchen island. Beside it, a tray of meats, cheeses, crackers, fruit and that whole charcuterie thing waited. A bottle of wine and two glasses sat beside it along with a bucket of ice. Inside the bucket, bottles of sparkling water and fizzy fruity drinks were decoratively arranged.

Soft music played in the background. A crackling fire snapped in the fireplace in the living room. And everything was so fucking romantic that I wanted to barf all over it.

Fuming, I took in the rest of the cabin. It was an open design. The kitchen, living room, and dining room were easily visible. A set of floating wooden stairs rose beside the kitchen, the entry way beneath it. A wreath was hung on the outside of the front door, visible through the door's glass pane.

My gaze traveled upward, taking in the short hallway on the second floor that the stairs met. The entire cabin was done in dark-brown woods, beiges, and creams with hints of cool-blue and navy.

It was as quaint as a picture, and the large couches with throw pillows and quilts draped along the backs of them made me think of hot cups of cocoa, good books, and snuggly socks.

"Ocean wanted to welcome you."

The Fire Wolf's quiet comment had me whirling around. He'd snuck up on me again, silent and still. "You didn't do this?"

"No." He was still carrying my bags, all of them, as if they didn't weigh a thing. With a thump, he set them on the floor and then waved toward the refreshments. "She's known to be a good hostess, and I see that hasn't changed."

"I thought this was your cabin."

"It is."

"Then she's not hosting us."

He shrugged. "Since I didn't think to provide anything for us, she obviously felt the need to."

I surveyed the food again, my stomach rumbling. I hadn't properly eaten since training with Prisha, and I still needed a shower, but all of that would have to wait. There were *so many* things that I wanted to know. And since the mate question wasn't going to be answered, I figured I would try a different route.

I crossed my arms. "Is Ocean your only sibling?"

"No."

I raised my eyebrows when he didn't elaborate. "Dude, seriously, why is getting information from you like pulling teeth?"

He flashed me a smile, highlighting those pearly whites. "All right. I'll play nice. What do you want to know?"

I tapped a finger on my arm. "How old is Ocean?"

"Thirty."

"How old are you?"

"Twenty-eight."

So my guess had been right. "What about your other siblings. Who are they? What are their names? How old are they? What do they do for a living? Are they married? Do they live here too? And how come that look on your face suggests you're not happy talking about them? And why the hell did you leave this place? It looks like Martha Stewart threw up in here. It's so . . ." I waved at it all. "Nice and welcoming."

He studied me for a moment, not replying. When I was about to throw my hands in the air, a small smile curved his lips. "You want to get to know me."

I rolled my eyes. "This is truly just basic information, you know. I know more about my employees at Practically Perfect than I do about you, and we've spent the past few days together."

He took a step closer to me, that infuriating smile still in place. "I don't usually talk about my family, but for you, I will."

I ignored how that declaration made my heart trip.

"I have two older brothers and an older sister. You've already met Ocean." The smile slid off his face. "My brothers are named Cameron and Gavin. Cameron's thirty-nine, married, and to be the next pack alpha. Gavin's thirty-seven and still single." His jaw locked, fire rolling in his eyes.

So the dude had issues with his brothers, okaaaaay. "What about your parents?" I winced after I said that. Something told me his dear mother didn't live here. She was a demon after all.

"My father, Paxton King, is the current alpha of the pack. He lives in the alpha mansion on the other side of town, and my mother . . . I have no idea. I've never met her." His voice stayed even, but his face went utterly blank.

My eyes widened. "You've never met her at all?"

"Not that I can recall. Obviously, she birthed me, but I don't remember any of that."

"And you've never visited her in the underworld?"

"Not . . . really."

A million questions burned through me at that declaration. I still wanted to know how his parents had met, how his father had impregnated a female demon, and how the hell this hunter also held sorcerer magic. But given the closed-off expression that had fallen over his face, the dude was no longer in the sharing mood.

"So now what?" I asked, gazing around.

"We unpack and settle in." He sounded a bit too happy about that.

"Don't you need to work? Surely, your pack can keep me safe while you're, you know, doing your hunter thing."

"I haven't taken on any new jobs, so no, I don't need to work." He grabbed my bags and headed toward the stairs.

I followed him 'cause I wasn't sure what else to do. "So we're going to be together, here, until they catch Jakub-Dipshit?" *Oh gods.*

He flashed me a smile over his shoulder. "Yes."

CHAPTER TWELVE

T he stairs creaked under the hunter's heavy weight as he climbed them, and my heart was racing way too fast for a simple jog up a flight of stairs.

"How long do you think it's going to take them?" I asked when he began walking down the short hall. Ahead, three doors lined the sides. *Please let this cabin have two bedrooms. Please have two bedrooms.*

The Fire Wolf stopped at the door on the right. It revealed what I guessed was the master suite. A large king-sized bed waited in the middle of the room. A wide chest of drawers sat in the corner, and two windows spewed sunlight across the floors.

I peeked into the room across the hall. A full bathroom. With quick steps, I went to the last door. *Surely, this is another bedroom.*

I swung the door open, but it revealed a quiet sitting

area. One small couch, two end tables, and a massive book-shelf was all it contained. The low, sloped ceiling held a skylight, and on the far wall was a sliding door to a tiny balcony.

"Is that a pull-out couch?" I asked hopefully.

The Fire Wolf grinned. "Nope. We'll share the bedroom." He hefted my bags over his shoulder before disappearing into the *only bedroom in the house.*

Heart thudding in my chest, I followed him into the room to find that he'd plopped my bags on the bed and was unzipping them.

I stopped mid-stride. "What are you doing?"

"Unpacking."

"That's my stuff."

"As I'm aware, but this still needs to be put away. Surely, you'd be more comfortable if you were settled." His hands dipped into my clothes in one of the bags, but then he stopped, as if suddenly aware of what he was doing and how *incredibly inappropriate that was.* His jaw slackened, and his hands dropped to his sides.

Yep, the dude had just realized he was about to unpack someone else's clothes, and that someone wasn't techni-cally his girlfriend. Hell, even if I was his girlfriend, that would still be a little weird, but doing a task like that wasn't unheard of in mated wolves.

Gah! This was going worse than I thought it would, because once again, his wolf was ruling him.

The hunter flashed me a tight smile and took a step back. I'd never seen the dude look unsure, but that was exactly how he appeared at the moment. Yep, so despite his love of teasing me, it was obvious he knew I was his mate, 'cause that look on his face was full-blown *must-make-my-mate-comfortable-and-happy*. This was true mating and courting shit.

Crap on a lap.

"I can unpack my things myself." I walked stiffly to the bed, and then slid my bag away from him. "But we can't stay in this room together. I'll sleep on the couch in the other room, but I'll keep my stuff in here since there's more space."

His brow furrowed. "No, you're staying in here."

I planted my hands on my hips. "We're not together, therefore, we won't be sharing a bed. End of story."

A rumbling growl worked up his throat before he said through gritted teeth, "You're not sleeping on a couch."

"Fine. Then you sleep on the couch."

"I won't fit."

"Not my problem."

His nostrils flared, and he stepped closer.

I hastily retreated, not liking that predatory look in his eyes, but he kept coming until he'd backed me into the corner. *Seriously? How did I end up here?*

He leaned down, his nostrils flaring more. "Release your cloaking spell."

"What? Why?" I sputtered. "What does that have to do with anything?"

"Just do it."

I sucked in a breath. "No way."

"If you stopped hiding and started showing the world who you really are, you'd be much happier and so would I."

"Why would you be happier? So you could walk behind me sniffing me all day? That's weird."

His body pressed closer, and he inhaled again. That damned fluttering began in my stomach once more. I fought the moan that wanted to slip from my lips. Just the feel of him so close to me . . .

This *really* wasn't good.

A hum of satisfaction came from him. "You want me, even now, I can scent it. You want me as much as you did yesterday morning. Remember, when I made you come? I could do that again. Why are you fighting this?"

My eyes fluttered closed. Dammit all to hell. I *did* want him. Even now, when I knew that his interest in me wasn't real, I wanted him. More than anything, I wanted to drop my cloaking spell, let him go all possessive, domineering wolf on me, and have me hauled against the wall with my legs wrapped around his waist as he thrust inside me.

Which was exactly why I couldn't let that happen.

I wanted him too much, and I would never be happy with someone whose animal side was the reason he'd chosen me.

I placed my hands on his chest. Warmth from his skin seared into my palms, and a deep purr sounded in his throat. Oh yes, the hunter liked that I was touching him.

I shoved him away. "You and I are not together. Why do I have to keep reminding you of that?"

That cheeky smile lifted his lips. "But we could be together."

Lord all mighty. I raised my eyes skyward. "For what? A few weeks? Is that why you wanted me here? So we could fuck like rabbits for the next month while the SF is out hunting Jakub-Dipshit? And then what, we go back to our normal lives? Me living in Chicago managing a magic shop, and you returning to your orgy factory in the Shadow Zone?" A tingle of jealousy snaked up my spine. I hated thinking about him returning to the Black Under-belly, where every female in the joint would be baring their breasts for him and offering to ride his dick.

His nostrils flared, then a slow smile spread across his face. "You're jealous again."

"No, I'm not."

"Your scent can't lie."

"Maybe your senses aren't working correctly."

He grinned, that lazy smile turning into an all-out Cheshire Cat grin.

Stupid man.

"Have I ever told you how much I enjoy talking with you?"

"Why? Because I constantly insult you?"

He chuckled. "I've never had that with a female before. It's quite . . . enjoyable."

"You've never spoken with other women before? If you weren't talking, then what were you doing?"

Oh my gods, I did not just ask that. Knowing what he'd most likely been doing made my insides fire like a cauldron with bubbling jealousy, because Carlos had claimed that the Fire Wolf was a womanizer. *Don't think about it. Don't think about it. Just* don't *think about it!*

The hunter stepped closer to me again, totally invading my personal space, and fuck me, if my stomach didn't dip at the feel of his hard chest pressing against mine. "What are you so jealous of?"

"Nothing." I ducked down under his arm before he could trap me and begin doing things to me that I was firmly committed to resisting.

He sighed, his head raising before he faced me. "If you don't want to fuck right now, then what do you want to do?"

Fuck right now. Yep, the dude totally just said that. And damn my vagina and the liquid heat that just pooled between my thighs.

I backed up even more. "First, I'm going to shower. Then, I'm going to eat all of that amazing food your sister very thoughtfully left for us, and then I'm going to town."

He straightened more. "To town?"

"Yep. I've decided I want to meet your non-pack after all." Before the Fire Wolf could question my plans, I snatched clean clothes from my bag along with my toiletries. Making a beeline for the bathroom, I slammed the door behind me and locked it. Not that the lock would stop him if he wanted to force his way inside, but I hoped he would at least give me some privacy to clean up.

Of course, I wasn't going to think about the thought of him showering with me . . .

A vision of the demon hunter's hard muscles dripping with water entered my mind. Then the scorching image of my tongue running along his chest while his erection brushed my entrance.

Nope. Not thinking about that, 'cause I wasn't interested in him. I snorted. *Just keep telling yourself that, Tala.*

Since my libido definitely needed some cooling off, I turned the shower to cold, then stripped before forcing myself under it.

I bit my lip to stop my squeal when the cold spray hit me, but at least any wayward thoughts about the Fire Wolf were extinguished. My teeth were chattering by the time I finally warmed the water up, but the icy plunge had done the trick.

Since my raging hormones had been vanquished and I could once again act like a sane person, I washed from head to toe using the expensive body wash that Tessa had packed in my bag. She'd either been feeling very generous when she tucked it between my clothes—since the stuff cost nearly as much as our rent—or she'd mistakenly put it in my bag.

Whatever the case, it felt good to scrub off the sweat from my earlier training session with Prisha.

When I finally finished, at least thirty minutes had passed and my skin tingled with the pleasant fragrance.

After toweling off, I took my time getting dressed, knowing that the hunter wouldn't mind since something told me the last thing he wanted to do was go to town. So I blow-dried my hair, lathered my entire body in lotion, and even applied makeup. If I was going to meet the hunter's non-pack, then I was going to make a good first impression. Because even though I wouldn't be the next alpha's wife birthing his pups, I sure as hell could show them that I wasn't some scumbag from America who reeked of sweat and had questionable hair choices.

When I finally emerged from the bathroom, I snuck a glance into the master bedroom. My bags still sat on the bed. Huh, he'd managed to control his mate instincts after all.

I quickly unpacked them, then put my suitcases in the closet. Out of curiosity, I opened the top drawers. Stacks of neatly piled male clothes sat in perfect rows.

It reminded me of when I'd been in the Fire Wolf's man cave and he'd used fairy charms to wash and fold my laundry following our run-in with the warlocks in the insane asylum. It seemed that the hunter did indeed have a domestic streak. I smothered a laugh. Who would've thought the scourge of society could be a housewife.

I finally shoved the dresser drawer closed and ventured back downstairs only to spot the Fire Wolf seated on a comfy-looking leather chair, his long body sprawled out in front of him, his feet propped on an ottoman. He held a book in one hand, and a glass of what appeared to be whiskey in the other. The fire still crackled in the hearth, and the food on the island remained untouched.

The corner of his mouth tilted up even though his gaze hadn't drifted from the novel he was reading. "Did you enjoy your shower?" His nostrils flared. "Is that perfume you're wearing?" He finally lifted his gaze, and when he spotted me, his jaw slackened, his book literally dropping at his side.

His gaze raked up and down my frame in a slow perusal. With every second that passed, the heat in my cheeks grew. The dude was checking me out like no tomorrow.

Forgetting his dropped book entirely, he rose to his feet. "You look . . ." He eyed me again, and I seriously felt like his favorite lollipop at a candy store. "*Fuck*, you look good."

My heart rammed against my ribs as the hunter stalked toward me. I spun to the island and grabbed one of the plates beside the tray of food. Maybe dressing up hadn't been a good idea, but I hadn't dressed up that much. I wore tight ripped jeans, cute suede ankle boots, and an off-the-shoulder thin sweater. The top's angled neckline and push-up bra enhanced my breasts, and the array of delicate necklaces I wore wasn't exactly helping as it drew attention to that entire area, but the sweater wasn't indecent or draping so low that one would stare.

Although, the Fire Wolf was indeed staring.

I just piled more food on my plate. "Aren't you hungry?"

"I was waiting for you."

Oh. Well, that was polite.

"What's the new scent you're wearing?" he rumbled from behind me.

"It's not perfume." I heaped even more meat slices onto my plate, then nervously popped a few cubes of cheese and some grapes into my mouth as I moved around the island.

"Then what is it?"

I shrieked when the hunter's voice came from directly behind me. I carefully set the plate on the counter. If I didn't, I would probably drop it or do something really graceful, like throw it in the air next time he startled me.

I spun around, my chest heaving. "You need to stop doing that."

He stood right in front of me, golden light blazing in his eyes as one of his dark eyebrows cocked upward. "Stop doing what?"

"Sneaking up on me. One of these days, I'm going to punch you involuntarily."

That sly grin lifted his lips. "I might like that."

I rolled my eyes even though a smile tugged on my lips. "There is something seriously wrong with you."

He leaned in closer, his hands drifting to the counter until he had one placed on either side of me, effectively caging me in. The desire grew in his eyes before his head drifted down and his nose trailed along my neck.

Goosebumps sprouted across my entire body, and it felt as if a meteor blazed all the way down to my toes. "What are you doing?"

"Scenting for that delectable fragrance of yours. While the perfume, or whatever you're wearing is nice, I much prefer your true scent. Now please, will you release your cloaking spell?"

Since his voice had turned all growly and deep, I once

again dipped under his arm until I was free of him and zipped around to the other side of the island. Panting, I stayed there.

His nostrils flared, but I just smiled sweetly now that the granite countertop separated us. Never mind that I was struggling to catch my breath. "That's not happening, and you seriously need to learn some boundaries."

"Since when do I need boundaries in my own home?"

"Since you tricked me into joining you here."

He smirked. "I never tricked you. You made the decision to come here of your own free will."

I snorted. "Says the cat who's about to pounce on the mouse."

"I'm hardly a cat."

"Really? I think I've heard a purr from you a few times. Are you sure you're not part kitty?"

He laughed, the chuckle rumbling from his chest. "Are you really planning to resist me the entire time we're here?" He prowled to the end of the counter, his steps steady and silent.

I swiftly sidestepped until we were once again on opposite sides of the island. "Yep."

He paused his prowling movements. "It's strange, the feelings you elicit in me."

"I'm not really sure I want to talk about our feelings. That seems a little too, you know, touchy-feely, and we're not really the touchy-feely type."

His eyebrows rose again. "So we're a type, hmm? But we're not *that* kind of couple?"

"That's not what I meant. I never said we were a couple."

"Then what did you mean?" He took another step closer, but I moved just as quickly so the hunter couldn't pounce on me again.

"I meant that I'm not one of those soft, helpless females that always needs to cry and have you listen to how I'm feeling, and you're not, well, you know—you're hardly the emotional sharing type."

"If you would like to cry in my bed, I'll listen."

"How touching, but the last time I slept with a man, that wasn't needed. I'm sure it wouldn't be needed with you either."

He stilled, and a glacial scowl descended over his features. "Who did you last sleep with?"

"That wasn't my point."

"Well, I'm making it a point. Who?"

"I don't know." Gods, it had been *months* since I'd last slept with a man.

"Was it Carlos?" A hint of fire rolled in his eyes.

I shrugged, and even though I knew better, I couldn't stop the taunt that slipped from my lips. "Maybe."

Granted, it'd been years since I'd slept with Carlos, but the hunter didn't know that.

The demon flames leaped in his eyes as golden light so bright it rivaled the sun flared behind it. "You're not with Carlos anymore."

"True, but if you don't want to know stuff like that you really shouldn't ask."

His jaw looked so tight now, I swear his bones were about to crack. "Are you planning to bed him again?"

"Only if I feel like it," I said, just because I was on a roll now and for once it was nice to see me irritating the hunter versus him getting under my skin.

But at least I was being truthful with my replies, although, the thought of having sex with Carlos when the Fire Wolf was more than happy to scratch that itch . . . I didn't think I could do it. Even though the sex with my ex had been fantastic, something told me it would be nothing compared to bedding the hunter.

Before I could blink, said hunter was in front of me, his chest pressing into mine as he bent me over the island. He had me angled back so sharply that my shoulder blades brushed the countertop.

Oh mother of all the realms, how could this be turning me on? My breath sucked in, as my insides coiled. Once again, I was reminded of the sheer power the hunter harbored in his veins, and fucking hell, it made me incredibly aroused.

His nostrils flared. "You will not sleep with Carlos. Understood?"

Heat flared in my core at the possessive rage strumming from the hunter. Damn him. Why did I have to react to him like this? It would be so much easier if I didn't find him so irresistibly attractive.

But did he seriously just tell me what to do?

My gaze narrowed. "You don't get to decide who I sleep with."

He snarled with such fury that goosebumps spread

across my body, but in my next breath, he disappeared from in front of me. The next thing I knew, he was standing in front of the fire, facing it as his chest heaved. One of his hands was propped on the mantel. His fingers twisted, and I swore the wood began to disintegrate under his fingers as sawdust flitted to the floor.

I watched him for a moment, my own heart racing. My gaze raked over his frame. His shoulders were so incredibly broad, and his back was sculpted with muscle that tapered to a toned waist. Thick quadriceps coated his thighs, and well, I'd seen his junk. The man was hung like a horse.

For a moment, I considered what it would be like if I gave in to this urge we obviously both felt. Truly, what harm could come from some mindless sex? It would certainly be an enjoyable way to pass the time, because I had no doubt it would be a never-ending fuck-fest as the Fire Wolf probably had stamina that rivaled a stallion's.

But then what? What would happen after our time here was done? I knew sooner or later the Supernatural Forces would catch Jakub-Dipshit and this would all come to an end, and where would that leave me? Either chained to a mated wolf who refused to let me go, even though his human side had never wanted me, or worse, I would be head over heels in love with him while he'd worked me out of his system.

Carlos's warning came back to haunt me. *Can't be a normal mate instinct.* My ex could be right. The Fire Wolf *wasn't* a normal werewolf. He was too demony, too quick to walk on that morally gray line. For all I knew, he didn't even believe in monogamy. What demon did?

Carlos might be onto something.

Because what the hunter felt for me didn't necessarily equate to what other male werewolves felt for their mates. For all I knew, his wolf just wanted to fuck me for the time being, but if his demon side took over, what then? Demons were not only known for being promiscuous but also for being assholes. And I'd seen firsthand how the hunter had treated some of the women at the Black Underbelly. He'd probably fucked half of the females in that bar, yet he was completely indifferent to all of them.

Who was to say I wouldn't end up in the same boat?

Forcing my gaze away from the hunter, who was still destroying his mantle, I smoothed my clothes and picked up my plate again. Making sure to keep to the opposite side of the cabin, I padded over to the dining table near the entryway and sat down. The drink I'd nabbed snapped open when I cracked the top, and I took a long pull of the fizzling fruity beverage. From there, I began nibbling on the food, my eyes widening at how good it all tasted.

Doing my best to ignore the pulsing energy emanating from the hunter, I quickly devoured everything on the plate since he made no move to join me. Once my stomach was full, I took my dish to the sink before rinsing it and putting it in the dishwasher.

The entire time, I felt the hunter's eyes follow me, that energy prickling from him so intensely that at times it felt as if lightning was hitting me.

"Tala." His voice was deep yet quiet.

My shoulders stiffened and my stomach dipped at the sound of my name on his lips. I closed the dishwasher, not turning around. "Yes?"

"I know I don't have the right to decide who you sleep with."

I arched an eyebrow in surprise.

"But I'm going to ask one thing."

"What?"

"Don't talk about Carlos again. And if you"—even from the distance, I heard his swallow—"*bed him*, please make sure I'm long gone."

This time, his voice came from right behind me. He'd prowled toward me once more on silent footsteps even though I'd asked him to stop doing that.

"Okay," I said a bit breathlessly. "But I'd like to ask one thing of you, too."

"Anything."

I paused. Strangely, I had a feeling he actually meant that. "Stop sneaking up on me. I don't like it." When I twirled around, he abruptly stepped back until he was two yards away.

"I can do that." His jaw locked.

We stared at one another. Rolling fire and luminescent gold bled through his eyes. His expression looked strained yet guarded.

My body responded, that desire pooling inside me again.

His nostrils flared, but he didn't advance. "Would you

like to train since you're no longer hungry?" He cleared his throat, and the rasp in his voice abated. "You need to learn to control your new power."

Train? A stone sank in my stomach. That was another way we could pass the time here, but at the moment, I couldn't even think about that. Images of the hunter shirtless and sweaty came to mind. Yep, definitely couldn't deal with that.

I crossed my arms, my chin jutting up. "I've already trained today. I don't think my muscles could handle another round, but I was serious earlier about wanting to meet your pack. So, what do you say, will you take me there?"

CHAPTER THIRTEEN

The hunter studied me, but his expression gave away nothing. "Why do you want to meet them?"

I shrugged. "Call me curious."

His cocky smile returned. "Does this have anything to do with you wanting to get to know me?"

A salty reply was on the tip of my tongue, but then I paused. Did it? Was that really what this was—curiosity about getting to know him on a deeper level because I *did* want to understand him?

And then it hit me. *Yes.* As much as I didn't want to admit it, I wanted to know him.

I kept my expression carefully neutral. "Maybe."

"If you want to learn more about me, all you have to do is ask. I'll answer your questions."

I snorted. "As you have so readily so far? Yeah, I've seen how that goes. I'll be lucky if I get more than one-word responses."

"I could be better."

"Oh, really?" I crossed my arms. "Then in that case, why do you never come back here?" I waved around at his cozy cabin and the breathtaking view through the window before crossing my arms again. "How come you haven't been back in ten years?"

He stared at me—a totally blank, leveling stare.

Le sigh. "See?"

He grumbled. "I don't really see why that's important. My pack has nothing to do with me. Why don't you ask something that's actually relevant?"

"Like what your favorite color is?" I asked sarcastically.

He smiled devilishly. "Black."

I rolled my eyes. "So original." I tapped my foot, trying to figure out why he was so cagey about this place, but of course, I didn't know. "What are you so afraid of me learning? Or are you hiding me from them? Do you not want them to meet me? Is that what it is?"

"No, I just don't want to see them. What's the big deal?"

I nibbled my lip, eying him again. "Did something happen here?"

A single flame appeared in each of his irises before it was extinguished. "My former pack is a worthless bag of shit that I want nothing to do with. It doesn't mean anything happened."

Right, and I'm Cleopatra. My eyes narrowed. "Did they do something to you? Hurt you or something?" My fingers curled into my palms at the thought. I couldn't imagine anyone hurting the hunter, but I only knew him as an adult. I'd never known him as a kid.

That tightness entered his jaw again, and—surprise surprise—he didn't answer.

"How old were you when you came to live here?"

"A baby," he replied in a clipped tone.

I didn't ask anything further. From the energy strumming from the hunter, it was obvious I was pushing into territory that he didn't want to enter, and as much as he'd claimed to be willing to answer my questions, he clearly wasn't.

Sighing, I ended with, "What about Ocean? If you don't want me to meet your pack, can we go see her?"

Some of the hard lines softened around his mouth. "Yeah, I'm always happy to see her."

I grinned. "In that case, let me grab my coat."

OF COURSE, we didn't venture to his sister's house in a car. Oh no, that would be too normal. Instead, the hunter pulled out his yellow crystal after I'd slipped my jacket on.

"What about the wolves guarding this place?" I fluffed my hair out of the jacket to trail down my back. "Don't we need to tell them we're leaving?"

"I sent them a text when you were upstairs. They know we'll be gone for a bit."

"And we don't need them at your sister's house?"

"No, you have me." He grinned wickedly, as if his

protection was all I'd ever need. And while we were awake that was probably true, but sleeping . . .

My blood chilled when I remembered the two supernaturals diving into my bedroom at night and trying to abduct me.

The familiar anger brewed in me again, that all of *this* was because of that fucker, Jakub-Dipshit. Taking a deep breath, I waved at his portal. "Don't you ever get tired creating those?"

"Not usually."

"How can you not? That takes an immense amount of energy. You're the first supernatural I've met that can conjure portals."

He grunted. "What kind of supernaturals do you hang out with?"

I bit back a smile. "Are you seriously saying that you have friends who can do the same thing?"

He chuckled. "I never said that."

"So you're admitting that you're the only supernatural you know of that can create his own portals?"

His eyes glowed wickedly. "Maybe."

I blew hair from my eyes. "Gods help me. And you wonder why I ask you so many questions. It's because you never answer anything."

He studied me for a moment, his portal swirling behind him. "You've learned more about me in a week than my closest friends learned about me in a year."

A flutter drifted through my belly again. *Ugh.* Why did

he have to make comments like that? Things that made me feel . . . special?

My eyebrows raised, and I tried desperately to hold on to the banter between us that, dammit, I was growing quite fond of. "You must have had very interesting and in-depth conversations with your close friends then."

He shrugged. "We spent most of our time drinking and talking smack when we first met, not baring our souls to one another."

I snorted a laugh as I stepped closer to his portal. Winds from it caressed my cheek as I asked more seriously, "Does that mean you think you've bared your soul to me?"

"Perhaps a bit."

"Does that mean we're friends?"

"I'd like to be a lot more than your friend." He gave me a seductive smile.

I raised my gaze skyward. "As I'm aware."

"But I'll settle with friendship. For now."

For now. A thrill ran up my spine despite trying to stomp it down. "Something tells me you and I could never just be friends."

He stepped closer, until his hand brushed mine. He cupped my palm, then entwined our fingers before tugging me forward. "No. You and I could never just be friends. I'd want to fuck you way too often for that."

A flood of desire shot to my core, and his nostrils flared.

So that was one thing we agreed on. The hunter and I were never meant for a platonic relationship. So what did that mean? That my body recognized him as *my* mate? But I wasn't a wolf, so how could it?

With that thought on the edge of my mind, he wrenched me forward until my chest was glued to his, and then the portal winds sucked us into their embrace.

His warmth was everywhere, and even though the twisting and popping sensations that accompanied magical transfers jolted through me, my brain was focused on one thing and one thing only—the Fire Wolf.

Heat from his body traveled through mine. It was impossible not to entwine my arms around his neck and hold on to him as we fell through time and space.

But it was over too fast for anything else to happen.

The early afternoon sun greeted us when the portal deposited us in the middle of a neighborhood. The hunter had his arm locked around my waist, but he didn't let go when the portal disappeared. Around us, small houses sat sandwiched together. The yards were tiny but well kept, and the neighborhood stretched for blocks.

The hunter dipped his head, and then whispered into my ear, "Now will you release your cloaking spell?"

A shiver danced along my spine. I was tempted. *So* tempted. Walking around with my cloaking spell in place added an extra weight to my very existence. It was something I was so used to feeling, but the times I released it, it was such a freeing experience.

"Nobody knows you here." His mouth drifted to my neck. His lips brushed along my skin, and it struck me that

I should be putting distance between us, but I didn't. "Don't hide yourself from me, *colantha*."

The foreign word slipped from his lips, and melted all over me like hot butter. I shivered. "What's *colantha*?"

His lips brushed my skin more. "A fae animal, like a lioness. She's queen of her jungle. A magical predator who no other animal dares cross."

"And that's how you see me?"

"That's how you could be. If you let yourself."

Another shudder racked my body when his grip tightened. His hands drifted to my hips. "Let me scent you, *colantha*."

My head tipped back, my throat exposed for the predator.

A rumble of pleasure came from him.

Oh, fuck it.

With whispered words, the thick spell encasing me fell away, as if a blanket had been dropped around me until it pooled at my feet. My power, my magic, the essence of who I really was, surged forth until the crackling power inside me vibrated along my skin.

I sighed. It felt so *good*.

A feral purring came from the hunter's throat. He inhaled along my neck, the feeling fluttery soft.

Another shiver ran through me, and I pulled back enough to see the golden glow in his eyes—the glow that I knew would be there. But instead of it shooting lust to my core, it had the opposite reaction.

I jolted from his grip, his wolf in his eyes only

reminding me that his desire for me was animal driven and animal driven only. It had everything to do with my scent. My magic. The strength that flowed through my veins. His wolf had obviously recognized it and decided we were compatible mates. He probably thought we would breed super-powerful, genetically enhanced uber pups.

This was Darwinism at work, plain and simple. Only, I had no desire to birth the next generation of magically charged children. I just wanted a normal life and a man who loved me as fiercely as I loved him.

And knowing that the hunter would never feel genuine love for me was like being dunked into a bucket of ice water. Frozen shards frayed along my nerves, like a needle constantly stabbing the edges of a quilt.

The hunter looked down at me with *want* and confusion in his eyes, as I put more distance between us.

I ran a hand through my hair, working through the blond strands.

"Does your sister live here?" I waved at the nearest home with its vinyl siding and peaked roofline.

"She does."

I kept my gaze on the house. "I'll follow you."

"Tala." He took a step closer to me, prompting me to hastily back up just as the noise of a banging door reached my ears.

"Kaillen!" Ocean jogged across her front yard, all smiles and flying mahogany hair.

I grinned, more from relief at her arrival than anything else.

She threw her arms around the hunter again, which reminded me how much wolves craved affection. Even though the Fire Wolf's eyes stayed locked on me when I finally looked him in the eye, he returned his sister's embrace.

Down the block, a few window curtains pulled back and curious-looking neighbors peered out. Then another neighbor appeared, trimming hedges from around the back of their yard, probably doing last-minute fall pruning.

It seemed that the Fire Wolf's appearance was causing quite a stir.

And I wasn't the only one who'd noticed.

The hunter's eyes narrowed in the direction of the prying next-door neighbor. The man hastily dipped back around the corner, his pruning shears bumping against his thigh. But that didn't stop the audience that was peeking through the windows of the surrounding houses.

"Do you want to come in?" Ocean asked.

"That's why we're here," he replied gruffly. He swung his attention from the nosy neighbors to me. His nostrils kept flaring, and the gold in his eyes hadn't receded, but if his sister noticed anything, she didn't comment.

Ocean grinned. "Perfect timing. I just made a pot of chili for supper. Want some?"

I patted my stomach. "None for me. I just gorged on all of that delicious food you left at the Fire—I mean, Kaillen's cabin. Thanks for that."

She beamed. "I'm glad you enjoyed it." She tugged her

brother up the walkway and beckoned me to follow. "Would you like a tour of my home?"

I grinned. "That'd be great."

She proceeded to show us the small three-bedroom house—a home the hunter had never seen before either. After the tour, she made a fresh pot of coffee, and the Fire Wolf accepted her chili offer, so she ladled him a heaping bowl topped with cheddar cheese, sour cream, green onions, and crunchy corn chips.

"Are you married?" I asked her, noticing a few framed pictures of Ocean and a handsome tall blond on a shelf in their living room.

She grinned. "That's Sven. We've been married three years." She patted her tummy. "No pups yet, but that could change soon."

The Fire Wolf's spoon stopped halfway to his mouth. "You're breeding?"

I somehow managed to keep a straight face at that very wolfy question.

"I am." Her entire face lit up. "We just started trying."

We settled more into our chairs in the living room, and the Fire Wolf accepted a second bowl of chili. I was still nursing my first cup of coffee but had started to truly relax. Ocean was proving to be genuinely kind and she seemed to truly care for her brother. But it was more than that. She doted on him, and not in one of those motherly ways, but more in a desperate-to-see-him and worried-it'll-be-the-last-time type of doting. I had a feeling she didn't see her brother nearly as much as she wanted to.

I finished the last of my coffee and was about to stand up to put my empty cup in the kitchen, when the Fire Wolf stiffened in his seat.

Heavy footsteps on the front porch came a second later, and then a knock. "Ocean? Open up! I hear you have company, and I'd like to let your visitor know a few things if he's going to be staying on my territory."

I took in the rage growing in the Fire Wolf's eyes, and something told me that it wasn't Sven at the front door.

CHAPTER FOURTEEN

A warning growl came from the hunter just as Ocean rolled her eyes and muttered something under her breath.

"Honestly . . ." She swung the door open, her emerald eyes flashing. "Is that any way to act after Kaillen's been gone for ten years?"

A tall, broad man stood at the threshold. He was easily six-three, maybe six-four, and had werewolf written all over him. Brown hair, similar in shade to Ocean's, was cropped close to his head, and his clothes looked new and expensive. Fisted hands pumped at his sides, and his dark eyes cut across the room until they landed on the Fire Wolf.

Dominant energy abruptly rolled off the man in steady waves. When it hit me, I felt the urge to fold my shoulders inward, but I called upon my magic, erecting a powerful shield spell around myself and gritted my teeth.

My shield wasn't strong enough to stop all of the energy pulsing from the visitor—shield spells rarely were from wolves this dominant—but it was enough to make me not wilt like a damned flower in his presence. I could still breathe, and I wasn't lying on the ground belly up. But the bottom line? The newcomer was *strong*.

The Fire Wolf got to his feet, his movements liquid and stealthy. If he felt anything from the newcomer's dominance, he hid it like a pro.

The man's jaw clenched when the Fire Wolf stalked toward him, then his lip curled.

"Brother, how nice to have you home," the man said sarcastically.

Oh. So this was one of the brothers. Now the question was, which one? Cameron, the oldest, or Gavin the second born?

"Always so welcoming," the Fire Wolf replied, menace dripping from his words.

"Is this her?" the hunter's brother said, jerking his chin in my direction. "Is she the reason my top fighters are all hiding around your little cabin in the woods?"

The Fire Wolf's lips twisted in a brutal smile. "*Your* fighters? Are you sure about that?"

His brother snarled. "Couldn't handle the heat on her own, huh?"

The hunter's smile vanished. "Still so charming, I see."

He snorted. "Coming from you, that's rich. So she's the bitch you're lusting after?"

In less than a blink, the Fire Wolf's hand was curled

around his brother's throat. "Pick your next words very, *very* carefully."

His brother didn't look concerned about being choked. Instead, he smirked. "She must be one hell of a good lay to get you back here. She's certainly gorgeous. I'd fuck that if I wasn't—"

A terrifying snarl ripped from the hunter's throat and in a blur of movement he launched his brother through the door and was on top of him outside.

My jaw dropped as I lunged across the room.

"Cameron! Kaillen!" Ocean yelled, also following them. "Stop!"

But it was too late. The Fire Wolf and Cameron were pummeling one another in the front yard, brawling and fighting in movements so swift I could barely see them.

The sounds of punches, grunts, and snarls came next, but just when I was about to call upon two binding spells to break them apart, an explosion of magic erupted.

In the next instant, two huge wolves stood facing one another. The Fire Wolf looked as I remembered him. Beautiful streaks of black, brown, cream, and russet-colored fur coated his body. His brother was of a similar beauty, but held no russet in his coat, and his wolf's build was a smidge smaller.

Shredded clothing lay on the brown grass around them, and since the Fire Wolf hadn't been wearing his quick-release garments, his clothes were utterly ruined.

In a flash, those terrifying snarls came from the two of them again as they turned into a flurry of fighting fur.

"Crap," Ocean whispered. "This is worse than I thought it'd be."

"What the hell is going on?" My chest was rising and falling so fast. I didn't know if I should intervene or let them fight it out, but now that they'd shifted, interfering could prove problematic. Dominant male wolves in the middle of a fight were not to be separated, or something like that. I struggled to remember what Carlos had told me about pack rules.

Ocean's eyebrows pinched together. "There's a reason Kaillen never comes back here."

"Is Cameron part of the reason?"

"Yes, him and Gavin are both awful to him."

"Do they always fight like this?"

"Unfortunately."

"So this isn't how it usually goes when long-lost pack members come back to Oak Trembler?" I asked, my tone sharp.

Ocean sighed. "No, I'm afraid this welcome is reserved for my baby brother and him only."

I scowled. "Does everyone treat him like this?"

She shook her head. "They don't fight him. They're too scared of him to do that, but despise him? Most do."

"But *why?*"

Ocean gave me a sad smile. "It's a long story, but it's not my story to tell."

I wanted to ask her more questions, to know how any pair of siblings could fight this brutally, but the brothers' attacks had grown so loud I'd barely heard her last answer, and she'd taken on a sickly color—pale and lifeless. Ocean looked resigned, but something else too, something deeper. Sad maybe? As if seeing her brothers act this way brought her more pain than a thousand deaths.

Swallowing the sick feeling in my stomach, I wrapped my arms around myself and hoped it ended soon. The Fire Wolf and Cameron were fighting so fast now their movements were a blur. Several times they paused long enough for me to catch sight of a swiping paw or the flash of a fang. But then they were locked onto one another again, snarls and vicious growls tearing from them as they swirled as fast as a tornado.

Blood flew, droplets sprinkling onto the dead lawn around them. My heart jumped into my throat when the two turned into a tumbling ball and rolled toward the street.

Curious neighbors drifted out of houses and from backyards, while some still peered through their curtains. A few had ventured to their front lawns as they boldly watched the spectacle. And as the fight wore on, many gathered closer, moving to Ocean's yard for a front and center view.

Most of the men had their arms crossed, hard expressions on their faces. A few kids were in the mix too. They were either cheering or covering their eyes when the snarls got particularly brutal. The women, however, shook their heads with barely concealed disgust. Disgust from the fighting or the fact that the Fire Wolf had returned to their town, I didn't know.

My nostrils flared at the thought, but I clenched my hands and didn't interfere even though my magic was heating inside me. I kept thinking their fighting would slow, that they would tire, get sick of tearing into each other, or just say enough was enough, but they didn't, and the longer it prevailed, the larger the crowd grew.

I didn't actually know who was a stronger fighter—both Cameron and the Fire Wolf were holding their own—but I did know that the hunter wasn't using everything in his arsenal. He wasn't casting magic, neither weaving spells nor throwing curses. And not once had he called upon his demon side by erupting into flames. Basically, the Fire Wolf was fighting as a werewolf only.

I eyed Ocean. "How much longer do you think they'll—"

"The bastard's back, eh?" A man shoved his way through the crowd. Like all the males here, he stood tall and broad. His lips twisted in a snarl, and his features made me do a double take. He and Ocean looked so similar.

"Let me guess," I said with a sick feeling churning my stomach. "That's Gavin?"

Ocean's face turned completely white. "Yes."

Gavin whipped his clothes off in one move, and in the next, he was shifting. His wolf appeared in an explosion of magic, his fur and coloring nearly identical to Cameron's.

The Fire Wolf whipped around just as Gavin's jaws clamped onto his hind leg. A vicious snarl erupted from the hunter before his body bent and he snapped at his other brother. He sank his teeth into Gavin and threw him off, but Cameron was on him again, sinking his fangs into the Fire Wolf's shoulder, the one that had been left open and unprotected.

My lips pressed into a thin line. "What the fuck is this?"

But Ocean didn't respond, and her face clouded in grief.

Cameron and Gavin circled the Fire Wolf, lunging and biting as the hunter met their strikes just as fast, but now that it was two against one, the older brothers were landing more blows and were able to tear more flesh between their teeth.

My hands turned into fists, the magic inside me near boiling. "They're ganging up on him."

"Yes," Ocean whispered. She wrapped her arms around herself, a pained sound coming from her throat.

On the lawn, Cameron slid at lightning-speed and snapped at the hunter's paw just as Gavin turned to the pack and howled. His long wail cut through the afternoon sky like a siren, and a shiver struck me, because something deep inside me told me that sound was more than just a howl—it was a calling.

The men watching the fight all eyed one another, their bodies beginning to tremble, their faces taking on expressions of excitement but something else, too, something darker and more primal.

"No." Ocean's face crumpled just as the first spectator shifted.

I took a step forward, my heart pounding. "What are they doing?"

Another man shifted, and then another. Since only men

could shift into wolves—female werewolves only carried the gene—the women stayed watching. Before I could blink, six more wolves were circling the Fire Wolf, all of them looking toward Gavin and Cameron.

Cameron snarled at them, then lunged at the hunter.

It was all the direction they needed. The six wolves descended on the hunter at once, their massive bodies becoming blurs of fur and malice.

My jaw dropped as rage strummed through me. Another commotion came from the crowd as more men appeared. They began to lift their shirts and unbutton their pants, all while the Fire Wolf became a spinning blur of jaw, fang, and claw.

"Oh no, you fuckers don't," I said, seething, and pushed against the porch, my legs carrying me as fast as the wind.

I reached the circle just as the newest men began to shift. Magic erupted from me in a hot wave of wrath and rage. My binding spell hit the men in a stinging roped tether. They all stopped mid-shift, their bodies distorted, their jaws partially realigned. Squeals of pain came from some. I could only imagine what halting mid-shift felt like, their bodies between man and wolf—bones not fully aligned, muscles partially torn—but I was beyond caring. What they were doing was bullying at its highest level, and I didn't give two shits if I ripped them all to shreds and was breaking every pack law in the universe.

With a fling of my arm, telekinetic magic skated down it in a full blast as I unleashed a huge well of power. When it hit them, the men flew through the air. Gasps and shocked whispers came from the women, children, and other men who hadn't joined the fight.

The half-shifted wolves landed two houses down, their bodies still twisted into those partially transformed shapes. Magic crackled around me as I swung around in a circle, daring anyone else to try to join in the fight.

The crowd all took a huge step back, their expressions turning from shock to disbelief to fear as they took me in.

Snarls and growls continued behind me, and I swirled around to the wolves, my palms tingling as my hair lifted with the energy crackling around me.

Cameron and Gavin, along with all of the other wolves, were biting and slashing at the hunter at every opening they could find. The hunter was still a blur, moving too quickly for me to see him, but he must have sensed me, must have known I was there, because he stopped mid-movement, just after he whipped one of the wolves off of him.

Fire raged in his eyes, and when he saw me striding toward him, the wind whipping my hair around my shoulders as the crowd leaped away from me, I could have sworn I saw a glimmer of pride in those blazing irises before his entire body erupted into flames.

The onlookers shrieked, stepping back even more as a flurry of whispers erupted among them. Words like *devil*, *demon-spawn*, and *abomination* reached my ears in those hushed comments.

With a sweep of my hand, I shot out a blast of power, knocking the three wolves closest to me to the ground.

They tipped over like bowling pins just as the hunter descended on the others, his flames licking their skin and singeing their fur.

Whines and yelps of pain came from those he burned, and I stopped, watching in awe as the Fire Wolf pounced and slashed, ripping and tearing his way through the remaining wolves, no longer fighting as just a wolf—because he wasn't just a werewolf. No, he was so much more.

Even his brothers didn't stand a chance despite their immense alpha power and magic, not when a demon wolf was raining his fury down on them.

Cameron let out a squeal when the Fire Wolf's jaws closed around his throat. The scent of scorched fur, then burning flesh, filled the air. Flames closed around his oldest brother as the crowd surged back even more, terror coating their faces.

A massive snarl abruptly cut through the crowd, coming from near the street. The entire crowd froze before they parted like an opening zipper as a huge middle-aged man barreled toward the fight. Murder shone in his gaze.

"That's enough!" the man roared. A wave of dominant energy shot out of him, firing like a weapon through the crowd.

All of the neighbors cowed, most wincing, before almost all of them dispersed and scurried back to their homes. They raced along the sidewalks and across the street, many of them glancing over their shoulders fearfully at the man who'd just appeared.

The half-shifted men I'd thrown did the same, finally changing back to their human forms, and they took off running, their bare asses mooning all who watched.

Another wave of power shot from the newcomer, and when it hit the Fire Wolf, Cameron, Gavin and those I'd knocked to the ground, all of the wolves ceased in their tracks, their heads whipping toward the old wolf.

My eyes widened when the newcomer's power hit me. And when it did . . . *holy shit*. If I thought Cameron was strong, he was nothing compared to the man who had just appeared.

I slowly backed up, keeping my attention on the old wolf as he stalked toward the brawling brothers.

"Let me guess?" I said to Ocean, who'd raced from her porch to get closer. My teeth chattered before I pulled my shield spell back up. "He's the alpha?"

Ocean nodded. "Yes, that would be my dad. Meet Paxton King, the alpha of the Ontario pack. Also known as Kaillen's father."

CHAPTER FIFTEEN

P axton didn't waste any time admonishing the other wolves who'd joined in the fight. With kicks to their rears and promises of retribution, he had them all scurrying away, their faces portraits of fear at the coming punishment their alpha promised.

And in two swift moves, Paxton had the brothers ripped apart—Cameron in one hand, Kaillen in the other, while Gavin's wolf bobbed to the side, his head bowed before he rolled to the ground, going belly up.

If the brothers' fight hadn't been so disturbing, I would have laughed at the comical sight. A fully grown, middle-aged supernatural werewolf held two, just as big, fully grown wolves by the scruff of their necks, dangling them in the air as if they were wee pups, while the third looked like a docile canine trying to avoid a whipping.

But the rage shining from the alpha's gaze smothered any amusement in me. Whatever was going on here, it was serious, and something told me it spanned decades. Because this had been far from a benign brotherly brawl, in which they could kiss and make up. Oh no, this went much deeper. It was obvious that Gavin and Cameron truly hated their younger brother.

"Shift back, now!" Paxton's command reverberated through the block and shook my shield.

Ocean, not having magic to protect herself, bared her neck, her chin jutting up as a strained expression formed on her face. Seeing all of this reminded me of how incredibly fucked up werewolf packs could be. Everything in them revolved around dominance, some packs still living in the old ways of male-dominated hierarchies where women were lowly servants or prized wives to be bred.

Luckily, most of the packs in North America had progressed, embracing a more modern way of life that was focused on the inclusion of women and the lesser dominant wolves, but they all still operated on dominance to some degree, and since I was new to Kaillen's non-pack, I wasn't entirely sure how this pack operated.

Another explosion of magic flashed on the lawn, and in a blink, Cameron, Kaillen, and Gavin were all crouched to the ground, naked and shuddering. Sweat dripped from their bodies, beady drops rolling past numerous cuts and bruises. But since all three were dominant wolves, their bodies began healing immediately. Any gashes or puncture wounds sealed over within a few minutes, and even though I didn't scent the Fire Wolf's magic that had healed him at lightning speed at the Black Underbelly, he still healed faster than his brothers.

Another middle-aged man jogged up behind Paxton and tossed the Fire Wolf, Cameron, and Gavin spare clothes.

"That's my father's beta," Ocean whispered.

Each brother tugged on a pair of pants, and the display was done so casually and easily, that I was again reminded of how nudity was not a big deal in packs.

My eyes glued to the hunter, raking up and down his frame as he stood to his full height and cinched the loose pants around his waist with the drawstring. The pants hung low on his hips, his ridged abs on full display.

None of the men bothered with a shirt, despite the air being cold and the wind blowing fiercely. The inky tattoo splayed across the hunter's upper back glistened with sweat.

I figured that the heat of the battle was still raging through their veins, or it was simply because they were werewolves with incredibly high metabolisms who were immune to the cold. Wolves were always known to be warm, as I remembered from my time with Carlos. But since the Fire Wolf also had those eternal flames inside him, I wondered if he burned even hotter than others.

My gaze slid over his impressive physique once more, taking in his rigid muscles and smooth skin. An aching pulse started low in my belly. My attraction to the hunter again fired through me, setting my nerves ablaze and my core on fire, even though it was an entirely inappropriate time to be having such a reaction.

The hunter's chin tilted toward me, his nostrils flaring. A knowing glint lit his eyes before his jaw locked and his attention shifted back to his father.

Paxton planted his hands on his hips, a heavy scowl covering his face. "What the hell is going on here?"

Cameron cast an irritated glare at his youngest brother. "He shouldn't be here."

If the Fire Wolf felt slighted, he hid it completely. In typical fashion, his face had turned into a stoic mask.

Paxton growled and took a step toward Cameron. "That's no way to treat your brother." His gaze swung to Gavin, too, who wisely kept his mouth shut.

Cameron's teeth gritted. "He's not our brother. He's worse than scum."

A pained sound escaped Ocean, and my hunter's gaze flickered toward her.

I watched the entire display, wide-eyed, and was beginning to see why the Fire Wolf had such disdain for this pack and didn't consider them his family.

Paxton glared at his eldest son, his eyes filled with deadly malice. "I was told you started this."

Cameron didn't reply.

"Apologize," Paxton snapped. "Right now."

Cameron's jaw locked. "No."

Paxton prowled a step closer to him, until his chest nearly brushed his son's. "Are you challenging me, boy?"

A muscle in the corner of Cameron's jaw flexed, and his

eyes flicked to Gavin, but Gavin looked down, his gaze on the ground.

Cameron went back to holding eye contact with his father, and a collective intake of breaths came from the few neighbors who had been brave enough to stay.

"Well?" Paxton bit out. A huge push of dominance shot from him.

Cameron's expression quivered, his muscles pulsing, but then he abruptly stepped back, bearing his neck.

Paxton glared again at his eldest son. "I'm still waiting for your apology to Kaillen."

Cameron's nostrils flared before he said through gritted teeth, "Sorry."

His father stared at him for a moment longer, as if to make sure his son wasn't getting any other ideas, before he shifted his attention to the hunter.

The Fire Wolf's outward expression hadn't changed, but his back grew straighter, his entire body stiffening.

"I'm sorry for this."

The hunter stayed quiet.

"You look well," Paxton added gruffly. "It's good to have you home."

The Fire Wolf gave a curt nod but still didn't reply.

"This won't happen again."

The Fire Wolf's eyes blazed, but his silence remained, and I wished so desperately that I knew what he was thinking.

Paxton glowered then barked at Cameron and Gavin, "Clean this place up. And I don't want to hear about any more fighting while your brother's here."

Cameron's eyes shot daggers at the Fire Wolf, and Gavin glared at him, but neither replied. Silently, they bent down and began collecting the shredded fabric on the lawn from the wolves who hadn't removed their clothing before shifting. They stuffed everything under their arms and stalked away.

Beside me, Ocean let out a sigh of relief as she shoved her hands into her pockets. "Looks like Kaillen's in the clear . . . for now."

I was still reeling from the entire brawl as the hunter and his father walked toward us. Now that the fight was over, the remaining neighbors retreated to their homes or backyards.

Paxton King stopped at Ocean's front porch. Up close, his face looked weathered. Deep grooves cut into the skin around his eyes, and his tanned complexion told me he spent most of his time outdoors. Like Cameron, his eyes were brown, but like the Fire Wolf, his frame was huge, similar in size to the hunter's.

The Fire Wolf's father cocked his head at me, his astute gaze assessing my frame. But unlike when Cameron had sized me up, the alpha's appraisal held no contempt or sneering hate. "You're Tala Davenport, the witch from Chicago that my pack is guarding?"

I nodded. "I am. And I hear you're Paxton King, the alpha of this pack?"

Surprise flickered in his eyes, even more so when my

gaze didn't lower. *That's right, sir. This lady isn't the submissive type.*

I continued to hold eye contact, and to his credit, he didn't shoot any dominant energy in my direction, which told me the Ontario pack didn't function entirely in the old ways. In other words, Mr. King didn't feel the need to have all women be subservient.

My respect for him grew, as did my relief at learning the Ontario pack wasn't archaic in its practices.

Still holding his gaze, I said in a friendlier tone, "Thank you for your pack's assistance. If I wasn't here, I would have been shipped off to who knows where by the SF."

"You're welcome," he responded. "Although, I have to admit, I was a bit surprised when Kaillen came to me with the request." His attention shifted from me to the hunter.

The Fire Wolf still hadn't uttered a word, but his back was as straight as an arrow while a small hint of a smile rolled across his lips as he watched me.

I tried to focus on the hunter's rigid posture instead of the fact that he was still shirtless, but, damn, it was hard. My fingers itched to touch him.

Paxton cocked his head at me. "I suppose I have you to thank for bringing my son home. It's been a decade since he's set foot on pack territory. How do you two know each other?"

"She hired me to find her sister." The Fire Wolf finally broke his silence, but he didn't elaborate past that simple declaration.

Paxton nodded. "I see. And I hear your sister is now safe?" he asked me.

"You heard correctly. Your son found her, but she's potentially still in danger. The SF believes the supernaturals your pack's guarding me against could attempt to abduct her again as a way of getting to me."

"And I hear they tried to abduct you, too?"

"That's right."

"So it's you they truly want, not your sister?"

"That's also right."

Paxton's attention shifted to his son. "Sounds like you and I have a few things to discuss."

The Fire Wolf's lips thinned. "I don't know if that's necessary. Tala and I won't be involved in pack activities, and I've already arranged the protection she needs with the men. Nothing else will be needed from the pack."

"But if the supernaturals who are after Tala are willing to use force to capture her, that could affect others in this pack. While we're happy to help, I also want to know exactly what we're dealing with."

"That's the problem. We don't know entirely who or what we're dealing with." The Fire Wolf's jaw tightened. "It's inevitable that they'll discover she's here if they have a seer, but they would be fools to antagonize the entire Ontario pack."

"Fools or not, it's a possibility we need to consider." Paxton stroked his chin. "From what Commander Klebus told me, this problem goes much deeper and broader than just you and your sister."

I nodded. "It does. Twelve other supernaturals are still missing, but with any luck, the SF will figure out what the hell's going on, catch all the bad guys, find the missing supernaturals, and wrap this up in the next few weeks. I don't intend to outstay my welcome here, and I'm sure you don't want your strongest fighters spending all of their time babysitting me."

A gruff laugh shot from Paxton. "You don't mince your words do you, Ms. Davenport?"

I shrugged. "You've already picked up on that, have you?"

A twinkle entered the alpha's eyes.

An amused smile lifted the hunter's lips. "If we're done here." The Fire Wolf stepped closer to me. "I'll take Tala back to my cabin. I'm sure this wasn't what she had in mind when we came to visit Ocean."

Ocean shoved her hands into her back pockets and shrugged. "But you only just got here, and now that Cameron's gone . . ." She let her words linger, and I raised an eyebrow at the Fire Wolf.

"She has a point," I said. "No offense, but hanging out in your cabin for the next few weeks doesn't sound like the most exciting way to spend our time."

The Fire Wolf's head dipped. "Are you sure about that?" A gleam entered his eyes, and a flush rose in my cheeks as Paxton and Ocean watched us with growing interest.

Paxton smiled. "So my son isn't just your hired hunter?"

"No!" I practically shouted. Mortification filled me as the Fire Wolf's gaze grew hooded.

"She and I disagree on that particular topic," the hunter added dryly.

Ocean's jaw dropped, and then a grin split across her face. "Do you mean . . ." Her attention shifted between the two of us, moving back and forth so quickly that she resembled a cartoon character with a spinning head. Her grin grew.

Oh gods.

"We're not together," I said with a sigh, bringing a hand to my forehead. "There's nothing going on between us and there never will be, so there's nothing to talk about. Really. This discussion is over."

A discontented frown came from the hunter as a twinge of curiosity entered the alpha's expression. His knowing smile came next.

Oh, for the love of all the gods. Not wanting to spend any time dwelling on this particular subject, I turned my attention to Ocean. "Do you want to show me around town? Your brother doesn't want to, and it would be nice to get to know the area better."

The hunter brushed closer to me, his hot skin beckoning me like the warm sun. "Tala, I don't think—"

"I would love to!" Ocean cut in. "Let me grab my keys."

CHAPTER SIXTEEN

Much to the hunter's consternation, Ocean gave me a thorough tour of Oak Trembler. Like the few other pack towns I'd visited, it was small but nicely kept. There was a large community center in the heart of the tiny city. Grocery and drug stores, clothing boutiques, and everything else in between that was needed to keep a community functioning, spread out around it. By the time Ocean finished the tour, darkness had fallen and the moon was shining.

I yawned, unable to help it as Ocean pulled onto the road leading to the hunter's cabin. "I'll take you back."

I nodded sleepily, somewhat embarrassed that I was practically nodding off, but it had been a long day, and I'd nearly died last night. Not to mention, I'd been running on fumes since Tessa's abduction.

A low rumble came from the hunter. "You need rest."

"I do." I didn't even bother arguing with him, because I did. I was bone-tired.

Ocean didn't linger when she pulled up to the cabin. She bid us goodnight, a radiant smile on her face that told me she'd enjoyed the time we'd spent together as much as I had.

"She's really nice," I said to the hunter as we waved goodbye while his sister disappeared back down the drive.

"She is. Ocean's the only reason I've kept in touch with this pack at all."

I gazed up at him as the moonlight touched upon his features, but he turned away and steered me toward the door. "You need to sleep."

My shoulders stiffened as I followed him.

He gave me a sardonic smile. "Don't worry. I won't force anything tonight. You'll take the bed. I'll take the couch. No more arguing."

Relief billowed through me knowing that I wouldn't have to contend with *that* tonight even though the hunter was still shirtless and, damn, it was hard to keep my attention firmly above his collarbones.

Still, it had been a long day so I gratefully took him up on his offer, and after brushing my teeth and changing into the questionable pajama choices my sister had packed for me—a black lacy nightie—I climbed into the huge bed in the master bedroom.

Within minutes, I was fast asleep.

~

THE SCENT of coffee woke me the next morning. It drifted into the bedroom, tickling my nose. My eyelids fluttered open as I stretched languidly.

A groan hit me when my sore muscles greeted me. *Ugh.* I was crazy stiff from training yesterday, but coffee? That, I would get up for.

I pushed the covers off me, noting the bright sunlight filling the room around the curtains. I'd definitely slept in. A peek at the bedside clock confirmed it. It was nearly ten in the morning.

After throwing a robe on, I padded on bare feet to the bathroom before venturing downstairs.

My footsteps slowed when I spotted the hunter. He sat in the same spot in the living room as he'd been in yesterday, legs stretched out, book in hand, while he sipped coffee from a large mug.

He paused his sipping, but didn't look at me, and continued to read his book.

I hurried past him, heading straight for the coffee pot on the counter, but called over my shoulder, "What are you reading?"

"A book about the history of supernatural wars."

Non-fiction. I cocked my head. That wasn't overly surprising. "Are you sure it's not a romance hiding behind a non-fic dust jacket?" I joined him in the living room but sat on the couch by the window.

A smile tugged at his lips. "I'm sure."

I sipped my coffee as the Fire Wolf continued to scan his book. He was legit reading it.

Settling more into the couch, I gazed outside, admiring the bare trees and rolling hills. Several minutes passed during which we both quietly sipped our coffee in companionable silence, and it struck me that it wasn't an uncomfortable solitude or one where a person felt the need to say something.

No, it was strangely one of those peaceful silences where neither person felt the need to fill the gaps with endless chatter.

I curled my legs beneath me and enjoyed my coffee as the hunter did the same, turning the pages of his book as he read.

When I finished my cup, I stood and eyed the outside again. "Can I go for a walk? Is that allowed?"

He set his book aside, his amber-hued eyes meeting mine.

My breath sucked in. The hunter's expression was open, his eyes soft, his dark hair tousled. He looked relaxed and at home, even though he didn't consider this his home, and I'd . . . never seen him look like that.

It struck me for the first time since meeting him that we weren't running hell-bent toward a fight, or chasing something, or avoiding the nagging attraction that sparked between us.

We were simply existing in a somewhat normal moment right now.

"I'll go with you." He set his book on the nearby table and stood. "I just need to change quick."

He still wore what I'd assumed he'd slept in. Loose

sweatpants and a T-shirt. I gulped as my attention shifted to the broadness of his chest when he rolled his shoulders. Somehow the man made sweats look sexy. I hastily looked out the window again. "Did you, um, sleep okay?"

He cracked his neck. "It was fine."

I eyed him. Something told me that he could have a giant crick in his neck but he wouldn't complain. "Thanks for letting me take the bed."

The corner of his mouth tugged up. "Don't expect it every night. That bed is big enough for two."

"Not if I sleep perpendicular."

"Oh, I'm sure I could accommodate that."

I bit my cheek to stop my smile as a twinkle lit his eyes.

Well okay then, the banter had officially started today.

With that twinkle still in place, he jogged up the stairs, a flurry of stealth, speed, and . . .

I jerked my gaze away. *I did not just check out his ass.*

But who was I kidding. I totally had.

WE VENTURED from the cabin to the surrounding hills, and even though I knew the pack's men were stationed around us, I didn't see any of them. The hunter and I walked leisurely, both of us quiet while chirping birds filled the breeze with their songs, dry leaves crunched under our feet, and bright sunshine warmed our faces.

The sky was blue, the air clear, and I realized it was the first time in years that I wasn't rushing to work, crafting spells, or running about in the chaos that was my life back in Chicago.

"This is nice," I said quietly.

"Good," he replied.

We carried on, and as the hills rolled around us, we began talking. It was the usual bantering at first, in which one of us was always trying to best or insult the other, but then it shifted and we actually settled into a more normal conversation in which I was surprised to discover that we had a few things in common. And since the subjects we were discussing weren't earth-shattering—books, music, movies, politics, cities we'd visited, that sort of thing—the Fire Wolf was forthcoming and his usual guardedness melted away.

Before I knew it, we were actually talking, laughing, and joking around like two normal people. Well, as normal as we could be. We still took sly jabs at each other every now and then, but from the grin stretching across the hunter's face, I figured he liked it as much as I did.

My mood was light when we finally returned to the cabin, and the walking had done my sore legs good. My stomach was another matter entirely, though. It was early afternoon and growling with a vengeance, reminding me that a cup of coffee for breakfast wasn't cutting it.

"I'll make lunch," the hunter said before prowling into the kitchen.

"I'm going to, uh, take a shower." I was still reeling that I'd just spent several hours with the menace of the Shadow Zone and now knew that his favorite city in the world was

London. Turned out the hunter had an affinity for history and mince pies.

~

WE WERE SEATED at the kitchen island, an array of food that Ocean had left for us last night spread out around us, as I inhaled everything in sight.

"You need to train," the hunter said out of the blue before popping a slice of ham into his mouth. His jaw worked, looking disturbingly sexy as he chewed the meat.

I forced my gaze away. "I know."

"So why are you stalling? There's no better time than now. You can't work here. There's not much else to do since you're still refusing to—"

"I know!" I cut him off before he could again hint at the fact that we hadn't ended up in bed yet.

He chuckled. "We should train today. I can help you."

My heartbeat stuttered. I forced the mouthful of food down my throat, then took a hasty drink of water. "How will you train me?" I asked hesitantly.

"I have a few ideas."

Of course he did.

He tossed the last pieces of food on his plate into his mouth. "No more stalling. We train today. You need to learn to harness your new power. If you could wield it, you would be unstoppable."

My heart rate kicked up, and not from the threat of Jakub-Dipshit. I raised my eyes to his, not surprised to find fire rolling in his irises. I swallowed the dryness in my mouth, knowing that he spoke sensibly even though I dreaded training with the hunter. But he was right.

"Fine. I'll train with you."

A slow smile spread across his face before it turned into a wicked grin.

I rolled my eyes. "Yes, once again, you win. Tell me, does your constant gloating ever get old?"

"Never. When it comes to you, Ms. Davenport, I plan to keep winning until I get everything that I want."

"So relentless," I muttered softly, shaking my head. "What the hell was I thinking when I hired the menace of the Shadow Zone who's known to be the most relentless hunter in this part of the world?"

He leaned closer to me. "I would say that made you quite astute." His lips drifted to my ear, and despite being determined to avoid the effect he had on me, a shudder ran through my body as a quickening curl of desire flooded my core. "I did find your sister, you know."

"At what price to me?"

"More like at what price to *me.* Now that I know you exist, you will forever haunt me."

After we'd finished lunch and changed into training clothes, the Fire Wolf transported us to the community center using his personal portal. It landed us in one of the huge rooms inside, and I knew from a quick perusal that it was a training room.

"We'll train here every day," the hunter stated. He was still wearing those damned loose pants, but at least he was wearing a shirt too. "But it won't be what you're expecting. Something tells me this new power inside you is less physical and more mental."

That comment snapped my attention away from ogling his physique. "Why do you think that?"

"Because you can't feel it when you're not under imminent threat. That tells me it's less connected to your physical body and more to your mental powers."

"How can you be so sure?"

"I know a thing or two about newly instilled mental magic."

His cryptic words had me frowning, then planting my hands on my hips. I gazed around at the large, airy area that was similar to the gym Prisha's family owned.

The Fire Wolf obviously sensed my hesitation because he added, "There are wards around this room. Even though wolves usually battle here, the Ontario pack employs several sorcerers and witches. These walls can withstand all species' magic."

"So are Canada's packs similar to America's? You obviously have community centers like they do."

"They are."

The times I'd visited Carlos's home with him in the States, we'd also ventured to his pack's community center. In most packs, the centers were huge buildings filled with classrooms, large dining areas, and training rooms. It allowed the entire pack to join together under one roof to mingle, care for the pack's young, hold pack meetings, and train.

I eyed the clock on the far wall. It was mid-afternoon. "You know, I'm still really sore from yesterday. Even if you think my new power is mainly mental, I don't know how much I'm capable of doing today."

"Relax, I promise to go easy on you for our first practice." He lifted his arms above his head, stretching. Muscles bulged everywhere.

My mouth went dry. *Lord, help me*. I crossed my arms. Forcing my gaze away from his very tempting appearance, I tapped my foot. "What makes you so confident that you can train me? My new power stumped Prisha's father, and he's been training me my entire life. Granted, he's never seen my new power in action or felt it like you have, but what makes you so confident?"

"I have a particular skill set that many don't share."

"And what exact skill set is that?"

He gave me another wicked smile. "Wouldn't you like to know?"

"Here we go again." I shook my head, and cast him an aggrieved stare. "I'm being serious, you know. This is only my life that we're gambling with 'cause I'm pretty sure Jakub-Dipshit doesn't value it."

All joking left his face. "I know that. I take this very seriously."

"Then would you answer my question?"

He held my gaze for a moment before replying, "It has to do with what I am."

"And what are you?"

He leaned down and began pulling mats together on the floor, the broad muscled plains of his back shifting and rippling. "I'm a supernatural unlike anybody else on earth."

"Meaning what?"

"Meaning, as you've pointed out several times before, I have a unique genetic mixture." His muscles bulged when he lifted an entire mat over his head before placing it beside the first. The scent of rubber rose around us every time he shifted the huge squares.

"What exactly are your genetics?"

"You already know that I'm part werewolf and part demon. But there's more to it than that."

"As I've surmised, since you're capable of casting spells." I tapped my foot again. "Are you ever going to tell me?"

His lips tilted up in a smirk, a low chuckle escaping him. "I don't know. I quite like when you constantly beg me. Your curiosity is amusing."

I advanced on him, intent on wiping that smirk right off his face.

An excited gleam grew in his eyes. *Ugh.* His demon side was running front and center right now, just waiting for the conflict. No, not waiting. *Relishing* what was about to come.

Seeing that brought me up short. I halted two feet away, realizing I'd almost fallen into his trap. He loved to provoke me, but what if I flipped the tables on him? I crossed my arms again. "How about this? I'll make a deal with you."

He straightened to his full height. Damn, why did he have to look so good? "I'm listening."

"If you tell me what you are, I'll tell you something in return."

"Like what?"

I shrugged. "Something that you're curious to learn about me."

"No deal."

My arms fell. "Why not?"

"Because that's not what I want."

"You're not interested in learning about me?" For some reason, that needled at my heart.

"On the contrary, I'm *very* interested in learning about you, but that's not what I want at this moment."

"Then what do you want?"

"You already know." Heat grew in his gaze.

"Oh my gods, you're such a male. *That's* not happening."

He sauntered away to grab the last mat by the far wall. I tried to ignore how those loose pants hung so low on his lean hips. "That's a shame," he called over his shoulder. "I know you're dying to know what I am."

My teeth snapped together as I glowered at his back. *Stupid, insufferable demony wolf.*

His dark chuckle rumbled in the room. "Careful. I can feel those daggers shooting into my back."

I cupped my mouth to project my voice. "Good. I hope they're painful!"

He laughed, the sound resonating around me.

I scoffed, and despite knowing that he was purposefully baiting me, I couldn't stop my curiosity. "Why can't you just tell me what your genetics are? How can you wield fire *and* magic?"

He strolled back, the last mat in tow. "I'll answer that if you give me what I want."

"No. I refuse to fuck you."

"But what if that's not what I was going to request?"

I eyed him warily. "Then what was it?"

"Sleep with me tonight."

I rolled my eyes. "Dude, what did I just say? I'm not fucking you, and I am *not* a prostitute. I'm not bartering sex for information."

"I never said sex. I said *sleep with*." He took another step forward, and his citrusy cedar scent hit me with such a vengeance that my entire body fluttered to awareness. When had his scent grown so strong? "You're the one who's wanting to strike a deal, and I just gave you my terms. I'll tell you exactly what I am if you share my bed tonight. Do you accept?"

I narrowed my eyes, not liking at all how my belly was tightening in anticipation. "Define what your definition of *sleep with* is."

"We share the same bed."

"And?"

"And we sleep beside one another."

"And?"

"There's no further *and*. We simply share a bed. That's all I'm asking for."

"You mean you're not insistent that I, you know . . ."

A devilish smile curved his lips. "Whatever are you referring to, Ms. Davenport?"

My cheeks flamed. "You're insufferable."

"You wouldn't have me any other way."

My breath caught at his words, because he was right. *Dammit.* As much as I didn't want to admit it, I liked his company. I liked bantering with him. I liked when his demon side made him entirely unpredictable. It put me on edge and set my nerves ablaze, and *excited* me. There was never a dull or ordinary moment around him—well, usually there wasn't. Our walk this morning had been relatively normal, but I'd enjoyed that too. He was wild and unpredictable, yet interesting and layered. And he was caring when needed, and oh-so fucking fuckable.

Crap. So I liked his company. I liked *him*. There, I'd admitted it to myself. And, gods, it would be so much easier to just give in to this desire to be with him. To let myself get swept up in the Fire Wolf's molten desire and heated promises.

But then Carlos's warning flitted to the front of my mind. *Can't be a normal mate instinct.*

If only I had a crystal ball. If only I could know what would happen if I did give in to these urges and took the hunter up on all of the tantalizing things he wanted to do in the bedroom. If my sister were in this position, she would do it in a second, never once thinking about the consequences or fallout of her actions.

But I wasn't her. I'd always been the more sensible, the more pragmatic. The one to carefully weigh the options and analyze the pros and cons, before making a decision that carefully balanced mitigated risk with a high yield. It was those traits that had resulted in Practically Perfect being a successful business.

With a firm press of my lips, I made up my mind. Nope. I wasn't going to have a mindless fling with the hunter. While the sex would no doubt be mind-blowing, I wasn't going to risk losing my heart to a man who'd never genuinely wanted me before his wolf caught my true scent. Because Carlos could be right. Even if I decided to ignore the hunter's initial lack of interest, and trust that he would still want me just as desperately after fucking me senseless because of the mate instinct, I had to remember that the hunter wasn't just a wolf.

He was a demon too.

And demons loved to fuck and forget.

Besides, even if the mate instinct didn't disappear after he banged my brains out, it would never change the reality of our situation. The truth was he'd never once wanted me before his wolf did. The man—the supernatural underneath all of his magic and power—hadn't wanted me. Only I had wanted him.

Pain again flared in my heart when I remembered that. *It is what it is, Tala. Don't dwell on it.* As long as I kept reality firmly in mind, I could meet his end of the bargain while finally learning what I'd been wondering about since we'd met. I could do this.

I squared my shoulders. "Okay, fine. You tell me what you are, and I'll sleep in your bed with you tonight, but all we're doing is *sleeping*."

A swell of triumph graced his features, smugness glittering in his amber-hued eyes.

I glowered. "You're doing it again."

"Doing what?" he asked with mocking innocence.

"Gloating."

"You can hardly blame me. Having you in my bed is something I've craved since the first moment we met."

Since the first moment we met? *But that would mean . . .*

I shook my head. No, he was mind-fucking with me. *Manipulative demony wolf hunter. Don't fall for it. You saw his amusement. He found your attraction to him comical, hardly sexy.*

Keeping that reminder firmly in the center of my thoughts, I said, "All right, I agreed to your terms, so tell me. What are you?"

"It's not a simple explanation."

I raised my hands. "Then good thing I'm not busy at the moment."

"Well, you should be busy. You should be training."

I rolled my eyes. "Just tell me already."

His brow furrowed. "It has to do with what happened to me after my father brought me here." He waved to the mat. "Do you want to sit down? This won't be a quick story."

CHAPTER SEVENTEEN

I settled on the mat beside the hunter, being careful to keep a few feet of distance between us. I didn't want him getting any ideas. Now that I'd agreed to spend the night in his bed—even though I'd made it clear we were *not* having sex—I also knew that I needed to keep my wits about me.

He leveled me with those amber eyes, his chiseled features growing carefully blank. "I'm half werewolf and half demon, but I also have sorcerer magic. My magic comes from a sorcerer that my father commissioned when I was young. After my father brought me back from the underworld, things were difficult, so now I have that particular sorcerer's magic inside me."

I sat up straighter. "How?"

He gazed at me, his expression turning deviously innocent. "I believe our deal was that I simply told you what I am. I just did. I'm a demon werewolf who possesses a sorcerer's magic. I've upheld my end of the bargain, and now it's your turn to uphold yours. Tonight, I expect you in my bed, beside me, until morning."

My core clenched at just the thought. Dammit, that wasn't a good sign. *Remember reality, Tala.*

A sizzling heat grew in his eyes. "I very much look forward to this evening. It's only a few short hours away." He inhaled, his pupils dilating when my true scent hit him. I hadn't put my cloaking spell back in place, and with a start, I realized it was the longest I'd gone without it since I was a child. "You smell so delicious, *colantha*. I can't wait to taste you again."

"There will be no tasting. Just sleeping!" Okay, so my voice sounded a bit breathless there, but I couldn't believe what I'd agreed to. Worse, I wanted to know more. Even though the hunter had revealed what he was, all that did was elicit even more curious questions in me.

He made a move to stand, and my hand shot out, locking around his wrist. I forced myself to ignore the feel of his hard muscles bunching beneath my grip, or the way his entire body grew still and ready, as if he were just waiting to pounce. "Why did you tell me to sit down? That was hardly a long story."

He settled back beside me, his large body moving with cat-like grace.

I inched back a foot. Funny how the hunter hadn't seated himself where he'd been a second ago. Oh no, he'd seated himself *right beside me* so our thighs brushed.

"You're right. That wasn't a long story." He grinned wickedly. "But it could be. I could tell you everything. Everything from the time I was born to now. Then you would know exactly what I am and why I turned out this way."

"I have a feeling that information comes with a price."

His grin grew. "You know me so well."

I rolled my eyes. "How many people know your story?"

"Only one."

"Who?"

"My father."

"What about your brothers and sister? Your non-pack? Your friends?"

"They know some of the details but not all."

My heart skipped a beat. "Yet you would tell *me* those details?" I shook my head in disbelief. "Why?"

"Isn't it obvious? I want you."

I forced myself to take a deep breath, because that dipping and rolling feeling in my stomach had increased a hundred-fold. "Why do you want me so much?"

He inhaled, leaning closer.

I backed up even more, knowing that if he touched me at this very moment, I would succumb to the heat sliding through my veins.

"Because I do."

I did my best to maintain an even expression, but that crestfallen feeling engulfed me again. It was the mate instinct, one hundred percent. It was the only reason he wanted me.

It is what it is.

Swallowing down my growing disappointment, I asked, "And what price do I have to pay to learn the whole story? And I mean *all* of it. I want to know what you are and how you ended up here in a pack that despises you, and how your father impregnated a female demon, and how a sorcerer's magic came to be inside you." I licked my lips, and the hunter's gaze fell to my mouth. A golden glow lit his eyes. "How much will that cost me? For you to share all of that? For me to know everything?"

His heated gaze grew. "That would definitely require me fucking you."

I slugged him in the shoulder just as he let out a deep laugh. He caught my wrist, his eyes darkening. "Have I ever told you how much I love your violent side?"

I stuttered. He'd seriously just used the L word. Granted he hadn't said he loved *me*, but he still used the word. I quickly brushed those thoughts off. It was the mate instinct talking again. "You just told me that I have to prostitute myself for information so, of course, I'm going to hit you."

"I was kidding about you having to fuck me. I only said that because I knew it would elicit your"—his lips curved in delight—"more *aggressive* tendencies, and I do so enjoy it when you hit me."

"You're deranged."

"Perhaps, but what I'm not is a paying customer. When you finally let me bed you—and you will—it won't be because I forced it from you. Instead, it will be because you'll be begging me to slide inside you. And I'll have you so wet, and so hot, that you won't be able to live another moment without me filling you." His voice dropped, his words turning husky.

My chest tightened, my breath catching. Just hearing him describe that, even *hint* at what it could be like between us . . . *Gods*.

His nostrils flared. "Even now, I can tell how much you want it, which makes me even more frustrated that you're fighting this so much."

"We're getting off topic," I said breathlessly.

"Perhaps, but you have to admit, *this* is a much more tantalizing subject and one I'd much rather be discussing."

"I disagree." I cleared my throat and tamped firmly down on the ache in my belly. "Now, back to what we were talking about . . ." Gods, my voice was *still* breathy. "What are your new terms? For you to tell me everything about you, what do you want from me?"

He watched me for a long moment, his gaze never wavering. That golden glow was still there, his wolf in his eyes. "I want you in my bed every night."

Every. Night.

Holy fucking tuna fish.

I cleared my throat again, determined to make this a clear business arrangement and nothing more. "Every night for how long?"

"For the remainder of our time here."

"And after we leave here that deal ends?"

Something flashed in his eyes, but it disappeared too quickly for me to decipher it. "Yes."

"Just to be clear, we won't be having sex. We will be sleeping beside each other every night and nothing more, and this will only be while we're staying here in Canada with your pack?"

His lips tugged up. "Have you made many fairy bargains?"

"Why do you ask?"

"Because if you haven't, you'd be quite good at it."

I shook my head but had to smother a laugh. Everyone knew how binding fairy bargains were. The less specific ones tended to get the supernaturals who'd agreed to them in a world of shit.

He held up a finger. "Also, to be clear, there's no reason we can't have sex, but like I said earlier, I won't be forcing anything on you."

I took another long inhale, feeling more than ever that I was making a deal with the devil. But as much as the hunter's demon side ruled him at times, I'd seen enough of him to know that he wasn't such a snake as to renege on our arrangement. He truly wouldn't force anything from me, but I also knew he'd be all over me in a second if I let him, which meant *I* had to be the strong one.

Surely, I could do that.

"Fine," I said briskly. "We'll sleep in the same bed every night while we're here, but *sleeping* and sleeping only. And if I want to put pillows or a big blanket between us to create a barrier, then I can. I reserve the right to do that."

He frowned, studying me. "No pillows. Or blankets between us."

My nostrils flared.

A smile slid across his face.

I opened my mouth to snap at him, but he beat me to it. "I know, I know. I'm gloating again, but that's only because I know that I have you. You *really* want to know what I am, and I *really* want you in my bed with nothing keeping your body from mine. So now the question is, how much do you want to know? Because I'm not budging. Every night. In my bed. No barriers. And then I'll tell you everything." He studied me, triumph building in his gaze. "You're going to agree. I can see it."

Irritation washed through me, but so did liquid desire. It shot to my core at the thought of sleeping with the hunter. His large body. His smooth skin. His hot muscles.

His nostrils flared again. He'd obviously detected my arousal. *Damn him.*

"Okay, fine. You win. Now stop being a demon-wolf and just tell me the damn story," I snapped.

He chuckled, the sound deep and rich, before he settled back, his hands splaying behind him as he leaned across the mat. Against my better judgment, I let my gaze dip.

His rounded shoulders bulged, and his pecs looked like smooth slabs of stone. And his abs. Lord almighty, the man gave washboard a whole new meaning.

The hunter was a freaking work of art. A dark angel sent from the black underworld. He was here to test my patience and inflame my senses.

Huffing, I looked away and called upon my practical side, willing myself to maintain control and *not* do something foolish. I could only hope that I didn't lose my head. "All right, I'm listening. Now spill it."

He grinned, an all-out Cheshire Cat grin. "I was an infant when my father discovered that he'd birthed a child to a female demon. He didn't even know about me until I was six weeks old."

All thoughts of desire and the hunter in my bed vanished. "You lived with your demon mother in the *underworld* until you were six weeks old?"

"I did."

"And you survived. She didn't eat you or kill you, obviously."

"She didn't, but I have a feeling that would have changed if my father hadn't found me." His expression didn't falter, but I couldn't help but wonder if knowing that hurt.

"And you don't remember her at all since you were so young?"

"Correct."

I shook my head. "Sorry, go on with the rest of your story."

He shrugged, not seeming to mind the interruption, and he'd freely offered answers when I'd asked for them—a first. The hunter was obviously pleased at what I'd agreed to, and as much as I wondered if I would regret it, I did feel a bit better that it didn't seem he'd hold back about his origins.

His hands splayed wider on the mat. "The problem was that my father didn't anticipate the challenges that would come with raising someone such as myself."

"What do you mean by that?"

He smiled devilishly. "Where do I begin . . ."

CHAPTER EIGHTEEN

"Start at the beginning. You promised everything, remember?" I reminded the hunter.

"Oh, don't worry, I haven't forgotten." That wicked smile grew. "Because of my mother's status in the underworld, caring for me on earth proved problematic for my father."

"What's her status?"

"She's Lucifer's daughter."

My mouth dropped open, and I gaped like I was trying to catch flies. But then I remembered his black flames and his cold words to Star Tattoo Guy before he'd killed him. *Don't you know who my mother is?*

"That's why you can create those black flames, and that's why you can control them and use them to kill other demons."

He nodded.

"But . . . how did your father meet Lucifer's daughter?

And how—" I shook my head, in complete disbelief that *any* of this was possible.

"Her name's Asuran."

I skimmed through my memories, trying to find what I could about demons. I came up blank. "I've never heard of her."

"Most haven't. Only some half-demons know of her. She's rather reclusive, never leaves the underworld, and given her power, she has high status down there. Not many have dared cross her."

"Then how did she end up pregnant with you?"

"Bad luck I suppose. For her, not me," he added quickly when my face fell. "She hadn't ever left the underworld as far as I know, and why she got inclined to leave the night she met Paxton, I still don't know, but she did. She entered the fae lands, and as demons typically do, she cloaked her appearance and went to one of the bars. That's where she met my father."

A lightbulb clicked on. "So it's the typical man sees attractive woman in a bar, they drink, then hook up, then oops . . . a baby was made scenario?"

"Not quite. My father was already drunk when she entered the bar, but he was drunk because he was trying to run from his pain. From what he can surmise, it was his pain that attracted Asuran to him. She entered his thoughts, and tugged at his memories until she learned what sorrows he was trying to drown with his fae drink."

I cocked my head.

The hunter's expression turned unreadable. "He was

grieving his dead mate, the female werewolf that birthed Cameron, Gavin, and Ocean. She'd been killed in a rogue wolf attack only six months prior, and he wasn't coping well."

"Oh." That would explain why his siblings all looked like werewolves only—because they were.

"So Asuran changed her appearance to look like my father's dead mate. My father only told me this story once, but when he did, I could tell that he'd been so destroyed by his mate's death that even though he knew the woman approaching him in the bar couldn't possibly be her, he pushed that aside and let himself drown in the fantasy of seeing her again." The Fire Wolf scratched his chin. "He said the entire night he was with her, he could feel his energy and magic being tugged and pulled at. Asuran was feeding not only off his pain and anguish, but also his ecstasy and hope that his mate was with him again. But, of course, in typical demon fashion, she didn't stick around. The next morning, she left, and it was only many months later that my father happened to hear about me. It was pure luck he'd even been made aware of my birth, because if he hadn't, I'm certain I would have died."

"How did he get you back?"

"He commissioned several half-demons to venture to the underworld to retrieve me, but taking me from Asuran was not as difficult as they assumed it would be." He gave a joyless smile. "She readily handed me over for a small price. Female demons are similar to their male counterparts in that aspect. She had no love for me. I was near starved when they found me."

I didn't know much about how demons mated or produced offspring, but the way they behaved toward their young wasn't like humans or supernaturals. The little I did know told me they were more like reptiles. Their offspring were born and then they were left to fend for themselves. Only the strongest survived.

"How did you survive at all? She must have fed you at times."

He nodded. "She did. We can only deduce that my werewolf blood triggered that in her, since demons don't normally feed their children. But my birth must have stimulated it because the half-demons who rescued me said she had full breasts that dripped milk, so Asuran must have fed me some, or I wouldn't have made it past a few days, but she didn't take care of me. I was barely breathing when they found me."

"So then what happened?"

"They took me back to my father, and that was when the problems started. My body wouldn't accept milk from the pack's wet nurse. It only made me sicker."

"But infants born of demon fathers can feed from their supernatural mothers or wet nurses."

"True, which means that something about coming from a female demon made me different. After days of me deteriorating further, my father sought help from the local council. One of them had heard of a sorcerer who possessed magic and knowledge that could help demon offspring. My father found him, hired him, and he was the one who ultimately saved me."

"How?"

"He created a synthetic milk, woven through magic and spells, that was able to sustain me. I began growing again, thriving in fact, but it wasn't until I reached toddlerhood that they discovered the side effect of creating that nutrition for me." He smirked when he caught my curious expression. "The sorcerer's power somehow also transferred to the synthetic milk he created. By accident or on purpose, I don't know, but his magically infused milk also gave me his power, and when he died, all of his magic transferred to me."

My lips parted. "Seriously? I've literally never heard of anything like this."

Amusement glinted in his eyes. "Seriously."

"He must have been very powerful."

"He was. One of the most powerful sorcerers in the world."

"Do you remember him?"

He cocked his head. "I have a couple memories of him, but he was old when my father found him and died when I was five. My father thinks he saw me as the son he'd never had and believes he purposefully gave all of his magic to me. That I was his only chance at leaving a lasting impression on the world."

"His legacy."

"Exactly."

And what a legacy he turned out to be. "So that's where

your magic comes from? This sorcerer who your father commissioned to save you?"

"It does."

I shook my head. "I didn't even know sorcerers could transfer their power."

"I don't think many can. Actually, it's possible *no* others can. He might have been unique in that aspect."

I studied him for a moment, trying to imagine what growing up with his genetics had felt like. "You must have felt very alone here in this pack since you weren't a pure-blooded werewolf like everyone else."

His expression clouded. "It created some challenges, mainly the discord with my brothers."

"So they hate you because you're a werewolf with sorcerer magic?"

"No, they hate me because I'm a constant reminder of their mother being killed and our father's betrayal to her memory. They're old enough to remember her. Ocean isn't. And they see me as the outcome of their father's fall from grace. No mated wolf male would ever sleep with another female as quickly as our father did. It's disrespectful to their mother's memory and what Paxton should have felt for her."

"But your father only slept with Asuran because she looked like his mate. It was his deep grief that drove him to do it."

"Try telling them that." He shook his head, a hint of bitterness curling his lip. "It didn't help that I grew up to be what I am. I'm stronger than them, more powerful, and they hate me for it."

I made a sour face. "That's ridiculous. You were an innocent child, even if you came from a female demon, and even if your father dishonored their mother by sleeping with that demon."

He shrugged. "They'll never listen to reason. I accepted that long ago."

"But what about the rest of your pack? Ocean said they all dislike you." From what I'd seen and heard yesterday, I believed her.

"They do. I'm an outsider. I always have been. To them, I'm the freak child of the alpha that they were forced to put up with, and of course"—his wicked smile returned—"it didn't help that I wasn't exactly a well-behaved child or teenager. Once I realized that it didn't matter how much I tried to fit in or how much I tried to please them, I stopped trying. But not only that, I went in the opposite direction. I made it a point to inflict as much pain as I could on all of them."

"By doing what?"

"Fighting. Stealing. Arson. You name it, I did it."

"You were rebelling because no one would accept you. How could they not see that?"

"Maybe they didn't want to."

"But a lot of kids do stuff like that before they outgrow it. Why would your pack hold that kind of behavior against you?"

He shrugged. "You have to remember that I'm the

youngest of my father's children. Cameron was always in line to be the next alpha, and if he backed out, there was Gavin. There was never any doubt that one of them would rise to the top. So not only was I different from everybody else, but I was inconsequential. With no hope of me ever leading this pack, the pack followed my brothers' lead. Since Cameron and Gavin hated me, everybody else did too, as you saw firsthand yesterday."

"But how could they possibly think you're inconsequential? You're stronger than all of them. I saw that much in the fight. You weren't even using half of what you're capable of, not even at the end when you erupted into flames."

He cocked an eyebrow. "Perhaps."

"So that means that you *could* challenge your father one day to be alpha of this pack. Surely, the others would have recognized that."

"They did, eventually, but I didn't come into my full powers until I was a teenager, and since I left when I was eighteen, there were only a few years where that fear came to light. But by then, the pack's mind had already been made up. I wasn't one of them. And since I showed no desire to lead them, my strength or power didn't matter because I wanted nothing to do with this place. The second I hit eighteen, I left and never looked back."

I sat silent for a moment, studying him again. He held eye contact, but his expression gave away nothing. It was tragic, really. He was the outcast of his pack, a unique supernatural that couldn't identify with anybody, and then to ostracize himself from his family on top of it . . .

"You must feel so alone." The declaration left my lips before I could stop it.

A small smile tilted his lips. "Don't tell me this is going to turn into a therapy session."

I chuckled, shaking myself out of my thoughts. "Hardly, it was just an observation. Do you though? Feel alone?"

His expression turned pensive, as though he were considering my words, almost as if he'd never truly thought about it. "If I was a full-blooded werewolf, I probably would, but I'm not, so no, I'm fine. I like leading my own life and not having the worry of turning rogue. And I've never felt the pull to this pack, or any pack. I am my own master. Nobody controls me."

As I had come to see all too well. "So that's why you've never turned rogue even though you don't associate with a pack? It's because of your demon blood and sorcerer magic?"

He nodded. "My demon blood is too strong. While I can shift into a wolf and can have werewolf tendencies at times, it doesn't rule me. I could spend the rest of my life never seeing another werewolf, and I would never turn rogue."

I nibbled on my lip, because his werewolf tendencies did rule him to some extent. How he felt about me was one hundred percent driven by his wolf side.

But I didn't go there. "So that's why your brother

attacked you at your sister's house. It was simply because he hates you."

"Yeah. Cameron's dislike for me runs deep." He sneered. "Gavin followed suit, even though there was a time when I thought that maybe Gavin and I could—" He shook his head.

"Were your brothers ever kind to you?"

"Cameron never was. Gavin was initially but that stopped long ago." His expression closed off, like a book snapping shut.

"Do you have any other siblings—half-demon siblings—from your mother's side?"

"Not that I'm aware of. As far as I know, she hasn't left the underworld again. Her venture to the fae lands, when she met my father and became impregnated, was her one and only dance outside of Lucifer's gates."

"Have you ever been curious to return to the under-world to meet her?"

He smiled humorlessly. "I tried once when I was a teenager and was feeling a bit sorry for myself. It'd been following a rather nasty encounter with my brothers and some other pack kids after school one day. That particular run-in didn't end well, for me or them. My injuries took several hours to heal, but once they did, I decided to run away to the underworld, thinking maybe I could live with Asuran. But that wasn't a good idea. I never even saw her. The other demons made sure of that, and it quickly became apparent that the underworld was no better than my pack." He smirked. "I haven't tried again to find her."

He said it all matter-of-factly, as if it were no big deal to be beaten up regularly, bullied, and made to feel so alone that you ran away *to the underworld* in search of a better life. My heart broke at the thought of a young boy feeling so alone and then trying to reach out to the one parent that he hoped he could perhaps identify with and find a home with. "Is that why you help homeless kids?"

He frowned, and then his gaze found mine. "I suppose it is."

"It makes sense. On some level, you identify with them."

He shrugged. "I suppose I do."

I was quiet for a moment, studying him, and then said, "You're brave and resilient."

He didn't respond, but a golden flare lit his eyes.

My heart cracked, and a feeling gushed into it that felt a lot like . . . admiration, and something deeper. I quickly sat up straighter. "Your father seems to care for you. Why didn't he put a stop to your brothers' behavior?"

"He tried." The hunter shrugged again. He looked away, and that emotion I'd seen in his eyes vanished. "You got a taste of that when he made an appearance at Ocean's house, but there's only so much he can do. Cameron and Gavin are headstrong, not surprising since they carry an alpha's bloodline, and my father can only control them so much. If he completely dominated them, the pack would never respect them, and then his sons would never rise to the top. At best, he was able to stop some of my brothers' malicious attacks. At worst, he never knew about them."

"How often did they beat you up?"

"Weekly. Sometimes more if my father was out of town and they knew they could get away with it. But since I heal quickly, he didn't know about most of them."

"And you never told him?"

He snorted. "And give my brothers the satisfaction of seeing that they could hurt me? Never."

"Such hatred." A bitter taste filled my mouth. Even though Tessa and I had our moments where we fought, I couldn't imagine treating her that way. She was my sister, my flesh and blood, and even though Gavin and Cameron weren't the hunter's full-blooded siblings, they were still his half-brothers. I made a sound of disgust, my mouth twisting in fury. "What assholes."

The hunter smiled. "You sound almost affronted."

"I am. It's bad enough they treated you like that when you were a kid, but it's even worse that they continue to do it as adults. They should've grown out of it by now. Actually, they should've realized how wrong they were to treat you that way and apologized years ago. The fact that they're still doing it—" I shook my head. "It makes me have no respect for them whatsoever."

His smile spread into a grin. "That makes two of us."

My nostrils flared as I tried to stomp upon the anger stirring around inside me. A cloud of the hunter's citrusy cedar scent hit me, sliding through my veins and folding around my senses. It was so strong again and felt as though I'd been wrapped up in the hunter himself. A brief sense of comfort flowed over me, dampening some of my rage.

"Is there anything else you'd like to know about me?"

His gaze burned into me again, those amber-hued eyes missing nothing.

My eyebrows shot up. "You're really willing to answer whatever I want to know?"

"That was the deal, wasn't it? I give you the full story and you sleep in my bed every night." That wild look of anticipation danced in his eyes again.

A flush stained my cheeks. Before my breathing could grow completely out of control, I glanced away and forced myself to take a slow, deep breath. "Nothing comes to mind at the moment. Everything finally makes sense now."

"Shall we train then?"

My heart skipped. "Right. Training."

I'd completely forgotten that was the entire reason we were here. I glanced at the clock. An hour had passed since we'd first arrived. Evening was just around the corner, and after that, it would be time to go to sleep—with the hunter.

"I suppose we should train." I made a move to stand, but the hunter's hand curled around my wrist, his sure grip and warm fingers causing goose pimples to sprout along my skin.

"The training I had in mind doesn't require standing."

I rolled my eyes. "If your training is some perverted demon thing in which I stay horizontal, don't even think—"

He laughed, the sound so sudden I stopped talking. "It's not, I promise. Sit down, across from me, and close your eyes."

I eyed him suspiciously.

"I'm not going to pounce on you." That wicked smile returned. "Yet."

I sighed and plopped down on the floor across from him as requested, but I didn't close my eyes. "If I get any hint of you using this training session to wear down my defenses and spring on me—"

He brought a finger to my lips. The abrupt contact of his body touching mine, even if it was only his finger, had me jolting upright, my spine snapping into a straight line.

"When we're in this room, I promise to only be training you. I won't cross any boundaries that you don't want me to."

His eyes promised that he would uphold that vow, but underneath it, I saw the heat and desire. He would maintain his boundaries as long as I asked him to, but the second I didn't?

Then all bets were off.

CHAPTER NINETEEN

"Keep your eyes closed and feel inside yourself for your forbidden power. Do you feel it?"

"I do." It swirled up and beckoned me to use it. "I can easily find that ability. It's the *new* power that's eluding me."

"What do you feel right now from your forbidden magic?"

My forehead puckered. "A bottomless well of strength and sparkling potential. There's so much."

"If you call for it, what happens?"

"It rises up, and I can easily wield it."

"What about your other magic—your witch powers?"

"They're separate to this one. They're always there, in my chest, but my magic that enhances power in people, that's deeper."

"Where is it in you?"

"Here." I placed a hand over my lower belly. "It's always down here."

"And when you're not using it, do you still feel it?"

I cocked my head, my eyes staying closed. "No, I don't usually notice it, but when I want to tap into it, it springs forward so I never have to search."

"I imagine your new power is similar, but since it's unfamiliar to you, you don't know how to locate or call it. Do you mind if I try to help?"

My eyes flashed open, then widened when I saw the hunter sat so close, although he wasn't touching me. "Have your eyes been closed at all?"

"No."

I glowered at him. "Have you just been staring at me?"

"I have. Is that a problem?" His voice dipped, turning husky.

My chest rose unsteadily. "We're supposed to be training."

"And we are. I haven't touched you, have I?"

"No, but you're watching me."

"I'm not the one who needs to be focusing inward, and besides, the view is quite delectable. It would be a shame not to admire it."

Gods, the man was . . . grr. I ignored the urge to squirm. "It makes me . . . uncomfortable when you watch me."

His nostrils flared, no doubt scenting the arousal that was again fluttering through my system. "Are you sure that's what it makes you feel?"

"Yes!" I snapped.

He smirked. "Fine, I'll close my eyes if you like, but I have an idea on how to help you. Can I try?"

"What are you going to do?"

"Trust me."

"Says the powerful demon lord offspring."

He chuckled. "Half demon lord."

"Sorry, your half-highness, but I still want to know your plan."

He smirked. "All right, my plan is to use your forbidden magic—as you call it—to find the new one. You'll need to use your forbidden power to strengthen my magic again, and I'm going to see if I can connect with you while you're doing it. I want to see if it helps us locate your new power."

"You're going to connect with me?"

"That's the plan. I'm going to try entering your body when I do it."

My mouth went dry. "You're going *to enter my body* when my magic is tethered to your power?" I'd literally never done anything like that with anyone. I was so used to hiding my forbidden power, not sharing it with others. "That sounds rather . . . intense."

"It could be. You're not scared, are you?"

Of course, he would taunt me. "Hardly. You give yourself too much credit."

"In that case, close your eyes and stop stalling."

Huffing, I did as he said.

"Now, use your power, infuse it with mine, but not so much that you pass out again. Are you able to do that?"

"Yes." I did as he asked, calling upon that incredibly

awesome magic which resided within me. It sprang forth, and I let out a steady stream, connecting with the hunter, until I felt his power begin to rise.

His breath sucked in, but unlike at the club, when we'd rescued my sister—where all of my power continued to flow out of me until I ran dry—I felt a slight push from his end. It was subtle at first, as if he was testing my magic, sensing how it felt and reacted, but then I felt a jolt surge into me.

An array of sensations flooded my insides. Burning fire. Crackling energy. Mind-blowing power. It wasn't like before, when I'd accidentally stolen his magic from him at Jakub's club, or when I'd sucked the magic and life out of the warlock in the insane asylum and the sorcerers who'd tried to abduct me. No. This was more controlled, but I wasn't the one controlling it. The hunter was simply using my magic that floated to him as a lifeline. He was inching his own magic along it, carefully maneuvering his power into me until it was inside me. But I still couldn't control his energy, I could just feel it.

I gasped. Gods, he was so powerful. My stomach clenched, the feel of him wrapping around me nearly overwhelming me.

"Don't fight me," he said quietly. "Let me fuse my magic with yours."

I forced my muscles to relax, the tenseness around my shoulders abating. Opening myself up more, I released the natural inclination to shield myself. More of his power soaked into me, flooding my cells and bathing me in his strength, but his power couldn't stray from my source. He couldn't consume me like I could him when I let myself become unleashed. My forbidden power kept him contained to that tether.

Still, it didn't lessen the sensations. The nerves along my skin tingled as my head swam with the *feel* of him. So much energy. So much power. And then I felt him reaching out, as if he were holding my forbidden power like a rope in a raging sea, but still swimming away from it, rope in hand, while searching for something. "What are you doing?"

"Using my magic to try to find your new power. Damn, *colantha*. You have so much magic inside you."

I kept the lid to my forbidden power blown wide open, but I also kept a strong hold on it so that it didn't surge out of me in one giant gush. Still, a sense of lightheadedness hit me. "Do you feel anything yet?" I asked.

"Not yet, but I sense something in you." I felt him searching farther and deeper, probing along that chest of power residing down low inside me. "It's near here, like a deep, dark cavern that's hidden but powerful enough that I can feel its void. Do you sense it?"

I shook my head. "No, all I feel is my witch magic and my forbidden power."

"Let me try to show it to you." His magic caressed me, dancing along my tethered cord. It sent a chill of goosebumps down my spine, like someone had swept a feather along my nerves but from the inside out. It was the strangest sensation, utterly foreign yet enticing.

"Follow the feel of me," he coaxed.

I did as he said, or tried to, and even though that feathery sensation didn't lessen, I didn't shy away from it. It was as I'd feared though. All of this felt so strangely intimate, as if I'd welcomed him inside me even though we weren't directly touching.

"Do you feel this here?" His magic tugged at me, probing me to sense whatever it was he was detecting.

"Where?"

"Here, to the side of where your forbidden power lies. There's something there. I can sense it."

I squeezed my eyes tighter, that dizzying feeling sweeping through me again. Even though I'd been careful not to wield too much of my forbidden power, it was still beginning to take a toll on me.

Willing myself to try harder, I scrunched my face up, reaching out internally. My magic brushed his, creating a tingling sensation like the soft stroke of a feather. A slight groan came from him.

I felt along his power, searching for the cavern he'd spoken of. Another strangled sound came from the hunter when my magic caressed his.

"Gods, *colantha*," he moaned.

I gasped, realizing that intimate feeling extended not only to me but him too.

"Do you feel it?" he rasped. "It's here."

I felt harder, willing myself to detect what he sensed. A moment passed, and then . . . a hint of something unfolded before me, like someone had brushed open a curtain before it drifted softly closed. A jolt of pure pleasure followed as his magic coiled around me in triumph.

My eyes flew open as another swirling rush of dizziness stole through me. I lurched back, breaking our connection.

It was too much—releasing my forbidden power while feeling him, wanting him, *craving* him. All of this while my forbidden power bound us together. It was just too much. This was more intimate than any sex I'd ever had.

"I can't." My forbidden power sucked back inside me, like someone had let go of a fully inflated balloon and it flew through the air until rushing into a storage chest before the lid snapped shut.

I brought a hand to my head as my arm reached out to the floor to steady myself. Another wave of fatigue filled me.

In a heartbeat, the hunter's hands were wrapped around my shoulders, holding me. "Tala? Are you okay?" That husky tone still filled his words, and I knew he was reeling too.

I nodded, and with each breath I took, some of the dizziness abated. "It's always like that with my forbidden power. It's so much, and it's so strong. Every time I use it, it tires me." Of course, I didn't mention the other part. The bit about feeling *him* being too overwhelming.

I felt him studying me, but I looked down. That was a mistake since my gaze landed on his crotch. The hunter was tenting big time. A huge erection strained against his loose pants.

I squeezed my eyes shut and concentrated on breathing

deeply and bringing myself back to the present. But my core still clenched with *hunger*. And it wasn't hunger for food.

Slowly, the swirling sensation of the room began to fade, and that pulsing and aching desire for the hunter lessened to something I could manage. I just thanked the gods I hadn't done anything stupid, because training with the hunter was even worse than I'd thought it would be. I'd been worried about battling and sparring, but that would be infinitely easier to deal with than what I'd just experienced.

"I think that's enough for today," I said.

"Did you sense what I did? Did you feel that cavern?"

I nodded. "I think I did, a little." I finally lifted my gaze to his. Raging amber eyes met mine. He was looking at me so intensely—heat running rampant through his irises like a raging inferno. I concentrated on the point of this training session so I wouldn't get lost in his fire. "Do you really think that was my new power? Do you think it resides beside my forbidden one?"

"It's possible. It was the only thing I sensed that felt untouched in you."

I shivered, unable to help it. Even though the hunter had kept his word and hadn't touched me physically until just now, it had felt as if he'd been touching *all* of me throughout that entire session.

I'd never allowed somebody else's magic to join with mine before. I didn't even know something like that was possible. My witch magic certainly didn't allow it, but my forbidden power? Apparently, that one did, and the hunter had sensed it and had the foresight to try it.

"How did you know that connecting with me could help?"

He shrugged and finally let go of me. I instantly missed the feel of him, but I refused to let myself acknowledge that. "When you used it on me in the club, I felt a connection to you. But in the heat of that moment, I obviously didn't explore it. However, it was enough for me to realize that you and I were fused. And I've been curious to try that again."

"So it was a hunch that you could find my new power? Or were you just wanting to cop a feel of my magic?" I asked, trying to lighten the mood.

He chuckled but then his voice dipped again, and damn, the hunter's erection was still fully apparent through his loose pants. "I won't lie, feeling you fused with me is incredibly arousing, but that wasn't why I wanted to try this today. You have to remember, I'm a hunter. I seek things that are lost. I think connecting my magic with yours is the key to helping you find it and learn how to access it."

My eyes widened. "You mean, we'll be doing this again?"

"If you let me. Until you learn where this power is and know how to access it, you won't be able to use it. I think the first step is helping you identify where it is. Once you have a firm grasp on that, you can begin playing with it."

"Playing with it how?"

"By using me. You can draw on my magic, suck it away from me, play with it, until you learn how to control your new magic better."

"You want me to play with you?"

He grinned devilishly. "It's almost as if that statement has a double meaning."

"Such a pervert." But I couldn't stop my smile.

"In all seriousness, yes, I want you to play with your new magic by using me, and you're welcome to use me in whatever way you please."

Heat rushed to my cheeks, but just as quickly so did a huge dose of reality. "But this new magic has *killed* other supernaturals. It's sucked the life and magic from them to the point of death."

"True."

"But what if I—" I shook my head rapidly. "What if I hurt you? Or kill you?"

He gave me a soft, seductive smile. "Well, *colantha*, we'll have to hope it doesn't come to that."

CHAPTER TWENTY

Somehow, I managed to stand from the mat without touching him while he conjured his portal. It was hard to believe that it was already evening. The day had slipped away so fast.

"Ready?" The hunter held out his hand while his portal swirled behind him.

I took it, and seconds later, we were in the woods just outside his cabin.

Night had fallen, the trees dark and bare, as the portal disappeared into a swirling gold void. I wrapped my arms around myself, shivering.

The Fire Wolf took a step closer, his large build predatory and silent. "I'm going to touch base with the pack members guarding you. Go on in and get warmed up. I'll be inside in a minute."

He disappeared in a blur through the trees, and I

thanked the gods that I had a minute alone. After that training session, I needed it.

Doing a one-eighty, I trudged toward the cabin, but while my body felt okay, my mind was another matter. I was mentally fatigued. What I needed was another good night's sleep without dreams or early wake-up calls.

I reached the porch steps and began to climb them when something tugged inside me. My gaze snagged upward, toward the shining waxing crescent moon. It gleamed brightly in the sky, like a curved pearly-white petal.

Lips parting, my feet moved hesitantly and then before I knew what I was doing, I was retreating back down the steps toward the forest's edge.

The tug continued to draw me, pulling me toward the moon's snowy light. The trees thinned, the meadow appearing. I stumbled into it, my eyes never leaving the moon.

It was incredibly alluring, shockingly beautiful, and so—

"Tala?" The hunter's sharp call snapped me upright.

I swung around to find him standing right behind me, his eyes shining amber in the moonlight. "Why are you out here? You're supposed to be inside."

His question cut through the fog in my mind, and with a shake of my head, I realized what I'd been doing. *Following the moon? Really, Tala? You need to get some rest.*

"I don't know," I said sheepishly. "Sorry."

A frown wrinkled his forehead, a groove appearing between his eyes. His nostrils flared, and he took a step closer to me. He inhaled, his frown deepening before he shook his head. "Come on. Let's get inside."

He held out his hand to guide me, but I strode forward without accepting it.

When we reached the cabin, I climbed the steps in a hurry and didn't slow even when I crossed the threshold. "It's late. I'm tired, and I'm—"

"You have to be hungry. I'll make us something to eat." He strode into the kitchen, and even though my gaze automatically drifted to the broadness of his shoulders and sexy roll of his hips, I forced my attention to the vaulted ceiling before fleeing up the stairs.

The sound of banging pots and pans came from below as I darted into the master bedroom. I paced a few times, my insides flapping like a caged bird since nighttime had come, which meant that my bargain with the hunter was just around the corner.

With clumsy movements, I went to my purse, needing to speak with Prish or Tessa and wanting to know if they were okay and how they were doing.

But then I remembered I didn't have my phone, and if I wanted to contact them, I had to write.

I pulled out the notebook I'd packed and began to scribble, writing the letter so fast that my penmanship was atrocious. But I needed some kind of distraction, and I missed my sister and best friend.

240

I sat on the bed and let myself get lost in my ramblings. I told them everything about the cabin, the small, quaint town, and how friendly Ocean was. I left out the details about the hunter's brothers and upbringing since that wasn't my information to share, but I ended the letters telling them that I missed them and hoped to see them soon.

When I finally finished, tantalizing aromas from downstairs drifted into the room.

A few minutes later, the hunter called, "Dinner's ready. Are you coming back down?"

I considered ignoring him, but then my stomach growled, reminding me that going to bed without dinner wouldn't be pleasant or wise. If my job here had become training my new power, I needed to keep my strength up.

Forcing myself to my feet, I trudged toward the stairs, my nose twitching at the delectable fragrances.

When I rounded the corner to the dining area, my eyes widened when I beheld the set dining table with a candle glowing in the middle of it, the warmth of the fire roaring in the hearth, and the corked wine bottle that sat beside two full plates. Steaming steaks, Brussel sprouts, and what looked like a rice pilaf were placed before me.

"I hope you like red wine," he said as he began filling two glasses.

"You made this?" I asked incredulously.

"I did."

"I thought you only ate nuts and cheese."

He chuckled and set the wine bottle back down. "The

food in my base is quite different from the food in my home."

"But you don't consider this home."

He held out a chair for me—well, okay then, this was *that* kind of meal—before saying, "True. This isn't my home. That's in Montana, but my sister knows what I like. She stocked the fridge with what I would have bought."

That statement brought to mind images of the hunter perusing the shelves at a grocery store, and holding up boxes of wheat pasta and sorghum pasta while trying to decide which one was the better choice.

I smothered a smile, laughing inside when I remembered that the hunter had a domestic streak. If only the Shadow Zone's inhabitants knew that.

"Thank you," I mumbled when he pushed my chair in behind me.

"You're welcome." He winked, an amused glint in his eye.

He seated himself, then handed me a full wine glass. I took a large swallow, definitely needing alcohol right now.

"I hope you're okay with medium-rare," he said as he cut into his steak.

"I'm a vegetarian."

His eyes widened to saucers, and a look of such horror streaked across his face, that I burst out laughing.

"I'm kidding, totally kidding." But I couldn't stop my snort.

It took a second for him to regain his composure, but then he laughed and took a few jabs at me, which helped quell some of the stiffness rolling through my spine. Cheeky banter with the hunter I could handle, but romantic meals and unquenched sexual frustration? That was much more challenging.

Somehow, we managed to make it through dinner without it feeling like a Hallmark movie, which of course was helped when—despite the romantic atmosphere and crackling fire—our bantering and needling continued.

But despite our less than traditional way of interacting, I was thankful for it. It helped keep my stomach from roiling with nerves, and the constant smiles and laughs from the hunter—and okay, who was I kidding, from me too—made the meal actually enjoyable, which was an entirely new level of crazy.

I leaned back in my chair when I finished the last of my steak, so full I wanted to curl up in front of the fire like a cat and go to sleep. If only Prisha knew that I'd just shared a candlelight dinner with the menace of society. She would get a total kick out of it. Perhaps I'd have to add a P.S. to my letter.

"Shall we go to bed?" the hunter asked as he collected the dishes.

That statement snapped me upright like a jack-in-the-box. "Bed? Right. Forgot about that." *Fuck a duck.*

A slow seductive smile spread across his face. "I haven't."

"I can do the dishes," I said, surging to my feet as my insides fluttered.

"No need." The hunter pulled something out from

under the sink, and with bulging eyes, I realized it was a fae charm. Sure enough, he tossed the charm into the air, whispered two words, and in a flurried magical cloud, the plates and dirty pans disappeared only to reappear a moment later stacked on the shelves, as clean and dry as the day they were bought.

"I see you brought your expensive cleaning products along."

"I don't leave home without them," he replied, totally deadpan.

Despite the anxiety swirling through my belly, I laughed.

The hunter prowled toward me, still not touching me, but his voice dipped when he said, "Time for bed. After you."

I swallowed the dryness in my throat, suddenly feeling like a blushing virgin on her wedding night, not that I actually knew what that felt like since I'd lost my virginity in high school, but I imagined it would feel similar to this.

Turning stiffly, I marched up the stairs, but then that march turned into a jog, and then an all-out run. How had the night come this fast?

"Are you that eager to join me in bed?" the hunter called from down the hall, a smile in his voice.

"Ha ha, very funny!" I called over my shoulder.

When I reached the master bedroom, I grabbed pajamas, then realized I was holding that black lacy thing Tessa had packed. Definite no to that one. Throwing it to the side, I grabbed an oversized T-shirt and dipped into the bathroom to get changed and brush my teeth.

When I emerged, my breath sucked in when I found the hunter in the bedroom. He stood by the window gazing outside. He wore nothing but loose shorts that hung low on his hips.

My gaze crawled up his back, over the broad planes and tantalizing muscles, across the swirling tattoo, then dipped down his bare arms, taking in the chiseled biceps and sinewy forearms. Despite trying desperately to keep my arousal smothered, I knew it was apparent when the hunter turned. His nostrils flared, and a slow smile curved his lips.

"I take it you like what you see?"

Since I wasn't dignifying that gloating comment with a response, I dove for the bed. I was under the covers with them pulled up to my chin before the hunter could turn fully around. I rolled to the farthest side of the bed that I could manage, but I was teetering. One misbalance, and I'd end up on the floor.

"Night!" I called shrilly.

The lights clicked off, and I heard the hunter dip into the bathroom. The sound of running water and brushing teeth came next, then the flush of the toilet.

My heart hammered as a thousand self-deprecating insults flew through my head that I'd been asinine enough to agree to this deal.

A moment later, the covers lifted and the bed dipped.

The hunter was in full predatory mode, moving as silently as the wind.

"Are you sure you're comfortable?" he asked, a smile in his voice.

"Yep. I'm good. Nighty night!"

"It's just that you look like you could roll off the bed at any—"

"I'm good!"

A long, heavy sigh came, then the feel of the mattress sinking further when he inched closer to the middle.

"Please stay on your side," I said formally.

A soft chuckle came from the dark. "We have sides?"

"Yes, we do. Think of us like an old married couple who ignore each other every night and give each other our backs when we turn the lights off."

"I can't imagine being an old married couple with you. I doubt we'd be that mundane."

I snorted. "Well, then you should stop reading romance novels. All couples end up that way."

"I don't read romance novels. I read non-fiction."

"Well, then don't start reading romance. It'll only give you wayward ideas of what reality's actually like."

"Does that mean you read romance novels?"

"Hardly." I snorted, even though, yes, I totally read them. But I wasn't going to tell the hunter that. I could only imagine the merciless teasing that would ensue.

"Are you speaking from experience then?" he asked. "Do you have memories of being an old married couple in your previous life?"

"No, but if I did, I imagine that's what it'd be like."

"You know, I've never seen or heard you look so tense before. Maybe I should massage—"

"Nope! Don't even think about it. Your side. My side. Don't cross it or I'll gouge your eyeballs out."

"Hmm." Another dip came from the mattress, then he purred, "There's that violent side I love so much."

"I highly doubt that you would love it if your eyeballs were hanging from your head by their retinas."

A strangled laugh came from him, before he said huskily, "So graphic. You're giving me a hard-on."

I whipped around to face the hunter, my mouth falling open. "Are you serious?"

He laughed—truly *laughed*—and I realized I'd fallen right into his trap.

"No, that particular image doesn't turn me on, but the thought of you attacking me and raking your nails over my chest, now *that*—"

"Goodnight!" I whirled back around, giving him my back once more, and even though he made a few more comments, trying to draw me in with his insufferable demony wit, I didn't fall for it.

Finally, a long sigh came from the hunter and he stopped moving around. Several minutes later, I heard his slow deep breaths, and I realized he'd gone to sleep.

He'd actually held up his end of the bargain and hadn't forced anything on me.

Once that shock had worn off, and I realized the hunter and I would truly be sleeping tonight and sleeping only, I allowed my rigid form to relax and drift back a few inches so I didn't actually fall off the bed. Then, I sank deeper into the mattress, letting the lull of sleep pull me under.

My eyelids drifted closed, triumph oozing through me as the heat of the hunter, only inches away, warmed me.

One night down. Only dozens more to go.

I could do this.

CHAPTER TWENTY-ONE

Blissful warmth and a cedar scent tingling my nose pulled me from a deep sleep. My upper body rose and fell as if I were on a ship at sea rolling over gentle waves. But what I lay on felt incredibly hard and hot, and something coarse tickled my cheek.

I slowly peeled my eyes open and came face to face with dark hair and a flat hard chest. It rose steadily beneath me —so, not an ocean then. Farther down, sheets bunched around a toned waist.

My face was turned, planted on the firm chest, and my body was half lying on top of said chest, my legs and limbs draped across the man's body.

And that was when it hit me.

Oh my gods, I'm cuddling with the Fire Wolf and lying on his chest.

A delicious thrill and a spark of razor-sharp embarrassment ran through me simultaneously. I made a move to scramble off of him and prayed that I didn't wake him. But the second my body lifted, a heavy arm clamped around my waist, holding me in place.

"Stay."

The single command fell with husky clarity. Turning my head, I peered warily upward and came face to face with the hunter.

Disheveled hair covered his head, and his beautiful lips twisted into a wicked smile. Too late. The Fire Wolf was already up.

"I'm sorry. I didn't realize that I'd—"

"I like it," he drawled. "It's good to see that in sleep you seek me even if you've yet to succumb to that desire while awake."

Heat bloomed across my face. "Well, good morning to you too. It's nice to see that you're already gloating." My heart raced, and I tugged at my shirt, trying to get it down since it had ridden up during the night. Even though my breasts were covered by my T-shirt, they were pressed flush against the hunter. My soft to his hard. *Gods.*

"You can leave that as well," he said when my T-shirt flashed a sliver of my abdomen. The damn thing didn't want to straighten.

"I'm sure you'd like that." I yanked on it more until I was completely covered again, but the hunter's arm was still locked around my waist holding me captive.

"Release me," I said curtly, or as curtly as I could manage.

He inhaled, his nostrils flaring. "You know you say those words, but I don't think you actually mean them."

So he'd detected my arousal that was already running full throttle. Not that I would ever admit it. I arched an eyebrow. "So no doesn't mean no? Is that what you're saying?"

"You didn't say *no*. You said *release me*."

"If that's going to be your argument in court, let me encourage you never to pursue magistrate school."

His lips curved, an excited gleam growing in his eyes. "First thing in the morning, and your sharp wit and delicious scent are already driving me mad. Did you know that's what you do to me?"

"I've kind of picked up on that." I stopped trying to move. He was holding me firmly in place, and even though I'd die before admitting it, waking up next to him felt more pleasant than I wanted to acknowledge, and I didn't actually want to move.

I wanted to press a kiss to his lips and run my fingers through his hair, to tangle myself up in his embrace and feel his hands on my thighs. I wanted him to settle between my legs and rub his—

My cheeks flushed more just as his eyes darkened. "I would love to know what you're thinking right now, *colantha*. Your scent just became mouth-watering."

I squirmed, my core clenching and aching. Perhaps I shouldn't be thinking about those things, but maybe I could enjoy this position. Just for a few minutes. Surely, there was no harm in that.

Tentatively, I propped my elbow on his chest and cupped my chin in my palm. "So, Fire Wolf, what are we doing today?"

His face tightened, an emotion clouding his eyes that I couldn't quite decipher. "Kaillen."

"What?"

"Call me Kaillen, not Fire Wolf. That name is for my jobs and the Shadow Zone, not for people I know."

I swallowed, thickness coating my throat. I absent-mindedly began to trace a finger along his chest, through the dark hairs on his pecs. "But do you and I really know each other? Has it even been a week since I accosted you at the Black Underbelly? And we met because I hired you to—"

He brought a finger to my lips, silencing me. The touch of him quickened my pulse and shot electric jolts down my nerves while halting my finger's progression on his chest. "You know me better than almost anyone on this planet."

His quiet declaration made me grow still, and with startling clarity, I knew he was telling the truth. That was how private and reclusive the demon hunter was. I, a woman who'd hired him in the Shadow Zone not even a week ago, knew him better than most alive.

That familiar tightening and tingling in my belly began anew, so I trailed my finger over his chest again, anything to distract myself from the dip in my stomach.

His breath sucked in when my fingertip grazed his nipple, his entire body shuddering. "Tala," he said huskily.

Before I could snatch my finger away, the hunter was upon me.

His huge body rolled me in a flurry of heat and fire as he pinned me to the mattress. I gasped, and then he was there, his lips molding to mine.

My back arched, my body jolting at the sudden feel of the hunter's mouth.

He growled, his weight sinking into me, and before I knew what I was doing, my fingers were threading through his hair, my hands beckoning him to move closer. Everything happened so fast, but then I was wanting, needing, *craving*.

Another low growl rumbled in his chest. Then, his hands were everywhere. Caressing up and down my thighs, over my hips, along the swell of my breasts.

I moaned as a deep aching need curled in my belly. My thighs drifted open, begging him to join with me.

The hunter sank between my legs, his hips gyrating against my core.

"Yes," I whispered.

I was too far gone to think, to care, to pull back. It was me and him. The hunter and his prey. The wolf and his mate.

His tongue plunged into my mouth, tasting and dipping, licking and teasing. I bit at it, nipping gently, and the heat from him burst to life until his magic swirled around us, caressing and teasing me.

I gasped at the feel of his magic touching mine, then tentatively relaxed the hold on my power. My forbidden magic surged forward, grazing my skin, then connecting with his.

A throaty moan worked from his throat. It was like last night when we'd been training, except now we were touching and biting, tasting and writhing. Gods, it was *incredibly* erotic.

"Tala," he panted. "I want you."

My power blazed unabashedly, his magic answering in turn, and the crackling aura that surrounded us grew until it was sizzling in the air, pulsing along with our tangled bodies.

"Kiss me." I wrenched him back to my mouth, eagerly seeking his taste and touch.

He groaned, sinking more into me, and I felt his insistence, his need to dominate, to claim, to make me his.

He tore his mouth from mine, kissing my neck and devouring my taste. He paused at that spot above my collarbone, the place a wolf inflicted his mark. He licked that sensitive skin as a possessive growl rumbled in his chest.

My body bowed, my fingers turning into talons in his hair. He shifted down again, my shirt riding up, then he tore my panties off and my naked body lay before him.

Molten gold shone from his eyes when his gaze feasted on me. "So beautiful."

And then he descended, his mouth pure pleasure and torment as he claimed each tit, rolling my breasts' taut peaks between his tongue, making desire pool in my belly so strongly that my folds slickened and dripped in need for him.

His arm snaked around my waist as he pressed hot, urgent kisses down my stomach, his fingers kneading into my flesh as I arched, welcoming him to do with me as he pleased.

I'd never wanted a man so much, this intensely, and my fingers released from his hair to grip the sheets. I dug and clawed at them as he pushed the sheet down until cool air flowed over my skin, my thighs, my core.

And then he pressed a soft kiss *there*.

"Kaillen!" I gasped.

His rumbled response was all I registered before his mouth was on my core, his tongue flicking across that bundle of nerves. I bucked as sensations bolted through me.

"So sweet," he murmured, a fierce possessive growl ripping from his throat. He licked again, and then again as he settled more between my thighs, his tongue a master of torture and torment.

Each breath, each suck, each lick from his demon tongue made me gasp and writhe at the feel of the hunter between my legs. A wave of pleasure built inside me, and then another. Gods, I was already approaching climax.

His finger parted my folds, then slipped inside me. Another fierce growl came from him, vibrating my clit and making me almost come right on his face, as his beast rumbled within him. "So wet, and you're wet for me." He pumped his finger into me again and again, while licking, sucking, and tormenting that taut nub.

I bowed again when he began pumping harder, scraping those spots of pleasure deep inside me, commanding my body like a symphony. Pure male satisfaction rumbled from his chest when the wave built higher, then higher.

I was so close to coming, so close to tipping over the edge, *so close* to screaming my release. I tangled my fingers in his hair, begging him not to stop.

His satisfied chuckle hummed through my core, and the mountainous peak loomed, right there . . . right there . . . and, oh gods—

"Kaillen!" a woman called from the main floor.

My eyes flew open as my climax died as swiftly as a vampire being staked. *Ocean.* I jolted upright, my entire body seizing as though I'd just been dumped in ice water.

A snarl tore from the hunter when his mouth ripped from my core. Fire rolled in his eyes as his gaze shot to the doorway. "Are you fucking kidding me?"

"Kaillen? Tala?" Ocean called. Then came the sound of footsteps on the stairs.

Heat flooded my cheeks, disbelief coursing through me that I was here, in the Fire Wolf's bed, so close to giving in to him, to coming on his face, to letting him fuck my brains out, and—*what the hell was I doing?*

I scrambled out from beneath him, his huge erection snagging my attention when he sat back on his haunches.

His rod stood stiff and throbbing, so incredibly thick it was pulsing, and—

I nearly tripped on the floorboards, then righted myself and flew across the room. Grabbing the first thing I saw, I flung it over my head just as Kaillen draped the sheet over his waist and Ocean appeared in the doorway.

"Hi!" she said cheerfully. "I brought pastries from the—" Her eyes flashed wide when she saw me standing in nothing but the hunter's sweatshirt, my hair no doubt in disarray, and her brother kneeling on the bed, the comforter bunched around his waist to hide . . .

"Oh." A hand flew to her mouth. "Oh!" she said more knowingly. "Oh my gods." She slapped a hand over her eyes. "I'm sorry, *so* sorry. I'm such an idiot!" She rushed from the room, her cheeks as bright as a cherry tomato.

"No, Ocean, it's fine!" I called to her.

"I disagree," the hunter grumbled, irritation washing through his words.

Ignoring Kaillen, I fled from the room after his sister, but she was already running down the stairs, her rich-brown hair flowing behind her. I finally caught up with her in the foyer just as she grasped the door handle.

"Ocean, stop! It's fine. Really, it is. I'm glad you came. You stopped—" My lips pressed together, but at least she'd let go of the door and turned to face me.

However, now that we stood looking at one another, my words died. How exactly did one say that she'd stopped me from fucking her brother? Um, yeah, not awkward at all.

Embarrassment burned in her emerald eyes. "I'm sorry. I thought you said you weren't together, and I always stopped in to check on Kaillen when he was younger. He never minded. He actually seemed to like it, so I didn't think anything of doing that again this morning, but gods." She smacked a hand to her forehead. "He's not a kid anymore, and I'm such an idiot."

"You're not. Really. Thank you for coming, and you're right, we're not together."

She cocked her head, her lips parting in confusion.

"What did you bring?" I said in a hurry, eyeing the bag she held as the desire that had been pulsing through my belly subsided. I sniffed, taking in the rich aroma of sugar and dough. Wow, whatever she brought must be amazing 'cause its scent was incredibly strong and mouth-watering. "Did you say something about pastries?"

She held up the bag sheepishly. "Yeah, I did. Apple fritters. They're Kaillen's favorites." She frowned. "Or they were. I guess I'm not sure now since I haven't bought any for him in years."

Heavy footsteps came from the stairway, then the hunter appeared at the bottom. He raked a hand through his hair, his gaze cutting to mine. Heat still lingered in his eyes, but thankfully his impressive boner had disappeared, and he was fully clothed. Yay for my clenching vagina. That bitch was being sidelined.

Still, I averted my gaze, too mortified that I'd almost done exactly what I said I wouldn't do.

"Did I hear someone mention apple fritters?" A crooked grin stretched the hunter's lips.

My insides fluttered. *Why, why, why, why?* Why did he have to look and sound like that? And why did it pull at me?

A knowing glint entered his fiery eyes, flickering like rubies, and I knew my arousal was hitting him full throttle.

"Yeah, I did." Ocean held up the bag. "You hungry?"

CHAPTER TWENTY-TWO

We managed to sit down at the table like three normal adults, eating apple fritters after Ocean had insisted on making the coffee 'cause she'd . . . you know.

But the entire time his sister fussed in the kitchen, I felt the hunter's gaze on me. Watching me. Assessing me. *Craving* me. The heat that smoldered in his eyes was enough to set me on fire, and I knew right then and there that if I didn't do something drastic, I wouldn't survive another night in his bed without riding that impressive cock of his until the sun rose. Especially if we were to be training each day, our minds and magic intertwining, which was intense enough as it was.

So, somehow, some way, I managed to start putting distance between us following that disastrous apple fritter breakfast. It started slowly at first, by keeping a few feet of space between us when we left or entered the house.

During training, I sat on one end of the mat and forced Kaillen to sit at the other. If he entered a room in the cabin, I would leave it. And at dinner, I would sit an extra seat down from him, just so our hands couldn't accidentally brush.

It was enough of a conscious effort on my part that he took notice. Each time I forced those distances, his brow would furrow, and his gaze would darken, but I made a point to continue doing it.

But by day four in Oak Trembler, I realized it wasn't enough. I still woke up each morning tangled up in the hunter, his erection hard and ready, my body aching and wanting. So I took it a step further, desperately doing everything I could to guard my heart and not give in to his wolf's mate bond. Sometimes when Kaillen would talk to me, I wouldn't answer. Other times, I would pretend he'd said nothing at all. And I began taking my meals separately from him, eating at outrageous times of the day just to avoid the sexy hunter. The odd hours didn't stop with the meals either. I began going to bed either much earlier or later than him, sometimes hours before or after. It messed with my internal clock, but some days I was so exhausted by the time I fell asleep that sex was the last thing on my mind.

And amazingly, despite the awkward wedge that had been born between us, my first week at Oak Trembler turned into my second week, and I found myself falling into a daily routine of survival and avoidance.

It was pretty much the same thing day after day. Sleep

until waking, then immediately dart out of bed so as not to be tempted by the hunter. Eat. Train all morning and into the afternoon. Eat again. Craft spells to send to Nicole and work on what I could for Practically Perfect remotely. Eat again. Write to Tessa and Prisha. Read their letters if any had come through that day. Then go to sleep with me on one side of the bed and the hunter on the other.

It was doable but barely. And whenever I felt myself start to cave or give in to the desire that scorched my nerves, I remembered Carlos's warning and Kaillen's feelings for me before I'd dropped my cloaking spell.

It was enough to snap me out of it. And thankfully, the near miss before that apple fritter breakfast had made me realize how easily I could succumb to Kaillen, so I made putting distance between us a priority. I only talked to him if I truly needed to, and I only allowed his magic to enter me during training.

Our training intimacy was bad enough since it affected the both of us, but he'd been right that it was necessary because each day, I sensed my new power a little bit more, and each time I felt it, I was able to call it out and wield it a tiny bit better.

But I knew the mental and physical distance I was forcing between us at all other times of the day was wearing on the hunter. His wolf thought I was his mate, and I was firmly rejecting him, day in and day out.

Consequently, each day Kaillen grew surlier and more irritable, and I supposed I had nobody to blame but myself. But I didn't know what else to do. I had to survive this.

"Again!" Kaillen demanded in the training room at the end of week two, his tone razor sharp and pulsing with magic. "Draw my power from me and don't stop."

My third week of training was nearly upon me, and I'd made enough progress that I was finally able to access my awakening magic somewhat readily.

"Now, Tala!" the hunter snapped when I didn't move fast enough.

Gritting my teeth, I pulled upon my new magic that I could now find almost as easily as my forbidden power. I'd finally learned where it nestled in my belly, in that deep, dark cavern that was black as tar and as invisible as a ghost. But with the hunter's help, I'd learned how to sense it, how to reach into that void and beckon it forth. It now only took me a few attempts to find it before I could tug on it. Because of that, we'd begun working on me pulling the hunter's magic from him.

The familiar feel of Kaillen's heat and flames entered me. I gasped, then slid my invisible tentacle-like claws along his power, getting a low groan from him in the process. I grasped at his magic more, pulling and stroking. A harsh breath parted his lips, a half moan, half snarl working up his throat, but since I'd only taken a little from him, I sucked more. Biting and clawing, stroking and taking.

"Yes," he rasped. "That's it."

A river of magic poured into me, barreling and rushing

as I grasped and yanked. Those invisible tentacles from me clamped onto him, sinking their teeth into his power, drawing more and more from the hunter until an ocean of potent magic, mind-altering power, and tantalizing heat filled me.

Gods, it was *so much*. It was enthralling in its intensity.

I still hadn't learned how to wield it, though. I could pull it out, yes, but when it came to harnessing his power and blending it with my own, I was still pretty clueless. But I had learned how to draw out Kaillen's magic slowly, controlling its flow. My awakening power was no longer a complete disaster of siphoning everything at once—killing the recipient in the process. Now, it was more of a gentle coaxing that flowed at the speed I commanded.

Fiery flames licked my insides the more I drew the demon hunter's magic from his core. Throbbing desire came next. Everything about Kaillen's magic was so hot and so vicious in its unfiltered potential. And when it wrapped around me . . . *gods*. I wanted nothing more than to settle on his cock.

It took everything in me not to climb all over him. Training was always like this. On one hand, it felt as if I were burning alive from the inside out, and on the other hand, I wanted nothing more than to fuck my training partner.

But part of mastering this new power was learning how to keep it from affecting me so much. On some days, I still fell to the floor, writhing in agony when I lost hold on that ability to tame it, but on most days I was able to corral it, as if my magic looped around it and kept it contained, which also kept me from grasping the hunter's impressive boner and doing all of the things I desperately wanted to do to his body.

And that was how today was going. A smile slid across my lips as I coaxed more of the hunter's power from him. It surged through my tentacles, my body drinking it in as I filled that well inside me. Desire made my core throb, but I kept it in check.

"Tala," Kaillen whispered. "That's enough."

A pang of panic hit me when I heard his weak and lethargic tone. My eyes flew open. Across the mat, the hunter's face was pale, his complexion waxy.

"Shit!" I quickly reversed course, nearly losing control of my awakening power in the process. My heart hammered, but I forced myself to take deep breaths and relax my tentacles' grip upon the hunter's essence. Sweat beaded along my forehead, but my claws slowly retracted, sheathing back inside my body as I stuffed my awakening power back into its cave.

My new power slowly drifted downward, like snakes slithering into their burrow.

Kaillen took another breath, but his eyes were still closed, his pallor now ashen. Pulse leaping, I called upon my forbidden magic, pushing all of the hunter's power back into him, reversing the surge so quickly that it felt as if my insides were being ripped out.

But my panic eased when his shallow breathing became deep and even. He slowly opened his eyes, and in the next instant, color appeared in his cheeks. He sat up straighter, rolling his shoulders, and a cloud of magic grew in the air around him, the scent so potent my nose scrunched up. His healing magic erased his sickly complexion and in seconds the hunter appeared healthy and alert again.

"Sorry," I said quietly. "I didn't know I'd drawn so much."

His jaw locked. "It's fine. It's necessary for you to learn how to control it and for you to understand what it feels like to drain a life."

"Were you . . . close to dying?"

"I had a few more minutes."

My throat worked a swallow, and I gave a swift nod as a horrible twisting sensation began in my stomach. I needed to learn better control, and I needed to learn to recognize when I was pulling too much.

When I glanced back at the hunter, he was watching me, but he quickly looked away. "Do you want to do another round?" he asked, his expression locked and guarded.

"Um, sure." And with a start, I realized the exchange we'd just shared was the most we'd spoken to each other all day.

"Give me a minute," he said.

I nodded swiftly, and even though my guts churned more at the thought of leeching his life again, I knew he was right. This kind of training was needed even if it took a toll on him. Because the more I worked with my awakening power, the more I recognized not only its feel but its purpose. It was the yin to my forbidden power's yang. The black to the white. The dark to the light. Like most things in nature, they were opposites that kept one another in check.

As for why it had taken so long for my new power to awaken, I didn't know.

"Are you sure you're up for it?" I asked, concern lacing my tone when he made no move to continue and instead hunched forward, placing his forearms on his knees.

"Yeah, it's just that you're getting quite good at that. It takes me a minute to recover."

A feeling of pride filled me, until I saw the huge erection pressing against the hunter's pants when he straightened again. Yep, the dude still got a boner every time we trained, even when I was sucking the life from him.

I couldn't blame him. It was impossible not to be affected by the intimate feel of sharing and connecting our powers. Every time it happened, tingles shot to my core and unquenched need filtered through my senses. Unlike the other times when my awakening power had yanked on another's magic, I was careful with the hunter. I wielded my power gently with him, always stroking and caressing his insides so I didn't tear into him. Of course, that care was also a double-edged sword.

Because every day, our training proved to be more intimate than sex, although it was sex without release. Yep, training was like blue balls on a daily basis.

A yearning ache filled me when I once again saw the

evidence of the hunter's desire, but I pressed my lips into a thin line. *Not real. His feelings for you aren't real.*

"Are you sure you're okay?" I pressed when he made no move to begin another session.

"I'm fine," he snapped. He rolled to his feet in one liquid movement and then stalked away, his shoulders tensed. As he'd begun doing lately, he put distance between us every time we took a break.

Since I'd refused to touch him, and had put an end to our bantering, and since I jumped away every time he prowled near, it was almost as though he was beginning to accept that nothing would ever happen between us. Because true to his word, he never forced himself on me. Every time I withdrew, he would growl but he would maintain his distance, which should have made me feel relieved, yet . . .

I watched him depart as he strode through the door at the end of the training room. A flush of disappointment hit me.

"Get a grip," I whispered to myself.

Since I knew that I'd have a few minutes alone before he returned, I headed to the training room's opposite corner where the water fountain waited.

Bending over, I began to lap at the arc of water streaming from the nozzle when the door opened behind me.

A newcomer's energy pulsed into my back. I straightened and whirled around to see Cameron. I wiped at the water dribbling down my chin, my eyes narrowing. "What are you doing here?"

Cameron took a step closer to me, his aura filled with menace. "Just came to check on what you two were up to. I hear you've been training here every day."

"What's it to you?"

He placed his hands on his hips, eyeing me up.

I looked over his shoulder into the hall but didn't see Gavin. "No sidekick today?"

Cameron scoffed, then crossed his arms as an air of arrogant nonchalance fell over him.

My magic whirled inside me, begging me to use it. He wouldn't stand a chance against me. Even before I'd been able to access my awakening power, I could have beaten him, but now Kaillen was right. I was a force to be reckoned with.

"So you're fucking that scumbag?" Cameron drawled as he leaned against the wall. A scent drifted toward me of earth and pine, underneath Cameron's cologne. *Weird.* "My pack tells me you sleep in the same bed every night, and this room reeks of sex."

I figured he'd detected all of the unquenched desire that flowed between me and the hunter, because we definitely weren't having sex in here. "Is this how you normally initiate conversations, by asking people who they're sleeping with? I'm guessing you were dropped on your head a few too many times as a baby."

His mouth tightened. "I'd be careful with your tone. I don't tolerate insolence."

"Really, what will you do? Bite me?"

He bared his teeth and made a snapping motion toward my neck. "Possibly."

I rolled my eyes. "Again, what do you want, Cameron?"

He reached into his pocket and extracted a letter. Holding it up, he waved it in the air. "Something came in the mail for you."

My eyes widened when I recognized the familiar SF envelope. Either Prisha or Tessa had written back. "Give me that." I moved forward and snatched for it, but his hand whipped back too quickly for me to grab it.

Cameron *tsked*. "Such manners."

"That's mine, and you know it. Hand it over."

He held it higher, like a schoolyard bully dangling something over a little kid. "Come and get it."

My nostrils flared. Well, if he wanted to play that game . . .

I called upon my magic, letting it rise to the surface, then whispered a maximizer spell so when my binding spell hit him, it would feel like a wall of concrete.

I unleashed my spells, and Cameron's eyes widened as his entire body grew rigid. I then did an old-fashioned punch to the gut, and he tipped right over like a falling tree.

He landed in a stiff plank position, only his body was supine.

"Whoops." I snatched the letter from his frozen fingers as he teetered horizontally on the floor.

Rage shone in his eyes, and even though his muscles

quivered, vibrating slightly beneath my spells, I still held him.

"You asked for it," I reminded him as I folded the letter and slipped it into my pocket. I let Cameron stew for a second longer before releasing him.

The second I did, he surged to his feet. "You bitch!" He leaped for me, but I dodged out of the way.

"Do you want me to do that again?" I snarled. "I could bind you for hours if you'd like."

His chest heaved, but he froze. Sniffing, his nose lifted, then his lip curled. "What are you?" he growled. "Not a normal witch from the smell of it. Are you like him? An abomination?"

Since I'd stopped cloaking myself days ago, my true scent wafted through the room. I arched an eyebrow. "Wouldn't you like to know."

Yep, that statement just left my mouth. I'd been hanging out with the Fire Wolf for way too long, although, admittedly, I hadn't heard a quip like that from him in days.

Cameron sneered, his gaze raking up and down my frame. "I suppose I can see why he'd want to fuck you. You have nice tits, and a decent ass."

His statement was so crass and filled with so much hate, but I knew what he was trying to do. He was trying to objectify and demean me. He was a true bully.

"Does your *wife* mind you saying things like that?" I bit back.

He shrugged. "She knows I'd never sleep with someone like you."

I snorted, then let my gaze rake up and down his frame, just as he'd done to me, except when my gaze landed on his junk, I gave him a withering glance. "I'm afraid I can't return the compliment."

Fury tightened his gaze. "You little bitch. I'm—"

The door on the opposite end of the training room opened, and Kaillen stepped inside. He stopped mid-stride, his entire face going taut. He waited, watching. He knew I could fight my own battles, but given the fisted hands hanging at his sides as rope veins curled up his forearms, I knew he'd be more than happy to intervene if I wanted him to.

"You better watch yourself," Cameron whispered, and then in a flurry of werewolf speed, he was gone, the exit door swinging closed behind him.

Kaillen blurred to my side, rage twisting his face. "What was he doing here?"

"Delivering this." I pulled out the letter.

He scowled. "How did he get that? Those usually come directly to you via an SF messenger."

"Beats me. Maybe he intercepted them." I rubbed the envelope and finally looked at it. My name was on the front, but the handwriting wasn't Prisha's or Tessa's. Frowning, I opened it only to pull out a letter that was written in a man's scrawl. My eyes widened when I saw the name at the bottom.

Carlos.

Holy fuck, my ex had written me a letter, and a rather

lengthy one at that. Carlos's handwriting was small and had covered the entire page.

I quickly stuffed it back into the envelope, but given the energy growing from the hunter, I guessed that Kaillen had seen who it was from.

The hunter's jaw snapped closed as a tidal wave of flames appeared in his eyes. "We should get back to training."

Guilt burned through me, which didn't really make any sense since I hadn't done anything wrong, but I knew from the hunter's furious expression that he felt I'd chosen Carlos over him. That perhaps he thought this was only one of many letters that Carlos had written me, and he was only now becoming aware of it.

"Kaillen." I grabbed his arm, and he stopped short. I didn't know if it was my unexpected touch, since it was the first time I'd touched him in days, or if it was something else, but his entire body stiffened. His gaze drifted to my hand that was clenching his forearm. Golden light flared in his eyes, but his face remained stoic, impossible to read.

I abruptly let go, already feeling the swirling energy rising between us, pulling and dancing, begging us to join and caress.

The breath rushed out of me, and I backed away. I tucked the letter into my pocket again and reminded myself that nothing could come of this. That none of this was *real*.

Kaillen's eyes continued to burn into me, that golden

glow growing. His gaze turned questioning, as if hoping that . . .

"Let's finish training." I stuffed my hands into my pockets. "I have to create more potions this afternoon when we finish. Nicole's expecting them."

I swirled around, intent on putting distance between us, but the entire time I made my way over to the mat, the hunter's energy pulsed into my back, and my own body's response begged me to give in.

CHAPTER TWENTY-THREE

Kaillen was still in the living room when my eyelids grew so heavy that night, I knew I couldn't keep them open for much longer.

Even though we barely talked now, I'd kept my end of the bargain. We continued to share the bedroom, even though the tension that rippled between us was enough to make me scream.

The moon was high in the sky when the clock chimed eleven. But Kaillen continued to sit by the fire, his body stretched out in his favorite chair as he nursed a whiskey and stared at the hearth's flames. It was his tenth drink. And even though his werewolf metabolism meant he didn't get drunk as easily as human men, I could have sworn he was doing his best to try.

He wasn't reading tonight either. In fact, I hadn't seen him read for several days now. Instead, if he wasn't exercising in the rigorous regime he completed each and every evening, he was spending his free time brooding, his eyes as flaming as the fire in the hearth.

This situation was obviously wearing on both of us. The desire that pulsed between us was still very much *there*, but since I refused to give in to it, I imagined his body had grown as tight as mine with unquenched *want*.

It didn't help that the SF still hadn't caught Jakub-Dipshit, and since they were so cagey about any information regarding him, neither the hunter nor I knew where things were with their investigation.

It was beginning to irritate me. Neither of us were used to sitting on the sidelines, and honestly, I wasn't sure how much longer I could, because this situation wasn't working. Even though my training was going well and I was improving at controlling my awakening magic, that was about the only good thing that had come out of this.

I didn't say anything as I began to climb the stairs, but the hunter's attention drifted to me, his eyes slightly glazed from the drink.

I felt that burning gaze follow me until I disappeared from view, and when I entered the bedroom and slipped into my nightclothes, a crinkling sound came from my pants' pocket when they fell to the floor. *The letter.*

I'd completely forgotten about Carlos's letter during the tense afternoon following Cameron's departure. Slipping it from my pocket, I climbed onto the bed and pulled it out of the envelope. The smooth paper felt like silk between my fingers as I stared at the black ink and began reading.

Tala,

I know it's only been a few weeks since we last spoke, but I've found myself missing you more and more each day. I wanted to tell you that in person, but obviously with the situation you're currently in, I couldn't. So I hope you don't mind that I'm writing this letter and sending it to you via the SF channels.

I feel the need to explain myself for what happened between us three years ago. I know that I left you. I know that I didn't keep in touch. There's no excuse for that. I got caught up in adventures and wanting to explore, but it doesn't excuse the fact that I never spoke with you properly about our relationship ending.

Because the truth is that I loved you when I left, and I still love you now. But I was young back then. I wanted to travel. I wanted to be free. I didn't want to be tied down, which is something I know you never asked of me, but in a way, it felt like if I'd stayed in Chicago, I would have been giving something up.

I needed to take that time to myself, to outgrow a few things and to work my curiosity out of my system, but I've done that now. I know who I am. I know what I want. And the truth is that I want YOU. I've always wanted you. It's always been you.

I hope you don't mind that I'm telling you this. But I wanted you to know the truth. I don't know how long it'll take to catch the supernaturals behind these abductions, but even if you need to stay in our protective services for the next few months, I'll wait for you. I'll wait for you to decide if you want me too, and if you do, nothing will stop me from being at your side.

Carlos

When I finished reading, I sat in numb silence. I'd known from Carlos's behavior that he had interest in rekindling our relationship, but I hadn't realized how much interest.

Stunned, I reread his letter, then read it again. *I'll wait for you.*

He intended to wait for me. But wait for what?

I folded the letter, my fingers trembling, before I tucked it back into the envelope and tossed it on the nightstand. My brow furrowed as I tried to contemplate how I even felt for my ex.

Honestly, I didn't know. But love? I knew I no longer felt love.

With a sigh, I quickly visited the bathroom before slipping under the cold sheets. That letter stared back at me from the bedside table, while below in the living room, the hunter brooded and the fire crackled.

~

I AWOKE to the feel of Kaillen beneath me and my body sprawled across his. Our limbs were entwined again, our breaths mingled. A shiver of awareness danced through me. It was how we often woke, as if we sought each other in sleep because while awake I wouldn't allow it.

Only this time, the hunter still slept.

I blinked, letting my eyes adjust to the early morning sunlight drifting into the room. Stubble graced the hunter's cheeks. He hadn't shaved in days. And despite the soft puffs raising his chest that let me know he slept deeply, dark smudges lined the skin beneath his eyes.

It seemed he was sleeping less and less each night. I had no idea what time the hunter had come to bed, but since a half-drunk glass of whiskey sat on his nightstand, I guessed it was pretty late.

For a moment, I studied him, letting myself take in his dark hair, the sharpness of his jaw, the smoothness of his forehead, and the angle of his profile. Gods, he was so beautiful. Achingly so. And his scent . . .

I leaned closer, taking in that aroma of cedar and citrus. I sniffed again, and caught an underlying scent of earth and pine, the same scent I'd detected from Cameron.

I shook my head. So strange. I sniffed again and still detected it.

For whatever reason, each day, Kaillen's inherent scent seemed to grow a little bit stronger, along with other smells and aromas. I had no idea if my awakening magic also affected my other senses, but I was beginning to think it did. It was the only logical explanation, because not only was my sense of smell becoming sharper but so were my eyesight and hearing, and I could swear that I'd grown physically stronger too. It was all so weird, but I wasn't complaining. It gave me an edge that I'd never had before.

The hunter stirred against me, shifting, until his leg locked around mine and his arm tightened around my waist. He pulled me closer, his head dipping, his nose nuzzling into the crook of my neck, all while he continued sleeping.

A flame of desire licked my insides, and I pressed my lips into a tight line to stop the breathy sound that wanted to escape from me. Pulsing need clenched low in my belly, and the unconscious hunter must have recognized it, even in sleep, because his rod stiffened, growing into a thick erection that strained against his shorts and speared my abdomen.

Gods.

A low growl came from him, and then his lips were pressing against the base of my throat, his tongue darting out to taste.

I knew I needed to push him away, to scramble back,

but he was still sleeping, and *oh my god*, it felt so good when he moved against me like that.

For a brief moment, I allowed myself to close my eyes, to let myself *feel* all of the sensations that came with being so close to the hunter, and I let myself pretend—pretend that for just a moment that he loved me for me and not just for my magic.

I shifted my hips until I rubbed against him. That aching curl increased low in my belly. A deep purr came from the hunter's throat, and his arm hauled me even closer.

I gasped, not able to contain the sound, and then Kaillen's eyes flashed open.

He gazed down at me, those irises still cloudy from sleep, but fire and *hunger* strained in them as his wolf's golden glow flared around them.

"Tala," he whispered hoarsely. His words were thick, and I wondered if he truly was awake or still sleeping because his eyes closed again before he inhaled deeply.

"*Mine*," he said in a deep, throaty growl.

Before I could stop him, his lips were crushed to my mouth.

I tried to scramble back, but it was too late. I'd allowed myself to get too close. After nearly two weeks of avoiding him, my body was wound so tight that one snip and it shot from my control.

My lips parted of their own accord, a breathy moan working up my throat. How? How could I possibly do this? Keep resisting him when I wanted him so much?

Because with him, I didn't have to tame my sharp tongue, or hide my true magic. He'd seen me—all of me—when I'd let my façade fall and behaved in a way that few in our community had ever seen before.

And Kaillen accepted those parts of me, reveled in them even. He'd encouraged me from day one to be myself without limits or restraints, even if those encouragements were driven by his wolf.

His mouth moved with mine, his hands gliding along my skin. My power hummed and swelled, and a low rumble of pleasure vibrated from him.

The hunter wasn't afraid of my strength even in sleep. He didn't covet my power. He simply admired it. Admired *me*.

And understanding that, *knowing* that he accepted me as I was, it . . .

My heart tore.

"I can't do this." I wrenched myself off of him, breaking his hold as that bone-deep knowledge hit me. Even though we were truly coming to know one another, this attraction between us, this want and desire . . . it wasn't real. No. It was only real *for me*. Not him. For him, it was entirely driven by his wolf. Hell, if it wasn't for his damn wolf, he never would have brought me here, told me about his childhood, trained me, kept me safe. If not for his wolf, the hunter wouldn't have given me a second thought after he'd rescued my sister.

I was halfway to the bathroom before a blur shot past

me and then he was there, standing right in front of me in the bedroom doorway, blocking my path.

"Tala," he said raggedly.

So he *hadn't* been sleeping.

"Get out of my way." The words hissed out of me, and for some stupid reason, tears began to fill my eyes.

"*Colantha*." Anguish streaked across his features. "Why do you fight this? Why do you run from me?"

But I couldn't respond. My tongue had tied itself into a knot as my belly ached from guilt and desire.

He snarled, his eyes glowing so brightly they were molten fire. "For days I've been living like this, barely able to breathe around you, and I know you feel the same attraction to me, so why, dammit? *Why?*" The last word shot out of him, more growl than language. His hands curled around my hips, locking me in place as his warmth seared into my skin. "Why are you doing this to me? To us?"

Harsh breaths lifted my chest, and I blinked furiously, hating these awful sensations strumming through me. Pain, tension, denial, regret, desire . . . it was all one big swirling mess. But I knew one thing with absolute stark clarity.

I needed to tell him.

I should have told him days ago, even before we'd come here to his home. Because he needed to know why we could never go down this path. And he was right. It was cruel for me to push him away while never giving a reason.

My hands curled around his.

He gazed down at me imploringly as I said, "Because it's *not real*. That's why I run from you." My words were so quiet, so broken sounding.

His head angled, his brow furrowing. "How is this not real?"

"Because it's *your wolf* that wants me. Not you. How can you not see that?"

His frown deepened. "My wolf?" The energy pulsed off him so intensely that it took my breath away.

"Yes, don't you remember back in Portland when I dropped my cloaking spell around you for the first time? You caught a hint of my true scent, and I saw something change in you, and the way you acted toward me changed completely after that. Remember the alleyway in New York?"

"I remember."

"But you *didn't want me* before then. You didn't desire me. It wasn't until you caught my true scent that you began to crave me. And it's all because your wolf has chosen me as his mate. *That's* why you want me so much. But before your wolf caught my real scent, you—*the man*—didn't want me at all. And so, this craziness needs to stop."

He stared at me. Hard. Those burning embers in his eyes flamed hotter. "You think the only reason I want you is because you're my mate?" His question was said with such venom and such disbelief.

"Yes!" I snarled. "I saw how you were before you caught my scent. You didn't want me. You—the demon hunter, the rogue sorcerer—*you* never wanted me before your wolf did. That's why this isn't real. Now let go of me. I'm going to shower. It's probably going to be another long day."

I didn't wait for him to reply, and instead ripped his hands off of me before stalking to the bathroom. Slamming the door behind me, I locked it and then sank against the frame.

I didn't hear any movement from him. I had no idea if the hunter was still in the bedroom or had prowled to the hallway and stood right on the other side of the thin door, waiting on silent feet.

But I did know that I'd finally been honest with him. Totally, brutally honest, and I told myself again that it was something I should have done a long time ago.

Sighing, I turned the shower on and stepped under the spray, hoping the streaming water would not only drown my body but also my heart.

CHAPTER TWENTY-FOUR

I didn't hear Kaillen when I emerged from the shower. All was quiet and still. After toweling off, I padded hesitantly to the bedroom, peering inside warily since I was convinced that I'd see the hunter standing by the window, waiting to finish our conversation.

But he wasn't there.

A bolt of relief ran through me that was quickly followed by a pang of sorrow. *Okay . . . whatever that response meant.*

As I shuffled toward the dresser, a flash of white on the bed's dark sheets caught my attention.

I turned to see the letter from Carlos open and lying on the bed. My lips parted. Lurching forward, I grabbed the letter. It was wrinkled, as if whoever had last read it crumpled it before throwing it on the bed.

Anger rose in me, swift and hard, at the thought that Kaillen had read a private letter, but just as quickly as that anger came, it left. No wonder the hunter wasn't here. He probably thought I'd decided to be with Carlos again.

"What a freakin' mess." I sank onto the edge of the bed, the letter in my hands. It was ironic in a way. The letter was from a past love who I was no longer in love with, but I did love someone else.

An image of Kaillen's amber eyes flashed through my mind. His dark hair. His sharp wit. His sexy smile. Gods. I loved him. Totally and completely loved him. Despite doing everything in my power to push him away in order to avoid a situation just like this, it hadn't mattered in the end, because I'd still fallen in love with him.

I sat like that for I didn't know how long, and since the cabin stayed quiet and the scent of coffee didn't waft through the air, I knew that Kaillen was long gone, and I had no idea when he was coming back. *If* he was coming back.

A part of me felt relieved about that, but the other part felt dread. I had no idea where we stood now. It was possible that since I'd now explained to him why I'd been fighting our attraction that he'd come to see that I was right. Perhaps, he'd even been able to make his wolf submit, and he no longer felt any desire for me.

It was possible. Since he wasn't a pure-blooded wolf, and since his demon side and sorcerer magic were so strong, I knew the mate bond could be fickle. Carlos could be right in that aspect, which meant that the hunter could have broken the bond since I'd told him I wasn't interested, which would essentially put us back to how we'd been when we'd first met.

Me wanting him. Him finding amusement in me.

Ugh. But at least I could hold my chin up high, knowing that I hadn't made an utter fool of myself by throwing myself at him and professing my undying love.

Still, it didn't make me any happier.

I finally dressed and went downstairs. As I'd suspected, all was quiet. No roaring fire. No uneaten breakfast. No discarded books. Kaillen had truly up and left. The only sign that he'd ever been here at all was the empty whiskey bottle from last night.

Shoulders drooping, I padded to the kitchen to make coffee. The pot gurgled and steamed, and once I had a much-needed hot mug in hand, I went outside.

The morning was cool, devoid of a breeze. A blue jay's trill came from the distance. I sipped the hot brew, my mind still feeling sluggish as I wondered where the hunter had gone off to.

A creaking sound came from the porch steps. My heart leaped, and I whirled around, expecting to see Kaillen.

But Cameron stood at the bottom of the steps.

My eyes narrowed.

"I'm here to see my dear brother," he said tersely.

"He's not here." I bristled and set my coffee cup on the flat railing.

"Where is he?"

"No idea. Should I let him know that you stopped by?" I

asked sarcastically. "I'm sure he'll be disappointed to hear that he missed seeing you."

Cameron prowled up the stairs, a smirk lifting his lips. "I see that you're just as rude as he is." He scoffed. "Figures. He would choose a woman as deplorable as his character."

"You mean as admirable as his character?"

He laughed humorlessly. "I see you're as cocky as that bastard demon too."

I crossed my arms. "What do you want, Cameron?"

He just snickered.

I rolled my eyes. This was the *last* thing I was in the mood for. "You can see yourself right down those porch steps and back to whatever hole you crawled out of."

His smug smile vanished. "Are you trying to tell me what to do on *my* pack lands?"

"Pretty sure they're not *your* pack lands, but rather Paxton's, and congratulations on mastering the English language. You're correct. I'm telling you what to do. Please leave." I gave him my back, intent on finishing my coffee inside, but then a low snarl erupted from him.

"I'm going to enjoy seeing what they do to you."

Before I could process that bizarre statement, his arms were around my chest, and he had a hand clamped over my mouth.

It all happened so fast. He must have used werewolf speed, but the second my shock wore off, instinct kicked into action. I called upon my magic. It swirled upward, but then I was suddenly whizzing through the air.

What the fuck?

Trees flew past my line of vision, and jostling sensations rocked my body. It took another second to realize that Cameron was *carrying* me somewhere. Using his damned speed to catch me unaware again.

Bastard. I coiled a huge dose of telekinetic power in my chest and flung it toward him, but the second it hit my fingertips, something cold and buzzing clamped around my wrists.

My magic slammed into an invisible wall.

"They said you might try to overpower me, so I came prepared," Cameron whispered darkly in my ear.

The trees abruptly stopped flying past us when he came to a jolting stop. The sudden halt made my heart slam against my ribcage.

Breathing hard, I struggled in his grip as I frantically felt inside me for my magic. *There.* My magic was roiling and heating in my chest. I tugged and clawed at it, but . . . nothing.

It was as if something contained it, like I was looking through a glass wall, fully able to see and sense my magic but not able to access it.

Heart beating faster, I awkwardly glanced over my shoulder to see glowing blue cuffs wrapped around my wrists. They were the same cuffs I'd seen before when—

Cameron shifted his hold. "Here she is. As promised." He abruptly let me go, and I fell to the ground, the cold, hard soil making it feel as though I'd been dropped on pavement.

I sputtered in pain as hair flew in front of my face, but

with my hands bound, I could only blow the strands out of the way, and that was when it hit me—Cameron had cuffed me with the same cuffs that Jakub's men had used on Kaillen in the New York nightclub and on me in my bedroom.

That could only mean one thing. *Fuck!*

"She looks so surprised," a man said.

My head whipped around to see two tall sorcerers standing side by side, leering expressions on their faces. Constellation tattoos were inked onto their necks.

Disbelief hit me like a freight train. "You're handing me over to them?" I spat at Cameron.

He shrugged. "The pay's pretty good, and it'll be nice to see your arrogant ass put in its place."

"You vile asshole!" I shrieked and rolled onto my back, kicking out at him, but he easily sidestepped me.

"Now, now," one of the sorcerers said.

Cameron smirked. "I thought you said she may be difficult to capture."

"We were told she could be. I hope she didn't give you too much trouble," the second sorcerer replied dryly.

"I caught her unaware, and my shitbag brother wasn't there, so that made it doubly easy. But you'll want to keep those cuffs on her. If I hadn't used them, it might have been more interesting."

For the first time since Cameron had showed up on Kaillen's doorstep, panic exploded inside me, but then I remembered that just because I was cuffed, I wasn't helpless. I could still use my new magic and forbidden power.

The cuffs had only contained my witch magic when they'd cuffed me in my bedroom during their last kidnapping attempt, and Kaillen had still been able to call upon his demon fire when they'd cuffed him at the club. The glowing blue device might drain witch and sorcerer magic, and werewolf strength and speed, but it didn't affect other-worldly powers. I'd still been able to use my awakening power, and Kaillen had still been able to use his under-world fire.

Smiling darkly, I tugged on that black cave within me, beckoning my awakening magic forth. It immediately responded, and I ensnared it from that deep, invisible cavern it slept in.

My body hummed and swelled, and a moment of complete triumph filled me as my awakening power's tentacles climbed and writhed, curling and clawing as if asking me who they should pounce upon.

"Hmm, it looks like she might be up to something," one of the sorcerers drawled.

The other one clasped his hands behind his back. "I dare say that you could be right."

Their confidence didn't stop my smile. I let it streak across my face as I said, "Just wait till you get a feel of this." I sprang my new power forth, shooting its tentacles right for the two sorcerers.

Those slithering talons shot down my arms to my fingertips, my smile growing. They reached my hands, ready to leap from my body, and—

Blinding pain. It hit me like a zap of lightning, electric shocks biting me so hard that I cried out.

My awakening power jumped back as I gasped. But I tried again in the next instant, surging that power forth, only to meet that wall of sizzling glass a second time. A terrible shock zapped me, my entire body shuddering under its strength.

WTF.

Panting, I peered up with wild eyes at the sorcerers.

No, no, no, no, no, no, no. This can't be happening.

The taller one dusted his fingernails on his shirt, his expression bored. "You'll find that we made a few improvements to those cuffs since we last encountered you."

The shorter sorcerer laughed, his little goatee dipping with the movement. "Look at her face. It's like she can't believe it."

They both laughed as my mouth grew dry.

I took in a huge lungful of air, getting ready to scream as I resorted to the last weapon I had to call upon—a yell for help. But then the tall sorcerer's hand shot out.

A tight feeling closed around my throat as an acid taste hit my tongue.

My voice *vanished.* I attempted to claw at my windpipe, but my cuffed hands didn't allow it. I tried to scream again, but that acid feeling grew. Disbelief tore through me.

A gag spell. That sorcerer had just cast a *gag spell* on me. It was just like the night when those other sorcerers had tried to abduct me from my bedroom. These new sorcerers were using the exact same spells and devices, only now, the cuffs were improved. They contained *all* of my power.

I lurched to my feet, despite being awkwardly bound, and desperately tried once more to access my magic. But the cuffs held, and without my voice or power, that only left my legs.

Run!

I stumbled away from them, my steps unsteady and clumsy, but then adrenaline infused speed into me. I sprinted toward the trees. If I could make it back to the cabin, I could barricade myself inside. It might buy me some time to—

A binding spell hit me.

I ceased in my tracks, my entire body going rigid. The binding spell was so strong that I toppled over like a tree, landing on my side and hitting my head against the ground. But the fucking gag spell kept me from moaning in pain or cursing the sorcerer who'd spelled me.

"Did she really think she was going to get away?" one of the sorcerers chuckled, amusement in his tone. "It would have been entertaining to let her run for a while. I do love when they think they can elude us, since it adds such a delicious *thrill* to the hunt."

Cameron's laughter joined theirs, and the three of them sauntered toward me. I could barely see them through the tall stalks of grass obscuring my vision. I couldn't move, couldn't sit up, couldn't speak. I was paralyzed, immobile, and helpless. A crushing sense of vulnerability hit me.

"Payment for this young lady should be in your account

by now." One of the sorcerers reached down to haul me up as he addressed Cameron.

Cameron pulled out his phone. "I'll check before you take her. Not that I don't trust you." He laughed and one of the other sorcerers joined in, as if we were all hanging out and having a jolly good time joking about my abduction.

My eyes shot daggers at all of them. *Fuckers.*

The sorcerer who'd picked me up grunted when he threw me over his shoulder. "Have you confirmed it?" he asked Cameron.

Cameron nodded and shoved his phone into his pocket. "It's there. Make sure you're discreet when you leave. The area is clear for the moment, but it won't stay that way. The wolves guarding her will be back shortly. It was hard enough to clear them out without raising suspicion." A snag of bitterness lifted his lips. "You'd think my pack was more afraid of my bastard brother than they were of me."

My heart hammered in my chest, thumping so fast and so hard that I grew lightheaded despite my head hanging down. Cameron had called off the werewolves guarding me? No wonder nobody was coming to help. Nobody was here.

I mentally fought as hard as I could against the binding spell, the gag spell, and the magical handcuffs again. But nothing I did worked.

Dammit, Tala, don't give up. Do something! Because if Kaillen and all of the wolves guarding me were gone, that meant . . .

"We'll be out of your hair within the minute." Goatee Sorcerer pulled a portal key from his pocket.

Oh shit.

Since a portal key was similar to Kaillen's ability, I could be *anywhere* in seconds, as portal keys created a one-time portal hop to wherever the bearer desired.

Goatee Sorcerer whispered the words to activate the key's spell, while Cameron retreated to the woods.

This can't be happening.

I squeezed my eyes shut and searched frantically inside myself for my new power again as the sorcerers stepped toward the glowing portal. Maybe, just maybe, I could break my magic free. This felt like my last chance, because once we stepped through that portal, I'd be transported to an unknown location and would be hundreds, if not thousands, of miles away.

I called upon my new magic again with everything I had.

My awakening power slithered upward, like an octopus searching and hunting. Its tentacles writhed and flowed, so I shot them down my arms, spearing them toward the sorcerers as hard as I could, and—

My new power hit that electric wall again, and it felt as if ice shards cut right through me. If not for the gag spell, I would have yelped. Panting from exertion, I reluctantly let my new power slink back inside, back to that cavern deep in my belly, hiding once more in its dark cave.

My chest rose and fell frantically. We were only *steps away* from entering the portal. I was screwed, totally screwed. The only chance I had was if Kaillen found me. I could only hope that the hunter tracked me.

But what if he couldn't? Or *wouldn't*? What if he no longer wanted to because he'd already made his wolf submit and had eradicated the bond? Then I would be just like every other female he'd encountered at the Black Underbelly—an irritating nobody to be ignored.

I squeezed my eyes shut again, the only things I could move since my body was still paralyzed from the binding spell. It was possible that I was on my own, that it would be hours before anyone knew I'd been taken. And even when they found out, it was possible that no one would come.

The portal winds blew across my cheek as panic and terror threatened to consume me, because I was on my own, and I had absolutely nothing to fight with.

CHAPTER TWENTY-FIVE

The sorcerers held on to me during the portal transfer, their hands clamping onto my body like vile leeches sucking blood from their prey. I shuddered and continued to mentally fight them, but it did little to help. I was completely useless without my magic, voice, or limbs.

The portal deposited us in a city, and we emerged in the back of an alleyway. It looked like every other alley in North America. Narrow lane, black asphalt, tall buildings on each side. For all I knew, we were in Chicago or Edmonton or New York or San Francisco. I had no idea.

"He's waiting." The tall sorcerer carried me toward a sedan idling at the street's curb. Its engine purred like a giant cat sleeping at the alley's mouth.

Goatee Sorcerer waved his arms, and a shimmering illusion spell appeared around us.

Great. Now anyone walking by on the street won't even see me.

Mentally, I fought again, clawing and screaming against my restraints, but as before, the sorcerers' binding and gag spells were too strong, and without being able to access any of my magic, I was no stronger than a human.

We reached the end of the alleyway, and the sedan's trunk popped open. A fresh bout of terror sliced through me when I realized they were going to *put me in a trunk*. It was everyone's worst nightmare.

Out of the corner of my eye, I saw the driver's car door open and a man step out.

"She's still conscious?" the man asked.

Since I couldn't turn my head, I couldn't see him clearly in my peripheral vision, but the cold detachment of his voice made goosebumps sprout along my skin. He sounded so clinical.

"She is, sir."

"Remedy that immediately. She shouldn't be awake right now."

"Yes, sir."

The sorcerer began to whisper a sedating spell, and dread filled my stomach. I was going to be drugged, tossed into a trunk, and taken to who knew where.

The sorcerer reached for me, his spelled fingers going for my neck, and a huge push of adrenaline had me fighting again. I squeezed my eyes shut and called upon every ounce of my power, bursting all of it wide open. A shiver ran through me just as the sorcerer's finger touched my skin.

His whispered words skated over my body when another jolt of my power hit the binding spell, zapping pain running through my entire frame when the cuffs activated again, still containing my magic

My eyes flashed wide open as the sorcerer's drugging spell began to weave around me, but then a glowing yellow portal appeared behind him and the spell abruptly stopped.

A ferocious bellow roared through the street as Kaillen flew through the glowing golden circle. He crashed into Goatee Sorcerer to my left, falling upon him like a dark angel.

The hunter had moved so quickly, and with such lethal precision, that in the blink of an eye the sorcerer was knocked to the ground, gaping in confusion.

Kaillen was on him before he could react, wrapping his hands around his neck in a blurred motion. A resounding crack split through the air around us, and my eyes turned to saucers when I saw that Goatee Sorcerer's neck was bent at an odd angle.

His illusion spell, which had hidden our activity, vanished.

"Shit!" Tall Sorcerer whispered a new illusion spell, then threw me to the ground.

Pain exploded in my chest when I hit the pavement like a sack of potatoes. But the haphazard throw had me rolling to face Clinical Dude at the car.

Another bellow came from the hunter as he descended

upon Tall Sorcerer, but the sorcerer was expecting him, not falling so easily.

Clinical Dude watched Kaillen and the sorcerer fight with cool detachment, and since I was finally able to see him, I took in his appearance all at once, committing his features to memory.

Short brown hair. Wide mouth. Medium build.

His expression didn't change or falter. Not even a hint of terror or disbelief coated his features. Instead, he calmly reached inside the sedan and pulled out a second pair of those blue cuffs. But the cuffs weren't glowing yet. That must only happen when they were closed and activated, but it was obvious Clinical Dude intended to put the second pair on Kaillen.

Grunts and the sound of sizzling casting magic continued to come from the hunter and Tall Sorcerer. Eyes widening in horror, I could only watch as Clinical Dude lifted a hand and wove it through the air. A *huge* cloud of magic began to swirl around him, and I fought anew against the binding spell holding me. Squeezing my eyes shut, I clawed and pulled at everything in me.

Rise, fight, break me free! Please!

Everything in me responded at once. My awakening power, my forbidden one, and all of my witch magic. It all swirled together, combining, and growing. I didn't even know they could be mixed, but I didn't hesitate. I let instinct guide me, and it was as though the final puzzle piece clicked into place. All of the days I'd been training with Kaillen aligned, and a sudden sense of *yes, this is what I can do* came over me.

My swirling magic exploded within me. Despite the cuffs, my power shattered the binding and gag spells like a cannonball flying through a glass wall.

My legs splayed out as though a rubber band holding them had snapped. I jolted into action even though my magic and powers swirled back inside me, drained and weakened from that cataclysmic use of power. But my legs could move even if my magic was once again contained.

The cloud of magic that Clinical Dude had woven was now a crackling tornado. Kaillen still fought Tall Sorcerer, alternating between using demon fire, sorcerer magic, and blurred werewolf speed, but the sorcerer was anything but weak. Even though Kaillen was driving him back, coming at him so fast I could barely see, the sorcerer managed to stay on his feet and kept punching spells at the hunter when he could.

But Kaillen dodged, dipped, and swayed. The expression on his face was twisted with such rage and terrifying ferocity that even I wanted to shrink back, but the sorcerer only bared his teeth at the hunter and hissed in exertion.

Rapid-fire spells shot from Kaillen's fingertips, but each time his magic collided with the sorcerer's, a bomb of power detonated, as though their magic cancelled the other's out.

Kaillen was so consumed with the sorcerer that he didn't see the cloud of magic Clinical Dude was weaving. It was so large now that I knew as soon as it was unleashed, the hunter would be knocked down despite his tremendous power—and then he would be cuffed.

Scrambling to my feet, I tried again to call upon my magic, but the cuffs still suppressed it. And the colossal power I'd managed to temporarily wield to break through the binding and gag spells had depleted me. I couldn't do it again, not right away.

So I did the only thing I had left.

Bending over, I ran at Clinical Dude full force, head-butting him right in the gut. He'd been so intent on his whirling magic that he hadn't seen me coming.

My head collided with his stomach so hard that I saw stars. I stumbled back, but so did he, landing flat on his ass. His eyes burned up at me in surprise, the first emotion I'd seen in him, as his cloud of sinister magic evaporated.

I smirked. Head-butting truly was underrated. "Did your magic not discharge as planned?" I taunted. Even though baiting him wasn't smart, it achieved what I'd set out to do. Clinical Dude's focus had left the Fire Wolf. Yep. It was now *entirely* focused on me.

Problem solved, but oh shit on a brick . . .

Clinical Dude stared up at me, a gleam in his eyes burning so deeply that for a moment, I couldn't move. There was something so terrifyingly detached about him. As if he weren't human or didn't have a shred of humanity left within him. It was as though I looked into the eyes of a cold-blooded alien whose only thoughts and actions were *kill, harness, control.*

But hopefully not in that order. A shudder ran through me, and I backed up.

"Interesting," he said quietly, as if sitting on the ground after being head-butted was a totally normal afternoon activity, but since he was talking, I guessed that meant he wasn't an alien. "I do believe you're the one I've been searching for."

Oh . . . That did not sound good. But then I registered his accent. It was harsher than the American accent, with a tongue-rolling lilt that perhaps heralded from Eastern Europe.

My jaw dropped. *Jakub?*

But I wasn't proficient in accents from Eastern European countries, so I didn't know for sure.

I took another step back as Kaillen and Tall Sorcerer's battle continued.

A quiver of excitement rippled through Clinical Dude's terrifying eyes, a second emotion that I could do without seeing.

Jakub-who-may-not-be-Jakub calmly stood, and when I dipped, bending myself forward so I would be ready to head-butt him again, he swirled his fingers.

A gust of magic punched me in the gut, sending me flying back. I landed on the rough pavement, my arms screaming in agony as they scraped across the asphalt since I was still cuffed and couldn't move them.

An explosion of magic came from nearby, and I whipped my head around to see a *ginormous* death curse blazing like a meteor toward Tall Sorcerer. Kaillen's curse tore through Tall Sorcerer's shield like a rock thrown through tissue paper. It hit the sorcerer square in the chest, a look of shock rippling across his face just before his chest split wide open.

Tall Sorcerer stumbled to the ground, his mouth opening and closing in death throes from the lethal gaping wound. With a crash, his body splayed across the sidewalk. Blood pooled onto the pavement around him as his head lolled, and then ceased moving. His unseeing eyes stared skyward.

The illusion spell that had shielded all of our activity from any surrounding humans vanished. Kaillen whipped a hand through the air, a new illusion spell appearing in a split second just as he rounded on Maybe-Jakub with murder shining in his eyes.

A hiss came from Maybe-Jakub as I gaped like a fish. "I'll be back for you," he said to me in that cold, clinical tone.

Um . . . that *definitely* didn't sound good.

I scrambled to my feet, ignoring the searing pain of my scraped flesh, and lunged toward Maybe-Jakub, but he dipped into his sedan. I wasn't sure how I would stop him or open his car door since my hands were still bound, and the cuffs once again had my magic contained, but if Clinical Dude was actually Jakub then we needed to prevent his escape.

His car revved and shot from the curb, colliding with me in the process. I flew back, and landed so hard on the street that I saw stars.

"Tala!" the hunter called.

New scrapes and cuts ripped through my flesh, and the scent of my blood filled the air. I would have hissed in pain, except I couldn't breathe. That whole wind being knocked out of me thing.

"Tala!" the hunter called again. In a blurred movement, Kaillen was at my side as Jakub drove away. "Where are you hurt?" he asked tersely. A golden glow, so bright it rivaled the sun, shone behind the raging scarlet fire in Kaillen's eyes.

"Jakub is—" I coughed because the lingering effects of being struck by a car were still making it hard to breathe, but I managed to suck in another breath and say, "Jakub! That might be him!"

Kaillen's attention swung to the fleeing vehicle.

"Go. Try to catch him!" I coughed again. "This may be our only chance!"

The hunter's gaze whipped back to me, his eyes skating over my frame, taking in the bound hands, the numerous injuries, my gushing blood, and my labored breathing. A wild look blazed across his face.

"I can't leave you. You're still bound and injured. You're totally vulnerable. I *can't*." He lifted me in his arms and whipped out his yellow crystal at the same moment.

In a split second, his swirling portal was open before us and then we were leaping through it.

CHAPTER TWENTY-SIX

In my next blink, I was back in the cabin in his living room. I lolled in Kaillen's arms, my head dipping. In two steps, he was at the couch, setting me down gently.

"Go!" I yelled, then coughed again. "Catch him!"

Kaillen's jaw locked. Fire was rolling through his irises so strongly that all of the natural amber in them had disappeared. And that gold rimming his fiery eyes shone as brightly as the sun. The dude definitely didn't appear stable right now.

"He's gone, Tala."

"But you're a hunter. Find him!"

His nostrils flared, no doubt scenting the blood running from my body along with the electric magic encircling my wrists. My muscles screamed in agony, and I could only imagine the emotional scents I was giving off, but if that was Jakub, we needed to catch him. Now. This could *literally be our only chance.*

Another burst of fire leaped into the hunter's eyes. "I'm not leaving you like this." A muscle ticked in the corner of his jaw. "We'll catch him but not today."

If I were standing, I would have stomped my foot, but then a rush of dizziness swept through me. Blinking, I realized this sofa looked and felt very differently from the couch I'd sat on before. Trying to clear my head, I peered around, and with wild-eyed shock I realized that I *wasn't* in his living room in Ontario. This was somewhere else. Somewhere new.

The room we were in was bigger and grander with mountainous views through the windows. But it had the feel of a cabin. Rustic wood railings graced a stairway that led to a large second-floor hallway. Oak floorboards ran the length of the room beneath my toes. A large stone fireplace sat cold and unused to my left. And the windows . . . *Gods,* so many windows. They rose to the top of a vaulted ceiling and captured the beauty of the wilderness outside.

Snowcapped mountains in the distance butted against an endless valley. Pine trees towered at the base of those mountains, and the rugged beauty was so enchanting that for a moment all I could do was blink, and then blink again as I stared at the view.

Where am I?

I sputtered, my head reeling. Everything had all happened so fast. It probably hadn't even been thirty minutes since I'd been enjoying a cup of coffee on the hunter's porch in Ontario, but now, I was in an unknown location. Jakub had tried to abduct me again. Numerous cuts, scrapes, and bruises covered my body, and I had *freakin' electric blue handcuffs* around my wrists with no damn key.

"I need to get those off you." Kaillen turned me slightly, being careful not to touch where my skin was torn as he assessed the cuffs. His fingers probed them, then he growled in angry frustration when they zapped him too. "You're going to have to use your forbidden magic on me. I'm not strong enough to break these on my own. It's going to be like in the club. You have to enhance my power so I can shatter them with sheer force."

My head lolled again. Dammit, I was so out of it. I wondered if these cuffs depleted more than just my power. Or perhaps I had an old-fashioned concussion since I'd been thrown like a bouncy ball so many times onto pavement. Who knew. All I knew was that everything hurt, and the world was beginning to grow fuzzy.

Trying to snap myself into coherency, I managed to shake my head. "I can't. My magic's too depleted, and these cuffs aren't like the ones they had on you. They're stronger. Better. It's amazing I was able to break through their binding and gag spells at all."

A low snarl came from the hunter that sounded a bit unhinged. Then there was silence, as if he were thinking. Or trying to.

"Wait here." The couch dipped when he stood.

"Well, it's not like I could really go anywhere," I drawled as a wave of dizziness swept through me.

He gave a small smile that didn't reach those crazed-looking eyes as he towered over me. Days' worth of beard still graced his cheeks. He'd been sporting that look for nearly a week now.

He pulled out his yellow crystal, and before I could blink, he'd created a portal and jumped through it.

"Kaillen?" I called to the empty room. Silence surrounded me, the only sound the soft ticking of a clock coming from somewhere in the house.

A minute passed, and I tried to sit more upright, realizing that even though nobody was harming me here, I was anything but okay. I was a freakin' invalid with these cuffs on. I couldn't even go to the bathroom like this.

But before I could contemplate that very embarrassing detail, another yellow portal appeared, and the hunter jumped back through it, reappearing in the living room.

My eyes widened at the huge ax in his hands. I recognized it. It'd been in his closet of weapons in his man cave back in Portland. It was pure black, huge, and deadly looking. Its sheer presence pulled at me, beckoning me to caress it and use it.

"What is that?" I managed.

"A weapon from the underworld. It's not supposed to be released from hell, and only demons can touch it, so I'd advise you to keep your distance."

"Do I want to know how you came to possess it?"

"Probably not."

"What are you going to do with it?"

"Break those cuffs. I think the ax's power will be strong enough to do it, but it may take a toll on you."

"Meaning what?" My eyes widened as he drew nearer. Those manic-looking flames still filled his irises, and I knew the hunter was still feeling a bit crazed and perhaps wasn't of sound mind right now.

I got awkwardly to my feet, and he assessed the cuffs, testing which angle to use the ax. "You may pass out, but you'll be okay eventually. I think."

"Right." That didn't sound promising. "Do we do this here?" I raised my arms behind me, positioning my wrists away from my body.

He guided me to the center of the room, which gave him more space to move. "Keep your arms raised, just like that. Don't move."

I squeezed my eyes shut. "Please don't miss. I don't really want to lose an arm . . . or a leg. No offense, but I have no idea how good your hand-eye coordination is."

I couldn't be sure, but I thought his lips twitched. "I won't."

I didn't question his actions or the wisdom of his decision further. It felt as if my entire body was going numb, and my mind was shutting down. *Too much. Too much.* Too much was happening.

All I could do in that moment was function on autopilot. I still had my eyes closed when the swing of the giant ax breezed against my back along my skin.

And then a huge *clang* of power sliced through the air,

like an enormous void had been ripped through the cosmos as it connected with the cuffs' chains.

An explosion of crackling vibrant power blazed through the room, heating my wrists right before the cuffs shattered. They disintegrated in a thousand blazing sparks, and then, I was free.

I sagged forward, my arms screaming in agony again at the sudden jolt, but at least I could move again. Shaking my hands, I tried to dispel that lingering zapping feeling.

Another wave of dizziness swept through me, but I tried to hold on, tried to fight it when my vision grew dark, but my head was *so* fuzzy.

Too much.

Too much.

Too much.

Gritting my teeth, I made one last attempt to stay conscious, desperately trying to escape the power of the ax and the lingering magic from the cuffs. But I was no match for the strength of the underworld.

"Tala?" Kaillen lunged for me.

I fell forward just as my vision went dark.

I woke to the feel of warm blankets cocooning me and the sound of a crackling fire. My eyes peeled open. Moonlight blazed through a window, bathing the room I slept in with silvery light.

I fixed on that glowing orb hanging in the sky. The

waxing gibbous moon shone brightly, just a day away from the full moon in the lunar cycle. A tug registered in my chest, snagging all of my attention to that beautiful ball of pearly light.

I should go to it. Out in the field. Open my arms. Bask in its light. I should follow the moon and—

"Tala, are you awake?" The soft question came from my side.

I snapped my attention away from the moon. My gaze landed on the hunter who sat on the other side of the bed, his back against the headboard, his long body spread out across the mattress. He was fully dressed and sat on top of the covers, as though he hadn't slept at all even though it was nighttime. That wild look was still in his eyes, those irises all flames and molten gold.

"Kaillen?" I asked, confusion strumming through me.

He pushed off the bed, and in a blur was kneeling on the floor at my side, only a foot away from me. A wild look covered his face, his expression so fierce that I wondered again how rational he was at the moment.

He brought a hand to my forehead, as if assessing me for fever.

I pushed up more, realizing my body was no longer sore, and the plethora of cuts I'd had before were gone. "Did you heal me?"

He gave a sharp nod. "I gave you a potion after you passed out, not my . . ." His jaw locked.

Not his blood. Right.

I ran a hand through my hair and grimaced. I could

only imagine what I looked like considering the snarl my fingers just encountered. "Was I sleeping?" I tried to make sense of everything, but a fuzzy feeling still coated my mind.

"You passed out after I broke the cuffs. You've been unconscious for nine hours. I didn't know how to wake you."

I frowned. My mouth felt like cotton and once again I was in a room I didn't recognize—it was a bedroom though. "Where are we?"

"My home in Montana. It wasn't safe to bring you back to Ontario, to those—" Roaring fire leaped to life in his irises. "Someone betrayed me and handed you over to those sorcerers, and from the scent on your clothes, I'm guessing it was my dear brother."

My lips parted when some of the dizziness cleared. "It *was* Cameron. He came to your cabin this morning. Or yesterday morning. Or whenever it was." I hung my head, still trying to make sense of everything. "He surprised me, then took me. I didn't have time to fight back before he put those cuffs on my wrists." My fingers curled. "If only I'd fought back immediately when he'd grabbed me, I could have annihilated that donkey's ass. But it all happened so fast, and I never thought he was capable of something like *that* even though he's a real fucker. He willingly handed me over to those sorcerers knowing they would probably kill me."

The flames in the hunter's eyes shifted from blazing red to deep-black. My breath hitched. I'd never seen them that color before. His demon shone fully through those irises as if rising from the depths of hell.

"I'm going to kill him," he said in such a low guttural tone, that I knew he was close to losing control, the rage or fear or whatever had been making him look so crazed when I'd been abducted was returning full throttle. "I'm going to kill him once and for all."

The mind-altering fury that strummed from the hunter was palpable. It flowed off him in hot, vicious waves that hit me again and again. And a scent accompanied it, a metallic scent of iron.

But I brushed that realization off, because I knew without a doubt that Kaillen had meant it. He would truly kill his own flesh and blood. He hated Cameron that much.

I shook my head, trying to dispel some of the whirling vortex of malice and death that swirled around the hunter. "Is there some water around here? I'm so thirsty."

My very uninteresting, mundane question seemed to snap whatever grasp the underworld had on the hunter. He blinked, and those black flames calmed back to the fiery red I was used to. They were still a bit crazed-looking, albeit not as much.

"Yeah, I'll get you a glass." In a blurred movement, he was up and gone. Not even a second passed before he reappeared at my side, a glass of water in hand. The water sloshed over the rim at his abrupt stop, but half of it stayed put, and at least his demon had receded enough that I was once again looking at the Kaillen I knew. "Here." He thrust the glass toward me.

With a shaky hand, I greedily gulped all of it, draining the entire glass in one go. "Thank you." I set it on the bedside table when I finished, and some of the dizziness swimming through me faded.

I tried to process my current time and place. I was in Montana, and it was obviously nighttime, but it felt as if I was jet-lagged, or had done too many realm crossings between earth and the fae lands. Everything felt discombobulated, disjointed, and it all rolled into one big swirling mess.

"Say, where did you go earlier this morning, or yesterday morning, when you left the cabin in Ontario after we . . . fought?"

His shoulders stiffened. "For a run. I needed to . . . clear my head."

"Right." I didn't press further. I could only imagine the guilt that was eating him. I figured he was blaming himself for my abduction since he hadn't been there. But it was *my* fault he'd left. My rejection. That letter from Carlos. All of it.

My head began to pound just thinking about that unfinished conversation.

I cleared my throat, shifting my attention back to the matter at hand, because one thing stood out clearly. I'd been with Kaillen's pack when I'd been abducted. I was supposed to have been safe there, but Cameron betrayed the hunter and me, and Maybe-Jakub had nearly caught me because of it.

An image of that man in the sedan came back to me.

Medium build. Short brown hair. Wide mouth. Detached, clinical expression. I shuddered. Had that truly been Jakub?

"We need to contact the SF," I finally said. "They need to know about the second abduction attempt made on me and those dead sorcerers that are probably still lying in the street."

"I've already spoken with them. They're in Philadelphia as we speak. Don't worry about the bodies. They'll take care of them."

"Philadelphia?"

"That's the city they took you to—where I tracked you to. The SF is there searching for clues about where Jakub went and who he is."

"But what about you finding him? Did you catch his scent while you were dueling Tall Sorcerer?"

"I did."

"Then *we* can find him." Um, okay, I'd actually just said that in spite of my realization earlier that staying side by side with the hunter *wasn't* a good idea.

Kaillen's entire body stilled. "You . . . want to stay with me?"

"Well, I dunno. I mean, it's been a bit, you know, and I mean, I—" I swallowed. *Awkward much?* I forced a deep breath. "I want to find Jakub and stop him. I know that much."

The muscle ticked in his jaw again. "But he's after you, Tala. I heard enough while battling that sorcerer to know that much. I don't know if you going after him is a wise move." That slightly crazed look entered his eyes again.

It struck me that he said *you going after him*, not *us*. I shrank back and remembered that agonizing moment we'd shared after waking in his cabin in Ontario. It was possible that things were over now for me and the hunter. Perhaps he truly had eradicated the mate bond, and from hereon I would be on my own.

"I see," I finally said, licking my lips. A rolling sensation dipped my stomach, and something a lot like pain flowed through me. But wasn't this exactly what I'd known was coming? That once he'd realized his feelings for me were merely animal driven, he'd snap himself out of it?

A growl came from the hunter. "It's not what you think," he said softly.

My head whipped up.

That golden glow rimmed his eyes again. The mate bond stared back at me bright and shining.

My heart thumped more. So he still felt it?

I straightened the sheet over me, anything to give my hands something to do. "If Jakub wants me, then I should be the one hunting him. He won't expect that. I've been hiding for days now and running every time he's showed up. But if I turn the tables, and begin seeking him out, I could catch him unexpectedly."

"The SF won't like that."

"The SF doesn't have to know about it."

A reluctant, albeit proud, smile kicked his lips up. "A *colantha* to the bone."

I snorted, then realized there were still so many things I didn't know. Like how the hell he'd found me for one. Now that I had a second to think about it, it seemed like a miracle that he'd been able to track me so fast.

I cocked my head. "How did you know I was in Philadelphia?" I sat more upright on the bed, intent on pulling our conversation away from all things mate-driven. The fact that the hunter still felt the bond after our explosive interaction before my abduction was something I was still processing. "I couldn't have been gone from Oak Trembler for more than fifteen minutes before you appeared. Did you do something other than scry? I didn't think you could do it so quickly."

His expression cleared, that proud smile that had been present a second before disappearing. He looked away, breaking eye contact. "No, I . . . scryed."

But I detected the deception in him. I sniffed, a new odor hitting my senses. It smelled bitter and *off*. And deep down, in some new part of me, perhaps where my awakening power lay, an instinct told me that he was lying. I didn't know how I was so sure of that, but I could *smell* it.

My lips parted, cold hurt biting me. Any warmth I'd been feeling for him vanished. "You're lying. You're *lying* to me right now. That's not how you found me."

He abruptly stood and went to the window before planting his hands on his hips.

I pushed the covers back, and despite the weakness I still felt from whatever the hell that ax and those cuffs had done to me, I forced myself to pad up behind him. His citrus and cedar scent hit me, nearly drowning me in its intensity—and that subtler earth and pine aroma was there too—but I shoved those details down.

I needed answers. *Twice* in the past two weeks abduction attempts had been made on me. And twice, this hunter had either saved me from death or saved me from falling into their hands.

And I wanted to know how.

"Kaillen," I said sharply. "Answer me. How did you find me?"

He stood rigidly, and I wondered if he was even breathing. I was about to open my mouth, to demand again that he tell me, when he spun around suddenly, his eyes blazing with black fiery embers. The depths of the underworld shone behind them again. His demon side looked at me front and center, and I instantly recoiled at the immense power roiling in those irises.

"Why does it matter?" he bit out.

I righted myself, anger swirling inside me that he was evading my questions. It was bad enough that we still hadn't figured out exactly where we stood, but if he was going to start lying to me on a regular basis, then the choice would be easy. It would be *sayonara* to the hunter, once and for all. Because I could put up with many things but outright lying wasn't one of them.

I took a step forward until we stood toe to toe. "It matters, because it shouldn't be possible. Nobody, not even *you*, can find somebody that quickly. How did you find me? Did you put a tracking hex on me?"

His head dipped, a guilty look streaking across his face.

"You did?" My insides stilled. That was such a grotesque breach of privacy. "How? When I was sleeping?" Fresh hurt cut through me.

"No," he snarled. "It's not a hex. That's not how I found you." His gaze shifted again as he continually refused to make eye contact.

"Then how?" I demanded. "*How?*"

A tense moment of silence passed between us. It was so thick I could have stabbed it with a knife. My fingers itched, wishing more than anything that I had a blade at my side. 'Cause even though I couldn't actually stab the air, I could sure as hell stab this lying fucking demon who was apparently keeping more secrets from me than his hoard of fairy charms.

"Tell me," I seethed. "Right *now.*"

He shook his head, silent again, and I was convinced he wasn't going to answer me, but then he bit out, "It was my blood." His words were so quiet I barely heard them. "That's how I found you. My blood bound you to me."

His blood? I shook my head. "What the hell are you talking about?"

He finally looked up, his jaw locked tight as black fire flashed in his eyes. "The blood I gave you on the night you nearly died following that first abduction attempt. It tied you to me. I can sense you now. *Feel* you. I know your whereabouts at all times. The second they took you from Oak Trembler, I knew."

My breath sucked in. "The blood I drank from you that healed me makes you able to *track me?*"

He didn't reply.

A second passed, and then another. "And you knew this? Or did you not know? When you gave me your blood and saved me, did you know this could happen?"

"I knew it would happen, if—" Guilt flashed in his eyes.

"*If what?*"

"If I spelled my blood as you drank from me. I knew you would have to take enough that it would fill you, and by spelling it as you consumed it, I could tie you to me."

I stumbled back, shock rippling through me. He'd tied me to him. Willingly *bound* me to him. All without my consent.

"What the hell does that *mean?*" I demanded. "Am I tied to you forever? Will you forever be able to hunt me? Feel me? What other ramifications does this blood bond have?" I nearly yelled.

A feral expression twisted his features, then he snarled and tore a hand through his hair. "I'm sorry, Tala. Okay? But the mate bond . . . I didn't fully understand what I was feeling when I first detected your scent. I know now that it was the mating instinct. It was pushing me, driving me. I was doing things I shouldn't have because of my fucking wolf. I know now that I shouldn't have bound you to me, but at the time, all I knew was that I needed you—*craved* you—and that pull was driving me crazy. It made me . . ." He shook his head, growling. "I'm sorry, okay? I fucked up."

But his apology fell on deaf ears. "Answer my questions. What else does it mean?"

He looked at me with pleading eyes. "I'm sorry."

I took another step back, fear and apprehension slamming through me. "Why? Why are you so sorry? What else does this bond do?"

The light from the moon streaked across the floor when I stepped into it. That tug pulled on me again, snagging my attention to it.

My breath sucked in. The moon. Its pull. My breathing sped up when I thought about the other new traits I'd been noticing in myself. Heightened senses. Increased strength too.

Were those traits *not* related to my new awakening power, but instead tied to the hunter's blood?

A flash of something Cameron had said that day at the training center collided with my thoughts. He'd sniffed and then uttered, *"What are you? Not a normal witch from the smell of it. Are you like him? An abomination?"*

Perhaps I was.

Tears of anger, pain, and betrayal pricked my eyes.

The hunter took a step toward me, but I took a much larger one back.

Kaillen glanced toward the window, toward the glowing orb in the sky. His expression turned pleading again. "I don't entirely know what else my blood could do to you, but I've—" His throat bobbed in a swallow. "I've been scenting a change in you lately. It's possible—" His lips pressed into a tight line.

My gaze drifted to the moon again, to that beautiful heavenly body that called to me. The tears grew in my eyes as a growing sense of dread filled me. "What have you turned me into?"

A look of absolute devastation rippled across his features. "I think you might be a werewolf now." Another bobbed swallow. "And I think you might shift, but we won't know for sure until your first full moon tomorrow night."

A strangled sob of disbelief tore from me.

My chest caved in.

My lungs shattered.

I stumbled back, my knees meeting the bed's edge before I collapsed and sank onto the mattress. "I'm a werewolf now?" I began shaking my head back and forth, the movement becoming faster and faster and faster until it felt as though my head would spin off.

He made a move to reach for me, to touch me, but I scrambled back.

"But female werewolves *can't* shift. They've never been able to. They only carry the gene."

"But you're not a born werewolf," he said softly. "You're a *made* werewolf. Men who are made can shift into wolves."

"But that's never been possible for females! You can't *make* a female werewolf!"

His expression turned so forlorn, so broken, as though sensing that the rage flowing through my veins precipitated the end of whatever had started between us. The end before the beginning. Because the blinding fury that I felt at having been transformed into something other than what I'd been born was *consuming* me, eating me away bit by bit, as if my soul were being devoured in its intensity.

The hunter's throat bobbed again. Guilt flooded his eyes, but that fire was still there, still rolling within his irises. It was enough fire to consume us both.

"I'm sorry, Tala, but I can't change what I did, and when the full moon hits tomorrow, I think you're going to become the first female werewolf that has ever shifted, and there's nothing I can do to stop it."

BOOK THREE
SUPERNATURAL CURSE

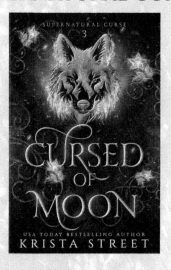

I'm going to kill my hunter. He's turned me into something that shouldn't be magically possible, so now I have *this* to deal with on top of everything else.

Well . . . I might as well make lemonade out of these freakin' lemons. Yep, that's right Mr. Broody Hunter, I'm going to take these newborn powers you thrust upon me and stop sitting on the sidelines. I'm done taking orders from others and you, and I'm done waiting for the Supernatural Forces to fix my problems.

I'm going to solve the mystery that's been weaving itself around me for far too long, especially when it becomes crystal clear that the key my nemesis has been seeking has been buried inside me all along.

ABOUT THE AUTHOR

Krista Street loves writing in multiple genres: fantasy, sci-fi, romance, and dystopian. Her books are cross-genre and often feature complex characters, plenty of supernatural twists, and romance in every story. She loves writing about coming-of-age characters who fight to find their place in this world while also finding their one true mate.

Krista Street is a Minnesota native but has lived throughout the U.S. and in another country or two. She loves to travel, read, and spend time in the great outdoors. When not writing, Krista is either chasing her children, spending time with her husband and friends, sipping a cup of tea, or enjoying the hidden gems of beauty that Minnesota has to offer.

THANK YOU

Thank you for reading *Bound of Blood*, book two in the *Supernatural Curse* series.

If you enjoy Krista Street's writing, make sure you visit her website to learn about her new release text alerts, newsletter, and other series.

www.kristastreet.com

Links to all of her social media sites are available on every page.

Last, if you enjoyed reading *Bound of Blood*, please consider logging onto the retailer you purchased this book from to post a review. Authors rely heavily on readers reviewing their work. Even one sentence helps a lot. Thank you so much if you do!

Printed in Great Britain
by Amazon